GRAND STREET 72

Detours

GRAND STREET 72

Detours

Grand Street (ISSN 0734-5496; ISBN 1-885490-23-2) is published by Grand Street Press (a project of the New York Foundation for the Arts, Inc., a not-for-profit corporation), 214 Sullivan Street, Suite 6C, New York, NY 10012. Tel: (212) 533-2944, Fax: (212) 533-2737. Contributions and gifts to Grand Street Press are tax-deductible to the extent allowed by law.

 Second-class bound printed matter postage paid at Trenton, NJ, and additional mailing offices. Postmaster: Please send address changes to Grand Street Magazine, 214 Sullivan Street, Suite 6C, New York, NY 10012. Subscriptions are $25 a year (two issues). Foreign subscriptions (including Canada) are $35 a year, and institutional orders are $30 a year, payable in U.S. funds. Single-copy price is $15 ($24 in Canada). For subscription inquiries, please call (877) 533-2944.

Grand Street is printed by Finlay Printing in Bloomfield, CT. It is distributed to the trade by D.A.P./ Distributed Art Publishers, 155 Avenue of the Americas, New York, NY 10013; and Ingram Periodicals, 1240 Heil Quaker Blvd., La Vergne, TN 37086. It is distributed to newsstands only by Bernhard DeBoer, Inc., 113 E. Centre Street, Nutley, NJ 07110; and Ubiquity Distributors, 607 Degraw Street, Brooklyn, NY 11217. *Grand Street* is distributed in Australia and New Zealand by Peribo Pty, Ltd., 58 Beaumont Road, Mount Kuring-Gai, NSW 2080, Australia; and in the United Kingdom by Central Books, 99 Wallis Road, London, E9 5LN.

GRAND STREET

EDITOR
Jean Stein

MANAGING EDITOR
Radhika Jones

ART EDITOR
Walter Hopps

ASSISTANT EDITOR
Michael Mraz

ASSOCIATE ART EDITOR
Anne Doran

POETRY EDITOR
James Lasdun

ASSOCIATE POETRY EDITOR
Justin Ginnetti

CREATIVE DIRECTOR (PRINT)
J. Abbott Miller, Pentagram

DESIGN (PRINT)
Jeremy Hoffman, Pentagram

WEBSITE DESIGN
Faruk Ulay

COPY EDITOR
Nell McClister

EDITORIAL ASSISTANT
Allison Smith

INTERNS
John Cochran, Leyla Ertegun, Aaron Hawn

ADVISORY EDITORS
Edward W. Said, Charles Merewether

CONTRIBUTING EDITORS
George Andreou, Jack Bankowsky, Mary Blume, Dominique Bourgois, Natasha Parry Brook, Frances Coady, Mike Davis, Barbara Epler, Kennedy Fraser, Stephen Graham, Nikolaus Hansen, John Heilpern, Dennis Hopper, Jane Kramer, Brigitte Lacombe, Alane Mason, Peter Mayer, Vanessa Mobley, Michael Naumann, Meghan O'Rourke, Erik Rieselbach, Robin Robertson, Fiona Shaw, Daniel Slager, Robert Storr, Michi Strausfeld, Deborah Treisman, Katrina vanden Heuvel, Wendy vanden Heuvel, Deborah Warner, John Waters, Drenka Willen

FOUNDING CONTRIBUTING EDITOR
Andrew Kopkind (1935–1994)

PUBLISHERS
Jean Stein & Torsten Wiesel

VISIT OUR WEBSITE AT www.grandstreet.com

Night, and Florida, the lonely road night of snow white roadsigns at a wilderness crossing showing four endless unreadable nowhere directions, and the oncoming ghost cars. And the roadside gift shoppes of Florida by night, clay pelicans stuck in grass being a simple enough deal but not when photographed at night against the oncoming atom-ball headlights of a northbound car.

JACK KEROUAC

From "On the Road to Florida"

Robert Frank, Kerouac with Flamingos, Florida, 1963.

Books Never Written, Journeys Never Made

ANTONIO TABUCCHI

Allons! Whoever you are, come travel with me!
Traveling with me, you find what never tires.

—Walt Whitman, *Leaves of Grass*

Na véspera de não partir nunca
*ao menos não há que arrumar malas.**

—Fernando Pessoa, *Poemas de Álvaro de Campos*

My Love,

Do you remember when we didn't go to Samarkand? We'd picked early autumn, the best season of the year according to our guidebook, when the leaves on the bushes and trees on the arid hills around Samarkand would be bursting with red and ochre yellows, and the weather mild—do you remember our guidebook? The one we bought in that little bookstore, Ulysses, on the Île Saint-Louis, that specialized in travel books, mostly used, often with underlinings or comments made by previous travelers; the notes were useful things like "Recommended tavern," or "Avoid this street, it's dangerous," or "They sell valuable rugs at a good price here," or else, "Watch out! This restaurant cheats on the bill."

There are several different ways to get to Samarkand according to the guidebook, of which the airplane is the fastest but certainly the least

*On the eve of never departing
At least there are no suitcases to pack

interesting. You could take off, for example, from Paris, Rome, or Zurich, fly direct to Moscow, where you have to stay the night, because there's no same-day connection for Uzbekistan. And did we want to spend the night in Moscow? We discussed it at great length one evening at Luigi's, the good fish restaurant where there was that amiable gay waiter who always gave us exceptional service. As far as I was concerned we shouldn't exclude that option. Why not, I said, remember? Imagine Red Square at night, seen from the windows of that big hotel Aeroflot uses for customers with next-day flights who have to stay over in Moscow: it's autumn in Moscow, already cold, the Place Rouge will be empty like in the Gilbert Bécaud song, I will call you Nathalie, we'll step out of a taxi, which in the Soviet Union all seem like the limousines for heads of state, I read somewhere that in the hotel restaurant they serve complimentary caviar made from Volga sturgeon, there might even be fog hovering around the streetlamps, like in a Pushkin story, and it will be beautiful, I'm sure of it, we can go to the Bolshoi, where one must go when in Moscow, and maybe see *Swan Lake*.

But that was the least interesting option, which was why we agreed to abandon it. It would be much better to go by land, by train, and that was what we decided on: the Orient Express to the Trans-Siberian, or else through Tehran. The Orient Express still manages to fascinate the snobbiest of intellectuals, and even if we didn't think of ourselves that way, maybe we were, and so that's why we concluded: by train, by train. Oh, the train! Did you know that in order to build the rails for his luxury express trains, Georges Nagelmackers had to negotiate first with France, then with Bavaria, Austria, and Romania, because they all worried the train service might threaten their national integrity? The inauguration was in 1883, and the journalist Edmond About, also a humorist and author of *The Notary's Nose*, recorded that first trip in minute detail. Nagelmackers never would have pulled it off without the patronage of Leopold II of Belgium, his partner in business too. And you might be surprised to learn that there were already some locomotives back then that could travel faster than 160 kilometers an hour and used compressed-air brakes, the British Rail Buddicom trains. Would you like to hear the menu for January 4, 1898? I've found one, it's a proper, prepared meal, not just a snack: there are oysters to start with, then tortoise soup or Potage à la Reine, then Smoked Trout Chambord, Selle de Chevreuil à la Duchesse, Chilled Partridge Salad with White Pepper Dressing, le Foie Gras de Canard aux Raisins, Champagne Truffles, fruit, and dessert. The sleeping cars, the muffled clattering of the wheels on the tracks penetrating the glass windows, as the trains sped through towns and loved them without ever touching them, like Chardonne, who told his friends, "*Si vous aimez une femme, n'y touchez pas*"—if you love a woman, don't touch her—and the wagon-lit let us touch places with our fingertips, like the poet who wanted to feel the harpist's gesture without touching her hand. I recited poems I knew by heart on the train and in the bistros near Gare d'Austerlitz, I declaimed Valery Larbaud: "Oh, Orient Express, lend me your vibrant voice, storm through worries, the pale easy breath of the locomotive, snaking four yellow cars branded with golden letters through the mountain solitude of Serbia, through Bulgaria full of roses . . ."

Where do you get the Orient Express? At the Gare de Lyon, the Gare de Lyon! And what else should be there in that marvelous station but Train Bleu, the very best restaurant in Paris! Do you remember? Of course you do, how could you not? Three enormous dining rooms, Pompier-style frescoes on the walls, red velvet chairs, Bohemian lamps, and waiters in little jackets and immaculate aprons greeting you "Bienvenus, Messieurs Dames" with the attitude of someone who couldn't care less. To start, we ordered oysters and champagne, because two people who aren't going to Samarkand on the Orient Express have the right to start out this way, am I wrong? Leaving is always to die a little, we said while we watched the people on the platform who were staying behind as they waved and talked to the passengers leaning out of their illuminated windows. Where was the elderly bald gentleman in evening dress headed, sitting, smoking his pipe and looking out the window with such nonchalance he could have been reclining in his own living room? And the lady in the carriage with him, her crimson hat and fur stole—was she his wife or a complete stranger? Would they have an affair during the course of their trip? Who knows, who knows—and in the meantime, we decide to start our own trip. The train leaves from Track L, at least as far as the schedule of departures is concerned, and the first stop will be Venice. Oh how you've dreamed of seeing Venice! The Grand Canal, San Marco, the Ca' d'Oro . . . Yes, all right, my dear, but I don't know how much you'll be able to see, for I'm sorry to say the train will only be making a short stop in the middle of the night at Santa Lucia Station, and the most you can see from there as the train passes through is the lagoon on the left and the open sea on the right—but you shouldn't forget that we're on our way to Samarkand, or else you'll start wanting to stop in every city the train goes through, first Vienna then

Istanbul, wouldn't you like to see Istanbul? Think of it, the Bosphorus, the mosques, the minarets, the Grand Bazaar.

In the end, the real trip not to make was to Samarkand. I have a vivid and unforgettable memory of it, such detail as belongs to that which is truly lived in the imagination. You know, I was reading a French philosopher who noted that the imaginary obeys strict rules of order much like the real. And the imaginary, my love, isn't illusory at all, but very much a different thing. Samuel Butler was quite a character, not just for the fantastic novels he wrote but for the way he saw life. One of his lines comes to mind: "I can tolerate lies, but I can't stand imprecision." My love, we've told each other so many lies in our life, and we've accepted them from each other, because they were what our imagination really did desire. But there was one, or if you'd rather, many, around the same real fact—and that lost us forever, because it was a false lie, it was based on illusion, and illusion is necessarily imprecise, existing only in the haze of self-deception. In dreams we've always been like Don Quixote, whose imaginary life presupposes madness—pushing imagination to the limit—the topography of the landscape he crosses in his imagination is as precise as a real landscape. Have you ever really thought of *Don Quixote* as a realistic novel? And then one day, you suddenly went from being Don Quixote to Madame Bovary, with her inability to identify the limits of her desire, to interpret where she'd ended up, to count the money she spent, to realize that the foolish things she did were real even though they seemed like air to her, not the other way around. Which is an enormous difference—one cannot say: "I was traveling to a distant city," or "A thoughtful gentleman kept me company," or "I don't think it was love so much as a certain kind of tenderness." One cannot say such things, my love, or at least one cannot say them to me, because that was your illusion, your poor, pathetic illusion; the city had a precise name, and it wasn't that far away, and he was older than you, this man you went to bed with. He was a lover who you thought was made of air, but he was made of flesh.

This is why I'm reminding you of the trip we never took to Samarkand, because that, yes, was true, it was ours, it was full, we lived it. And thus I continue our game. The philosopher I was telling you about says that memory brings back lived experience; it's precise, exact, implacable, but it doesn't create anything new—that is its limitation. The imagination, however, can't evoke anything because there's nothing to remember, which is its limitation, though in compensation, something new is created, something that wasn't there before, something that's never been. And so I'm combining these two faculties hoping that together they can evoke once again for you the trip we never took to Samarkand, the trip we imagined in the most precise detail.

Our traveling companions were a disappointment and a delight, respectively. That fine gentleman who looked so elegant turned out to be a base salesman who tended toward the squalid, and we never did figure out what kind of import-export business he actually had in Turkey, but we weren't talking about anything particularly upright—as far as you were concerned it smelled fishy, you winked at me a couple of times, don't you remember, and even breathed a sigh of relief when he got off in Istanbul, because his flattery had grown rather too gallant considering he was a stranger on a train and you were at your wits' end because in the meantime I'd quite unfairly extricated myself from the whole scene. The lady, on the other hand, turned out to be much more than her appearance had promised. I mean, her appearance in the Chekhovian sense in that it represented her character, which was your impression whispered to me out in the corridor. And I've never encountered quite such a Chekhovian. We started with the subject of the little girl's age in "Sleepy." We ended up trying to identify the point at which the physiological need for sleep might drive a person to homicide. My goodness, this depends, explained the lady with an irresistible competence, Have you people, for example, ever studied sleep, biologically speaking that is? Well then, the waking state has a tolerance threshold similar to the pain threshold, which varies according to one's age. The age, for instance, at which the need for sleep is indomitable, when it controls every other sensation and function especially in females, is the onset of puberty, and one of the reasons that the little maid suffocates the newborn baby she is supposed to be comforting is that his crying keeps her from sleeping; and that night, or the night before, she'd had her first menstruation and was exhausted.

This summary of our conversation is rushed and meager, because as you probably remember better than I, the lady had a very precise way of speaking and a fantastic ability for exposition, and her expertise in Chekhov was certainly not limited to picturesque or academic anecdotes like this one. You remember, for example, the conversation we had about Chekhov's last words? Of course you remember, we were both stupefied, neither one of us had ever heard that while he lay dying Chekhov said, "*Ich sterbe*." That's right, he died in a language other than his own. Isn't that strange? He loved in Russian, suffered in Russian, hated (rarely) in Russian, smiled (a lot) in Russian, he lived in Russian and died in German. The explanation that unknown woman provided as to why Chekhov died in German was stupendous, and I will never forget the expression on your face when she said good-bye and got off the train in that unknown station: it was an expression of marvel, surprise, and maybe you were even moved. Then there was that wonderful, extraordinary day I watched you come running toward me, where I was waiting in our old café, you cut through the crowd, excitedly waving a little book and you cried out, "Look who that old lady was!" The book had just come out and the critics hadn't gotten to it yet, but you didn't miss it; you never miss anything—oh, that wonderful old lady with her great kindly voice whose golden fruit flavored our journey without ever revealing her identity before she disappeared into the horizon. And the inappropriate use we made in Samarkand of Chekhov's last words! Of course I was the one who started it and then you started imitating me even though you had said right off, "You're blasphemous! Really blasphemous." The first time was in that variation on the Tower of Babel, the Siab Bazaar: where the smells, the spices, the head scarves, the rugs, the shouting, the throng, the crush of people all mixed together, Turks, Europeans, Russians, Mongolians, Afghans—and I stopped, terrified, and screamed, "Ich sterbe!" And from that point forward "to sterb" entered our lexicon, an obligation, almost a vice. We sterbed together in front of the Gur-I Amir Mausoleum, the teardrop steeple perched atop the cylindrical tower that was all inset with verses from the Koran; there were onyx tiles on the inside, and a jade tombstone decorated with carved arabesques and colored with yellow and green mosaic tiles. We sterbed again in the Registan Square, before the towers of the Madrasahs while the crowd lay prostrate in prayer. The binoculars we'd brought were critical—that had been your suggestion, you were unparalleled at times in things practical. Without those we never would have been able to decipher the mosaics that decorate the courtyard of the Ulugbek Mosque, the flowers with twenty petals set in a twelve-point star radiating geometric patterns that become a kind of labyrinth. Will life be like this? you asked, beginning with a point, like the petal of a flower, and then dispersing in every direction? What a strange question. In answer to your question, I brought you to Ulugbek's Observatory, with its enormous planetarium, the arc of the dome more than thirty meters across, where one can determine the positions of the stars and planets simply by observing the way the light streams in onto the floor from apertures cut into the ceiling. Is it reflective? I asked you. What? you answered. I wanted to know if the sky reflects what you've revealed about yourself, I told you, it isn't an answer, I answered your question with a question. Then, in a market a little later you were sterbing for a buckram the color of lapis lazuli, but you didn't sterb for long, because you said we didn't have enough money and we'd have to skip at least two meals and what if we found a prettier one in Bukhara that would cost less? But, wouldn't you know it, we never got to Bukhara. Who knows why we decided not to go there in the end—do you remember? I really don't. We were tired, that's for sure, and our journey so far had been intense, packed with emotions and images and faces and landscapes; we might have felt as if we were exaggerating had we gone on, like when you're at a museum that's too big, too full, and you decide to skip some rooms even if they're beautiful because nothing could possibly add to the beauty you've already seen and you don't want to run the risk of having too much and blotting out the memory of everything. And then life called us back to reality, that daily life which sometimes allows a crack, but even those cracks close up right away again.

This crack opened again for me only now, after all these years. And that's why I've started thinking over all the things not done, this difficult but necessary taking stock that can provide a kind of lightness, a childlike, even gratuitous sense of well-being. As if one were a consequence of the other, I started thinking with the same childlike, even gratuitous sense of well-being about the books I never wrote and that I nonetheless recited to you with the same exactitude I used to tell about the trip we didn't take to Samarkand. The last one I didn't write, the last one I told you about, was called "Looking for You," and its subtitle was "A Mandala." The subtitle referred to the search for a character in the sense that the hunt is a concentric, spiral journal and the characters, as you know, weren't my characters—I'd stolen them from another novel. You remember how intolerable I'd found the ending of that novel full of dissolute and happy ghosts while the two protagonists, the Him and Her, never find each other. Can it be possible that He, in whom a manifest sarcasm masks a real, incurable melancholy, and She, so generous and passionate, will never meet again, almost as if the author were making fun of them, or taking pleasure in their misery? And then I thought that She hadn't really disappeared at all, which was what the author was trying to make us believe; She hadn't vanished from the landscape but, rather, it seemed to me that she was in perfect evidence, at the dead center of the portrait, and the reason we couldn't really see her was that she was too obvious, hidden under a detail, hidden, even, under herself, like Poe's purloined letter. And this is why I set him back on the hunt for his beloved, and circle after circle, in diminishing circles, just like a mandala, he manages to get to the center, to the meaning of his life, which is finding her again. It was a little romantic, maybe too romantic for a novel, right? But that's not why I didn't write it, for in truth, that novel would have been the masterpiece of all my unwritten novels, the masterstroke of silence that I had chosen for my whole life. A little masterpiece, I mean, nothing like those monumental tomes that are such a delight to editors and that I never even considered not writing, but a slim book that wouldn't end up being longer than ten chapters, a hundred pages, the golden mean. It took me exactly four months not to write it, May through August—I remember the date because San Lorenzo has always been a special night for us, even more for you, because of the wishes you like to make on the falling stars that fill the sky on that one night. And then, I came to see you that very evening, you'll remember, after having spent four months in the country house, in this terrible heat that clogs a person's throat and gets into his bones, while you called me every day and asked me why I wouldn't come home, I told you, I repeated, I told you that I am not writing a very complicated novel and it makes me sweat like a dog even more than the infernal heat of the countryside, but it's going to be beautiful, I promise you, or at least weird, weirder than me, a weird creature like an unknown reptile fossilized in a rock—as soon as I get there, I'll tell you all about it.

I told you that night, standing on the balcony of the house at the sea, watching the falling stars that left white streaks in the dark sky. I remember very well what you said when I finished, and yet I still want to repeat a chapter for you. But I won't summarize this time like I did that night, I'll transcribe it for you as if I were copying word for word from memory as I imagined it. In concrete terms it only exists in my memory, of course. In the end it doesn't really matter where as long as it's nowhere. And you know what it costs me to betray this secret pact with myself, rendering written and visible, thus in existence, words that came out as air, light, winged, resisting capture—free to be while not being, just like thought. How aggressive they become on the page, almost vulgar, fat, getting irreparably arrogant, as words do. It doesn't matter, I'll transcribe it anyway; deep down, you used to love the cracks between things too, even if you ended up choosing the whole and perhaps you did well, because it's one kind of salvation, or at least a way of accepting what we are. Ah! *Que la vie est quotidienne!*

I'll try to spare you the descriptions and narrative passages. I didn't love them when I wrote them mentally, why in the world would I want to read them for real? Only strictly necessary information: We're on to Chapter Eight, and his hunt for her has brought him to this strange place in the Swiss Alps, a community of Zen Buddhists, or something like that, because he's intuited that she's caught up in the sorts of things that now seem "New Age" but many years ago, when I wasn't writing this, would have struck another note entirely. He eats and spends the night in this place as a pilgrim looking for something, which in and of itself is true. And, during dinner, he starts talking to this lady who is sitting beside him at the table, French, not a young woman anymore. The decor there, as you might remember, is Easternized, there's Indian raga music playing in the background and Indian dishes like gutshaba and vegetable samosas, details that I'll spare you because I know they irritate you. And at a certain point the lady makes a strange comment, she says she's there because she's lost the limit of things. Now I must resort to quotation marks, and I can't tell you how sorry I am about it.

"There are rules here, it's true; rules are useful when you've lost all the limits, and then, deep down, the practical reason I've come here is that this is a shelter."

"What does having lost all the limits mean? I don't understand."

"If we keep on talking, you'll come to understand, but in the meantime, we should order dinner, if you'll permit me to explain the evening's menu."

[*Omitted* . . . the music changes, now a drum starts beating. *Omitted* . . .]

"Pardon me, but I really would like to understand what you mean by having lost the limits."

"I mean that the universe has no end, and that is why I'm here, because I too have no end."

"Which is to say—"

"Do you know how many stars there are in the galaxy?"

"I haven't got the slightest idea."

"There are somewhere around four hundred billion. But in the known universe there are hundreds of billions of galaxies, the universe has no end."

[The woman lights an Indian cigarette, the spicy kind, rolled in a single tobacco leaf. *Omitted* . . .]

"I had a son many years ago, life took him from me, he was called Denis, nature had been unkind to him, and yet he had his own sort of intelligence. I understood it."

[Omitted . . .]

"I loved him as you only love your own child. Do you know what it's like to love a child? So much more than you love yourself—that's how you love your children."

[Omitted . . .]

"He had his own way of knowing and I learned it. For example, we worked out this code, one of those codes that they don't teach in the kinds of schools where children like my Denis went, but the kind of code that a mother might be able to invent with her own son, just between us, tapping a spoon against the side of a glass, do you know what I mean? Tapping a spoon on glass—*ting ting*."

"I'm not quite sure I understand."

"You must be able to hear the frequency and intensity in order to understand the message—and I am an expert of frequency and intensity, it was part of my job, studying the stars at the observatory in Paris—but that wasn't what guided me, it was because I was a mother, and a mother loves her son more than herself."

[Omitted . . .]

"Our code functioned perfectly, we'd created a language that no one else could understand—he could say, Mamma, I love you, and I'd know how to tell him, You're my whole life, and then other things, too, more daily things, things he might be needing, or more complex ideas, like that I was sad or happy, or if he was sad or happy, because even people to whom nature has been cruel know as well as we do what happiness and unhappiness are, melancholy or joy, everything we feel, everything we consider normal."

[Omitted . . .]

"But life isn't just cruel, it's wicked—what would you have done?"

"I don't know. Really, I don't know. What did you do?"

"After he passed away, I spent the days wandering Paris, looking in store windows, watching other human creatures all dressed up and strolling the sidewalks, sitting on park benches or at tables in cafés. And I thought about how we organize our life on planet Earth. I spent my nights at the observatory, but the telescopes weren't strong enough for me anymore. I wanted to look at enormous interstellar spaces, I was the minute dot who wants to find the limits of the universe, it was the only thing that held my interest, as if it were the only thing that would ever give me peace of mind. What would you have done in my place?"

[*Omitted* . . .]

"The highest observatory in the world is in the Chilean Andes, it's also one of the best equipped, and they were looking for an astrophysicist, so I sent off my CV, they called me, and I went—"

"Please go on."

"I was stationed at the radio-telescope in order to study extra-galactic cloud formations—Do you know what the Andromeda Nebula is?"

"Of course not."

"It's a spiral system like the Milky Way, but it's tilted in such a way that the tracks of the spiral are not perfectly visible. We weren't even sure until the first part of this century that we were seeing beyond the Milky Way itself—it wasn't until 1923, when a scientist studying the Triangulum constellation figured out where the limits of our system lie, the limits of our universe."

[*Omitted* . . .]

"You use the radio-telescope to capture radio-galactic emissions by sending modulated signals with the idea that any intelligent life form will send back modulated signals . . ."

[*Omitted* . . .]

"You can't know what it's like to stand on one of the highest mountains in the world while there's only storms and snow outside, and send messages out to the Andromeda Galaxy . . . and then one night, it was windy and the ice had caked over the windows of the observatory dome, an idea came to me. It was an absurd idea, I don't know why I'd tell you about it . . ."

"Oh please do, really."

"As I said, it was a ridiculous idea."

"Please go on."

"Well, I was sending my modulated signals and that night I wanted to use a code from my memory, and I chose a code, one that only I knew, and I translated it into mathematical modulations and sent it . . . This is ridiculous. I told you."

"Please go on."

"I don't know if you realize this, but a message sent to the Andromeda strain, counting in light years, takes over one hundred of our calendar years to get there and then another century again to receive any kind of response. This is absurd; you're going to think I'm crazy."

"No, I don't think so at all, I believe that anything is possible in the universe, please continue."

"It was night, the ice crystals were melting on the glass and I was standing there behind the telescope feeling very foolish for what I'd done, and a message came back from Andromeda, a modulated message, and when I went to decode it I recognized it instantly; it was the same frequency, the same intensity that I'd heard for fifteen years of my life given in mathematical terms, it was my son, Denis. You think I'm crazy."

"No. I think maybe the universe is crazy."

"What would you have done?"

"I don't know, frankly, I wouldn't know what to tell you."

"I discovered in a sacred Indian text that cardinal directions can be infinite or nonexistent, the way they are on a circle, an idea that distresses me, because you can't take cardinal directions away from an astronomer. That's why I'm here, because you can't ever think you've reached the end of the universe, because the universe has no limits."

You know, my love, I wouldn't have transcribed all this for you if it weren't already so late, if I weren't already on the far side of summer, the sunny days of December. But the pages of that novel I didn't write stirred memories in me of the journey we never made, maybe because they speak so much about the stars, and there are so many stars in the sky that it doesn't make much difference when one falls, and we tried to understand the topography of the sky, September 24th, so many years ago, because one whole night of the trip we never took to Samarkand we spent in Ulugbek's Observatory. Isn't it foolish to study the stars? Look to the earth, toward the earth, because life obliges us after all to keep our heads lowered.

Recently, I've been studying a little Uzbek. But not seriously, just the way you study languages in the useful-phrase section of guides for the perfect traveler, and you know, I'd read that studying languages at a certain age helps prevent the onset of Alzheimer's. Don't you remember how silly Uzbek sounded to us? For example, *alvido*, the word for "see you later" and also "farewell," sounds silly because it could easily be Spanish. But the silliest expression of all is *Men olamdan ko'z yaemapman*. Which is nevertheless a literary expression. The more simple, rather, familiar version is *Men do'z o'ljapman*. Do you know what it means?

It's a verb. My dear love, it means "Ich sterbe."

Translated from the Italian by Minna Proctor

An Orange Light in the Windows

CHARLIE SMITH

. . . of course there are cranberry bogs for sale
and rich partial distractions
you experience when a neighbor's carried off,
poisoned by his wife. You say we all deserve it

or wash the windows and sit in the truck listening
to Crawdaddy sing his blues,
but the interference you sense, the dusty needle points
and delays in your release date

are real, as real as anything is. Where will it come from
this time? Your check's
lost like an expedition to discover
the source of the Nile. Speculation used to be fun,

but you're overextended, gripped
by nervousness now.
The rainout lasted for weeks.
And then an infestation of varmints,

something dissociated from itself, from the crew,
and things were hazy
and tasted of flavored salt.
Where did you put

the thingamajig that was going to save you?
A disputed set of values
didn't look right.
What did she mean, about the smell?

Clean

Flattened, sprawled out, snuffling like a dog,
I sniff the expectorate and the feculent lost phenomena,
the shavings and culls, the drifted apart discards
and answers become complications heaved into the grass.
I slide on my belly over the damp places
where old men lay down to try the earth on for size.
In misused areaways behind buildings, among the grassy footings
and slippery spots where disgusting practices ended up, I find
a kind of happiness. My body's covered with what's down there.
Mottled and stained, I've become one with the particulate, the crumb,
the soiled and ineradicable section, the sulcated and unattended spot.
I follow the hog trail of longing. The lowdown is my fortune.
The fundament, the footing, the radicle, the rhizoid, the parquet.
Mouth stuffed with dirt, I chew the bulletins of governance and desire
and take comfort in the filth, in the place
of failure and exudation. I am at home among fistulas
and burned patches, down there with the stems, the shrieks that failed
to arouse pity, the exogenous hopes tossed out with the trash.
What I gather about me was there before I came.
It is often slick and pulpy like a mango,
hot like the scrap of cat hide the sun shines on,
and in its capacity to represent the likelihood of a life beyond
integrity and consummation, I am solaced.
I make small flapping motions, I scurry
my feet and spirate, dragging myself forward,
paying a manifest attention to the tiny voices of ant wings and drying spittle,
and I repeat what they say. In the faint resettlings
of dust and endlessly reducible fractions
I recognize my own voice. Like them I am not saying anything important.
Like them—like the torn-off bee abdomens and locust petals,
the crusts—I have left behind the designs
and purposes I was built for. I am free to inch along,
without meaning. Among the lost
I'm found. I present to myself the unoccupied remainders and
disarranged failed circumstances, the painted tin receptacles
and scuffed flooring of transience: among the discarded, discarded:
among the deserted, the marooned, the forsook, I am part of things.

Now the casual elimination is acceptable to me,
the object hurled down in fury or bitterly tossed aside,
the letter torn to pieces,
the wedding ring in feckless ceremony placed
between two slightly larger stones and covered with moss,
the torn away excess
and deliveries that failed to reach their destinations—
all are acceptable, as are the messy discharges and the exuviation.
Relinquishments, the scattering of pieces, erasures and jettisons,
the fatally incomplete, are equal in my sight.
I flutter and scramble, I drag myself overland,
leaving a trail, abreast of the trash,
keeping up with dereliction, equal with the failed repairs,
the designs growing more marginal as we speak.
It is here I find the endings that in their perfections of absolute loss
have become beginnings again, the bitten-off phrases and
inconspicuous wadding of spoiled opportunity about to start over.
I see the lost revamped. The mortified recast.
The crapped-out recombined with the useless to make the futile.
All the old possibilities—corrigendious, bone-headed and radiant—are here.

WILLIAM EGGLESTON

MEMPHIS BUNGALOWS & NIGHT PORTRAITS

2200

William Eggleston

I've seen a picture of William Eggleston as a child that was taken by his maternal grandfather, Judge May, who lived in the tiny town of Sumner, Mississippi. It's a black-and-white print from the early 1940s, and a black house servant named Jasper Staples is holding the young Eggleston, then about two years old, in his arms. The baby has a little camera, and he is taking a picture of his grandfather at the same time as his grandfather is taking a picture of him.

By the early '60s, Eggleston had taken up photography seriously. Although he would ultimately be celebrated for his work in color, his first photographs were in black and white, and from time to time, especially in the '70s and '80s, he has returned to that format, particularly for serial projects. Eggleston's night portraits, ca. 1973, were taken with an unusual 5x7 camera set up to use infrared film. With it, Eggleston could shoot in virtual darkness in the juke joints and clubs around Memphis. Almost all of these pictures are of people who were unaware that he was photographing them. Eggleston's camera, which he would rest on a table, looked like just a plain rectangular box. The portraits are offhand and spontaneous but insistently stark; their brutality is heightened by the absence of color.

For his Memphis bungalows, ca. 1969, Eggleston sought out houses that resembled one another as much as possible, then shot them head-on with a 35 mm Leica. He made over one hundred of these pictures and used to carry them around bundled up like stacks of money in a large black photographer's-equipment case. I remember his bringing them to the home of a mutual friend, the artist William Christenberry, in Washington, D.C., where he kept me up most of the night inspecting them. As soon as I thought I'd exhausted all there was to see in one image, he'd point out something new.

The night portraits and the bungalows share a commitment to portraiture. The bungalows, with their curiously anthropomorphic quality, look like passport shots of one person after another. The portraits also have a leveling effect—whether biker or debutante, the people Eggleston photographed are clearly denizens of the same realm. But if the similarity between the subjects in each series is immediately apparent, it's the distinguishing details that linger, as if Eggleston is reminding us: look closely, each of these individuals is subtly different.

WALTER HOPPS

Phone Calls

ROBERTO BOLAÑO

B is in love with X. It is, of course, an ill-fated love. B, at one time in his life, was prepared to do anything for X, more or less what everyone in love thinks and says. X breaks up with him. X breaks up with him over the phone. At first, of course, B is in anguish. But eventually, as is usually the case, he gets over it. The years pass.

One night, when B has nothing to do, he manages, after making two phone calls, to get in touch with X. Neither of the two is young and this can be heard in their voices that cross Spain from one end to the other. Their friendship is reborn and a few days later they decide to meet again. Both carry the baggage of divorce, new illnesses, frustrations. When B takes the train heading for X's city, he is still not in love. They spend the first day holed up in X's house, talking about their lives. (Actually, it is X who speaks; B listens and asks a question now and then.) At night X invites him to share her bed. Deep down, B has no desire to sleep with X, but he accepts. When he wakes in the morning, B is again in love. But is he in love with X or is he in love with the idea of being in love? The relationship is problematic and intense: X borders on suicide from day to day, is in psychiatric treatment—pills, lots of pills, which nevertheless do nothing to help her. She cries often and without any apparent reason. So B takes care of X. He cares for her tenderly, diligently, but also awkwardly. His ministerings imitate those of a person truly in love. B realizes this right away. He tries to lift her out of her depression but only succeeds in leading X down a dead-end street or one X judges to be a dead end. At times, when he is alone or when he is watching X sleep, B also believes the street to be a dead end. He tries to recall his lost loves as a kind of antidote; he tries to convince himself that he can live without X, that he can save himself on his own. One night X asks him to leave and B catches the train and leaves the city. X goes to the station to see him off. Their farewell is affectionate and desperate. B travels in a sleeping car but is unable to fall asleep until very late. When at last he goes to sleep, he dreams of a monkey made of snow walking through the desert. The path of the monkey is bordered off, leading most likely to failure. But the monkey prefers to ignore that and its cunning turns into its will: it walks by night when the frozen stars sweep the desert. When he wakes up (now in the Estación de Sants in Barcelona), B believes he understands the meaning of his dream (if it had one) and is able to make his way somewhat consoled. That night he calls X and tells her his dream. X says nothing. The next day he calls X again. And the next. X's attitude is getting cooler and cooler, as if with each call B were receding in time. I am disappearing, B thinks. She is erasing me and knows what she's doing and why. One night B threatens X that he will take the train and be standing on her doorstep the next day. Wipe that thought from your mind, X says. I am going to come, says B. I can't stand these phone calls any longer, I want to see your face when I talk to you. I won't open the door for you, X says, and then hangs up. B doesn't understand a thing. For a long time he thinks, How can a human being possibly go from one extreme to another in her feeling, her desires? Then he gets drunk and seeks comfort in a book. The days pass.

One night, a year and a half later, B calls X on the phone. It takes X a while to recognize his voice. Oh, it's you, she says. The coldness in X's voice is enough to put his hair on end. Nevertheless, B senses that X wishes to tell him something. She's listening to me as if no time had passed, he thinks, as if we had spoken yesterday. How are you? B says. Tell me something, says B. X answers with monosyllables and after a while, hangs up. Bewildered, B dials X's number again. When they are connected, however, B prefers to remain silent. At the other end, X's voice says: Hello, who is it? Silence. Then she says, hello, and is quiet. Time—the time that separated B from X and that B was unable to comprehend—passes through the telephone line, is compressed and stretched, reveals an aspect of its nature. B, without realizing it, has begun to cry. He knows that X knows who is calling her. Then, silently, he hangs up.

Up to this point it is a familiar story—sad but familiar. B understands he must never call X again. One day he hears a knock at the door and standing there are A and Z. They are policemen and wish to question him. B asks what the reason is. A is reluctant to tell him. Z, after awkwardly beating around the bush, explains. Three days ago, at the other end of Spain, someone has murdered X. Initially B collapses, then he realizes that he is one of the suspects and his survival instinct puts him on guard. The police ask him about two days in particular. B doesn't remember what he has done, whom he has seen during those two days. He does know—how couldn't he—that he hasn't left Barcelona, that in fact he hasn't left his neighborhood and his house, but he can't prove it. The police take him away. B spends the night at the police station. At one point in the questioning he believes they are going to transfer him to X's city and he finds the possibility strangely seductive, but in the end that does not happen. They take his fingerprints and request his permission to do a blood analysis. B agrees. The following morning they let him go home. Officially, B has not been arrested, he has only agreed to work with the police to clear up this murder. When he gets home, B gets into bed and immediately falls asleep. He dreams of a desert, of X's face. Just before he wakes up he understands that they are one and the same. It is not hard for him to conclude that he is lost in the desert.

That night he throws some clothing in a travel bag and heads for the station, where he takes a train whose final destination is X's city. During the course of the trip, which takes the whole night, from one end of Spain to the other, he is unable to sleep and spends the time thinking of all that he could have done and didn't, of everything he could have given X and hadn't. He also thinks: If I were the dead X, I wouldn't have taken this trip in the other direction. And he thinks: That's precisely why I am the one who's alive. During the sleepless trip, he contemplates X as she actually was for the first time, he once again feels love for X and scorn for himself, almost unwillingly, for the last time. When he arrives, quite early, he goes straight to X's brother's house. X's brother is surprised and confused, but nevertheless invites him in, offers him a cup of coffee. He has just washed his face and is half dressed. He hasn't showered, B notices. He's only washed his face and splashed some water on his hair. B accepts his offer of coffee, then says that he just found out about the murder of X, that the police have questioned him, that he should explain to him what happened. It's awfully sad, says X's brother as he makes the coffee in the kitchen, but I don't see what you have to do with all of it. The police think I could be the murderer, says B. X's brother laughs. You always had bad luck, he says. It's funny he should say that, B thinks, when I am the one who's alive. But he is also grateful that X's brother doesn't doubt his innocence. Then X's brother goes off to work and B remains in his house. A while later, exhausted, he falls into a deep sleep. X, as one would expect, appears in his dream.

When he wakes up he thinks he knows who the murderer is. He has seen his face. That night he goes out with X's brother. They go to bars and speak of trivial things and no matter how hard they try to get drunk, they fail. As they walk down the empty streets heading home, B tells him that once he called X and didn't speak. Son of a bitch, says X's brother. I only did it once, says B, but then I understood that X was getting these kinds of calls. And she thought it was me. Follow me? says B. The murderer is the anonymous phone caller? asks X's brother. Exactly, says B. And X thought that it was me. X's brother frowns. I think, he says, that the murderer was one of her ex-lovers. My sister had many suitors. B chooses not to respond (X's brother, it seems, hasn't understood a thing), and they are both silent until they get home.

In the elevator B feels like he is going to throw up. He says, I am going to throw up. Hold on, says X's brother. Then they quickly walk down the hallway, X's brother opens the door and B takes off like a shot for the bathroom. But when he gets there he no longer feels like throwing up. He is sweating and his stomach aches but he can't throw up. The toilet bowl, with the lid up, looks to him like a mouth full of gums laughing at him. After washing his face he looks at himself in the mirror: his face is white as a sheet. He can barely sleep the rest of the night and passes the time trying to read and listening to X's brother snoring. The next day they say good-bye and B returns to Barcelona. I will never visit this city again, he thinks, for X is no longer here.

A week later X's brother calls him to say that the police have caught the murderer. The guy had been harassing X, the brother says, with anonymous phone calls. B doesn't answer. An old lover, X's brother says. I'm happy to hear it, says B. Thanks for calling me. Then X's brother hangs up and B is alone.

Translated from the Spanish by Mark Schafer

From Grand Street 68,
in memory of Roberto Bolaño, 1953–2003

CYNTHIA CRUZ

The Kingdom

We three girls in the Kingdom at the end
Of an endless table, grasping our hands out to
Mother. Exquisite in her mandarin coat and lace-
Stitched satin pajamas. Every afternoon,
And a myriad of allergy tests.
Seaweed green glass bottles and
The poking of needles up and down our backs.

Nepenthe

In mother's sable, I've been
Waiting in your old room, in that
Collapse, the mishap that was
Your boyhood with its lit-globes.

Handsome in your blond suit,
Leaning against a wall of silk
Ribbons. A blur, your pale face, a saint's
Turning away from the light.

And the hush of dusk as it drops in the hills
Like the drug of sleep. How you consumed it:
Piloting against the fenced-in-night of it.
Then let it slip—milk bleeding from the stalk.

Goleta

Lady Murasaki was mother's mare and Flying
Cloud was father's, his favorite, a pale strawberry roan.
Little Fox was mine, upon whose back I broke
Loose those locked rooms, that
House. The Ranch. Goleta,
The impossible fire. A field, a World, a winter
Of singing that would not stop. At night,
Even now, I can hear the sound
Of great flocks passing overhead.

Little Fox in Ghostweed

Little Fox was mine, a dappled gray pony I raced
One morning among the sweep of steeple and
bindweed,

Then crashed. Fox's mouth split and
Hoof crushed against stone.

Rocking in the ghostweed so as not to start
The weeping.

The Report on Horses II

Then, the final season of my brother's last visit.
His long dark hair in his face, and shirtsleeves
Concealing his thin white arms. Like a girl, he was always
Trading in what little he owned
Of his life. Already he was
Too fragile for this world.

In my mind I have been hiding
Among the ruinous thistle of last winter:
Fox, my girlhood horse, wasting away in the barn,
Her weak limbs at rest along the tremendous dark
Of her body.

ISAMU NOGUCHI

UNITING TRADITION & MODERNITY:
A POSTWAR PHOTOGRAPHIC JOURNEY

On May 2, 1950, the sculptor Isamu Noguchi arrived in Tokyo on the final leg of an eighteen-month journey. His faith in the meaning of art had been shaken by World War II, and he was seeking a new role for sculpture in the nuclear age. "If the world would postpone blowing itself up," he wrote years later, "I wanted to find out what sculpture had once been, and to what purpose, to what end it might aspire in a world in flux." His travels, sponsored by the Jungian-oriented Bollingen Foundation, had taken him from his Greenwich Village studio to the megaliths of Brittany, the ruins of Italy, Greece, and Egypt, and farther east to India, Sri Lanka, Indonesia, and Southeast Asia. He ended his journey of spiritual regeneration in Japan, where he had spent his childhood but to which he had not returned since 1930. In Tokyo, Noguchi was welcomed as an emissary of the international avant-garde by a delegation of Japanese artists, among them Kenzo Tange, an architect and assistant professor at Tokyo University. Nine years Noguchi's junior, Tange had recently been selected as the chief architect for Hiroshima's Peace City, a commission that would become the symbol of postwar reconstruction in Japan.

At Tange's invitation, Noguchi designed three projects for Hiroshima between 1950 and 1952: two maquettes for a bell tower; the railings for the east and west bridges on either side of the planned hundred-meter-long Peace Boulevard, linking the city to the park; and a cenotaph in memory of Hiroshima's dead. Only the bridge railings would be realized. They were designed and built within a year, while Tange's centerpiece, the Peace Memorial Museum—a rectangular box perched on *pilotis*—struggled for funding and remained under construction for years. Noguchi's cenotaph—a thick black granite parabola that would have enclosed a subterranean core with the names of the dead—was rejected by the committee that oversaw the project, and Tange was asked to produce a replacement: a simple arch on axis with what would come to be known as the Atomic Dome, the ruins of an exposition hall left standing after the bombing. As Tange explained to Noguchi, his nationality was the problem: although his father was a celebrated Japanese poet, his mother was American. Noguchi—the quintessential cosmopolitan—was tainted by his blood. The

Yuku (To depart), West Bridge railing, designed by Isamu Noguchi, Hiroshima, ca. 1952–53. Peace Memorial Museum, designed by Kenzo Tange, under construction in background.

shining augur of modernity had come to represent modernization's alien face—the *locus genus* of overwhelming destruction.

The East-West problem, constantly internalized by Noguchi and embodied in his work for Hiroshima, tends to be configured historically on the one hand as an encounter between the forces of conservative tradition and reactionary nativism, and on the other hand the impulse of progressive modernity and globalism. However, it is no coincidence that Noguchi's initial involvement with Hiroshima took place during the American occupation, or that the rejection of his cenotaph occurred in 1952, as the occupation was drawing to a close and the protocols of the East-West paradigm were becoming oppressive. In May 1956—the year Tange's Peace Museum was finally completed—a dialogue was published between Noguchi and Tange that reveals the already altered perspectives on this opposition. Two groups of photographs taken by Noguchi during his recent travels in India provided the point of departure for their discussion: a rural village in northern India and Chandigarh, the Punjabi capital built from scratch in the 1950s from the designs of modernist architects Le Corbusier and Pierre Jeanneret and their team (which included Maxwell Fry and Jane Drew). The failure of modernity was unthinkable for Noguchi and Tange; still, looking at Chandigarh, they noted a catalog of faults. Tradition, represented by Noguchi's photographs of rural architecture in India, disputes modernity by transfiguring daily life. Many of his photographs show an architectonic order that sutures East and West, old and new, but other images emphasize the fragility of rural beauty, the abjection of poverty, and the disarray of daily life that resist transformation. The comments made by Noguchi and Tange in the course of this dialogue might be read as a set of questions that are still urgent: How do we face the past when history itself has become traumatic? How can we rebuild the world once we have shattered it?

NEIL PRINTZ

Secretariat, designed by Le Corbusier, under construction. Chandigarh, Punjab, India, ca. 1953.

NOGUCHI: People say that there are great temples in India, but no architecture. Most visitors, though, only see India's big cities. . . . On my recent trip, I went to a small village called Khajuraho, and it was there that I suddenly realized the beauty of Indian architecture: it is closely associated with people's lives. In a typical house, you enter a huge dark room with almost no windows. Glass is scarce and making windows is difficult, so the room stays dark and is used mostly for sleeping. People spend their time outside, talking to each other or working together. They find pleasure and fulfillment in communal activity.

TANGE: In Japan, all the houses basically look alike, but the inhabitants of each house make it their own. Residents really develop their homes; they are not restricted by them. The effect is different from what happens when an architect designs specifically to a certain taste, in which case each house is unique from the outset. Often in modern architecture we analyze one type of lifestyle and draw up a plan to fulfill it. However, a person's way of life can change within an hour. These ordinary houses, though they look alike, retain that kind of freedom.

When Le Corbusier and Jeanneret planned new architecture in India, they considered harmony more than any other architects had before then. But that alone can't make up for tradition, for the gradual impact over the years of ordinary people living their lives in a house. One single architect can't accomplish that. I believe that a long tradition supports the beauty of accident.

NOGUCHI: In the village I visited, the courtyards were covered with a beautiful geometric pattern, made out of cattle dung, that is reminiscent of tatami mats [see pp. 43 and 48]. Everyone who lives there knows the technique to fix broken sections and create new designs. When I arrived, people welcomed me into the courtyard and asked me to take off my shoes to avoid spoiling the pattern. If even a little part of it got wet, it would be damaged.

PP. 43 AND 48 (TOP AND BOTTOM): Rural village, probably near Imphal, Manipur, India, ca. 1956.

ABOVE: Minister's house designed by Pierre Jeanneret. Chandigarh, Punjab, India, ca. 1956.

LEFT: Rural village, probably near Imphal, Manipur, India, ca. 1956.

NOGUCHI: Le Corbusier designed the wall patterns for one of his buildings in Chandigarh out of unevenly placed bricks, thinking that the shade would protect residents from the heat. Europeans have the impression of India as being an incredibly hot country, based on what they see in photographs. Indians don't necessarily share that impression. Le Corbusier also made the streets wider for better ventilation. But from the Indian point of view, a wider street would just make its inhabitants feel lonesome, since each house would become more distant from the others.

Visiting new apartment developments in Delhi or Chandigarh, you find people sitting around outdoors, using sewing machines on the street, because they can't adapt to these city neighborhoods. I think modern architects who design residential houses should pay more attention to the lifestyles of the people for whom they're building.

TANGE: When I look at an Indian farmhouse or private house, I find something that we lack in Japan. Japanese architecture's connection with nature is often praised, but its dependence on nature lacks the strong human desire for definition of our own space, separate from nature. When I see buildings like the ones you photographed in India and notice the way the wall cuts off the interior from the exterior, I realize that the space is annexed from nature. In general, Japanese architects don't show that kind of will to overcome nature. . . . Private homes in Europe, India, and China take an oppositional stance. They fear nature, but they fight it all the same. We need to learn more about that attitude.

High Court, designed by Le Corbusier, Chandigarh, Punjab, India, ca. 1956.

All photographs by Isamu Noguchi.

from The Yellow Rain

JULIO LLAMAZARES

Like sand, the silence will bury my eyes. Like sand that the wind will no longer be able to scatter.

Like sand, the silence will bury the houses. Like sand, the houses will crumble. I can hear them moaning. Solitary. Somber. Smothered by the wind and the vegetation.

They will all fall little by little, in no particular order, without hope, dragging the others with them as they fall. Some will collapse only very slowly beneath the weight of moss and solitude. Others will collapse suddenly, violently, clumsily, like animals brought down by the bullets of a patient, inexorable hunter. But all of them, sooner or later, some resisting longer than others, will, in the end, restore to the earth what has always belonged to the earth, what the earth has been waiting for since the first inhabitant of Ainielle first stole it.

This house will probably be among the first to fall (possibly with me still inside it). Now that Chano's and Lauro's houses are gone, now that the walls and all memory of Juan Francisco's and Acín's have been overwhelmed by scrub and bushes, mine is now one of the oldest of those still standing. But who knows? It may well resist. It may well follow my example and hang on to the bitter end, desperately and tenaciously, watching as it grows more alone with each day that passes, watching the other houses gradually abandoning it as my neighbors abandoned me. It might even be that, one day, years from now, Andrés will come back to show Ainielle to his family, in time to see his house still standing as a memento of his parents' struggle and as silent testimony to his neglect.

But that's very unlikely. If Andrés does come back, he will probably find only a pile of rubble and a mountain of scrub. If he does come back, he will find the roads blocked by brambles, the irrigation channels choked, the shepherds' huts and the houses fallen. Nothing will remain of what was once his. Not even the old alleys. Not even the vegetable plots planted by the river. Not even the house in which he was born, while snow covered the rooftops and the wind whipped along the streets and roads. But the snow will not be the cause of the desolation that Andrés will find that day. He will search among the brambles and the rotten beams. He will rummage in the rubble of the former walls and will find perhaps the odd broken chair or the slates that clad the old fireplace where he so often sat at night as a child. But that will be all. No forgotten portrait. No sign of life. When Andrés comes back to Ainielle, it will be to discover that all is lost.

When Andrés comes back to Ainielle—if he ever does—many others will have done the same. From Berbusa, from Espierre, from Oliván, from Susín. The shepherds from Yésero. The gypsies from Biescas. Its former inhabitants. They will all gather like vultures after my death, in order to carry off what remains of this village in which I leave my life. They will break the bolts, kick down the doors. They will ransack the houses and the shepherds' huts, one by one. Wardrobes, beds, trunks, tables, clothes, tools, implements, kitchen pots and pans. Everything that, over the centuries, we, the inhabitants of Ainielle, so painstakingly gathered together will end up in other places, other houses, perhaps in some shop in Huesca or Zaragoza. That was what happened in Basarán and in Cillas. And in Casbas. And in Otal. And in Escartín. And in Bergua. The same will soon happen in Yésero and Berbusa too.

As long as I have been here, no one has had the courage to come to Ainielle to take away the things left behind by the other inhabitants. After what happened with Aurelio, no one even dared to cross the frontier that they knew existed between them and me. I occasionally saw someone prowling the roads or watching the village from afar, from among the trees, but they all fled as soon as they saw me. They were probably afraid that one day I might carry out the threat I made to Aurelio outside his own house.

What they did not know—and will never know—is that I too felt afraid when I saw them. But not of them. Nor of their shotguns. I was afraid of myself. Afraid of not knowing exactly what my reaction would be if one day I came face to face with one of them in the hills. What I had said to Aurelio had been a warning, pure and simple, a threat made with the sole intention of frightening him so that no one else would come bothering me again. I never thought that I might actually have to carry it out. I did not even consider—not then at least—whether I would be capable of shooting him in cold blood if he did come back one day. That is why, whenever I saw someone prowling the roads or watching the village from the hills, I felt afraid of myself—afraid of my shotgun and of my blood—and I would hide.

But I will not be alive much longer. In a few minutes' time, or a few hours perhaps—before dawn at any rate—I will be sitting with the other dead around the fire, and Ainielle will be left completely empty and defenseless, at the mercy of the eyes that are watching it now. Perhaps they will wait a while yet before approaching. Perhaps they will wait to make sure that I really am dead and won't suddenly appear with my shotgun to greet them. But as soon as the people in Berbusa find out, the day after my body lies at last beneath the earth, all of them, beginning perhaps with the people from Berbusa themselves, will fall like wild beasts on the defenseless stones of this village which, very soon, will die with me. And so, on the day that Andrés comes back, he will find nothing but a pile of rubble and a mountain of scrub.

But perhaps Andrés never will come back. Perhaps time will pass, relentless and slow, and Andrés will still remember what I said to him the night before he left. Perhaps that would be for the best. Perhaps I should have written to him this morning—and left the letter on the bedside table for the men from Berbusa to find—and reminded him once more of what I said: Never come back. That, at least, would spare him the sorrow of seeing his village in ruins and his house buried beneath moss, just like his parents.

But it's too late for that now. It's too late even to think about what might have become of this village, what might have become of this house and of myself if, instead of leaving, Andrés had decided to stay here with me and his mother. It's too late for everything. The rain is erasing the moon from my eyes, and, in the silence of the night, I can hear already a distant, desolate, vegetable murmur, like the murmur of nettles rotting in the river of my blood. It is the green murmur of approaching death. The same murmur I heard in the rooms of my daughter and my parents. The one that ferments in graves and in forgotten photographs. The only sound that will continue to exist in Ainielle when there is no longer anyone to hear it. It will grow with the night, just as the trees do. It will rot in the rain and in the March sun. It will invade the corridors and rooms of the houses while they fall, while the solitude and the nettles slowly erase all trace of their walls, their sunken roofs, and the distant memory of those who built them and lived in them. But no one will hear it. Not even the snakes. Not even the birds. No one will stop to listen—as I am listening now—to that green lament of stone and blood when vegetation and the cold of death invade them. And one day, in years to come, perhaps some traveler will pass by these houses and never even know that once there was a village here.

Only if Andrés comes back, only if one day he forgets my old threat or if his own old age finally awakens in him some compassion and nostalgia, will he search among the stones for the remains of this house, track through the grass for the memory of his parents and, who knows, perhaps find among the brambles a stone with my name carved on it and the shape of the grave in which, very soon, I will lie sleeping, waiting for him.

Translated from the Spanish by Margaret Jull Costa

ARTHUR BISPO DO ROSÁRIO

ABOVE: Arthur Bispo do Rosário wearing
Manto da apresentação (Presentation mantle), 1984.

RIGHT: Abatjur (Lamp), n.d.

ROSANGELA MARIA

SERGIPE
PERNAMBUCO
BAHIA
GUANABARA
PARAHIBA
RIO GRANDE DO NORTE
PIAUI
PARA
AMAZONIA
CEDONIA
MAJESTADE
SUA ALTEZA REALFILHA
ESCOLA APREDIZES MARIN
HEIROS
CUJO
ALIJÔ
LEADER
MIMOSO
ENTRE NAVIOS E ESTABELECIMENTO
SAHIR DA ILHA PAQUETA 25 M
VILLEGAIGNON

ABOVE: *434 como é que eu devo fazer um muro* (434 How should I make a wall), n.d.

LEFT: *Navios de guerra* (War ships), n.d.

ABOVE: *A 57 arraia* (The 57 ray), 1972.

LEFT: *Planeta paraizo dos homens* (Planet paradise of men), n.d.

ABOVE: *Dicionário de nomes—Letra A-I* (Dictionary of names—Letter A-I), n.d.

RIGHT: *Onze cetros* (Eleven scepters), n.d.

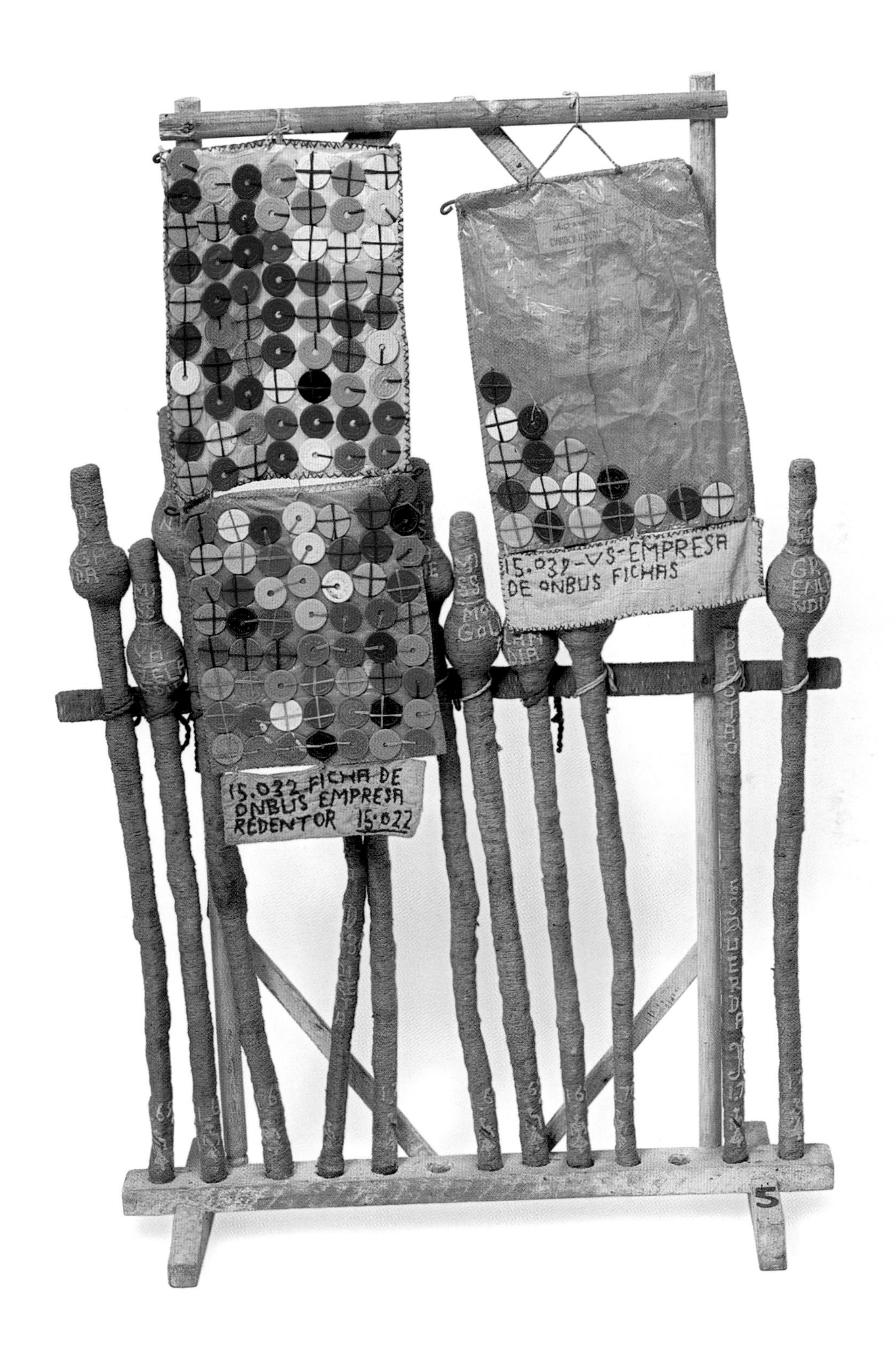
15.022 FICHA DE
ONBUS EMPRESA
REDENTOR 15.022
VS-EMPRESA
DE ONBUS FICHAS
5

Arthur Bispo do Rosário in blue jacket with two assemblages, 1984. Left: *Bolsa vermelha—Farmácia da praça* (Red purse—Drugstore on the square), n.d. Center (blue jacket): *Sembrantes—Eu vim 22.12.1938 meia noite* (Faces—I came 22.12.1938 at midnight), n.d. Right: *Garrafa térmica* (Thermos bottle), n.d.

Arthur Bispo do Rosário

Brazilian artist Arthur Bispo do Rosário, now known simply as Bispo ("bishop" in Portuguese), was born in 1911 in the northeastern state of Sergipe. He served in the Brazilian navy, and after being discharged in 1933 he worked in a variety of occupations: electric company employee, housekeeper, doorman. Five years later, after two days of delirium in the streets of Rio de Janeiro, he was arrested and committed to a psychiatric hospital. In 1939, Bispo was transferred to the Colônia Juliano Moreira, a poor state-run asylum in Rio, where he was diagnosed as a paranoid schizophrenic. He would spend the next fifty years there making artworks with whatever material he could gather.

Recognition arrived a few months after Bispo's death in 1989, when a major exhibition of his work opened in Rio's Escola de Artes Visuais do Parque Lage to critical acclaim. Since then, Bispo's works have appeared in several major shows, including the 1995 Venice Biennale. Almost all of his work, which belongs to the Brazilian Ministry of Health, is kept at Rio's Museu Bispo do Rosário. The collection includes mummified objects, banners with embroidered texts, drawings, assemblages, wood constructions, and found objects. The materials Bispo used were valuable goods in his milieu: cups, sneakers, plastic bottles, cutlery. His signature material, which he used to wrap objects and to embroider, is the blue thread that he unwove from his asylum uniform. There is a striking similarity between some of Bispo's work and that of Marcel Duchamp, On Kawara and other Conceptual artists, and French sculptor Arman and the Nouveau Réalistes. What is perhaps more significant is how influential Bispo's work has been on contemporary Brazilian art, from the work of young artists such as Sandra Cinto and Marepe to that of veteran Nelson Leirner and cult figure Leonilson.

The title of Bispo's 1989 exhibition, "*Registros de minha passagem pela terra*" (Records of my passage on earth), points to his rigorous conceptual spirit. Bispo did not call the objects he made art. He claimed that a voice once told him, "It is time for you to reconstruct the world," and his works are records of that comprehensive project of reconstruction. His banners catalog words and stories gathered either from his own environment (the names of people he'd met that began with the letter A, for example) or from the outside world (countries and their flags, governors, presidents). One senses a full-blown "archive fever" in Derrida's terms, the development of a radical encyclopedic task that perhaps only a visionary could fully realize.

ADRIANO PEDROSA

Franco-Ethiopian Railway,
Gota, Ethiopia, ca. 1950s.

Conte de fer

ABDOURAHMAN A. WABERI

The sea is a savanna of water.

—Tchicaya U Tam'si

Ultimately it will stretch across 784 kilometers. It will pass through deserts, plains, savannas, and high plateaus. A condensation of history. It will span a great distance. Two parallel lines of blood will link two countries and a thousand different landscapes. A difficult gestation: it will take twenty years to be of use. It will come into being one day in 1897—at first on finely ruled graph paper. It will destroy those whom modernity has trampled. It will leave the land of thirst. It will climb, climb, climb all the way to an altitude of 2,350 meters. It will climb from the flat, blue-tinted sea to the foothills overrun by the dark green of the eucalyptus:

> It will cross the land of reality.
> It will cross the land of dreams.

It made history from the outset, piled up dates and deeds of arms, accumulated successes and failures. It built a castle in the mind, a palace of memory where every clan, every person involved—from French engineers to Swiss designers, Afar sultans, Somali workers, and Abyssinian soldiers—comes to shop at the self-service souvenir stand. Statistics were on its side, irrefutable numbers, as solid as the steel that built it: 784 kilometers in length, 2,350 meters in altitude, 1,355 bridges, 31 tunnels, 1 bankruptcy, a capital investment of several hundred million. How many human lives lost? Nobody counted.

It will bear the label "Designed and built by French ingenuity." People will examine it, photograph it, ask its advice about the psychology of the natives, about the ultimate effects of the trampoline of history: Adwa,* "pacification," the thousand and one conquests of the Abyssinian ogre, and so on.

* Historic defeat of the Italians by the Abyssinian emperor Menilik II.

Big brothers will be found for it, rich uncles brought direct from the American frontier and the Far West:

> It will cross the land of reality.
> It will cross the land of dreams.

It sprang into being one day in 1897. It terrorized more than one nomad, though they are not easily impressed. The two rails traced out a Dantean circle. It wounded the land of reality. Just one example: at the place known as *Jab Issa*,* warriors of the Issa tribe massacred railway workers who insisted that the monster's perfidious rails must pass through the sanctuary of a venerated ancestor. The vengeance exacted by colonial troops lived up to their reputation. Three years passed before work could be resumed.

* Defeat of the Issas.

It will span wadis. It will tunnel into the flanks of burnt mountains. It will count the stones that crackle under the halo of a fulminating sun. Tumefaction. It will eat the heart of the region of creation's fourth day. Putrefaction. The Issas, stunned, will end up on their asses in the dust. Then they will lift up their heads: *Ciisow Sarakaa! Ciisow Sarakaa!** They will rouse their scattered brothers and launch attacks and raids. The monster will be vanquished for a while. A sign will caution: "Work halted." The natives will prove to be tough. The sun will shit on the comatose monster's organs of steel.

* "Issas arise! Issas arise!"

At a snail's pace the work will resume. Campfires will be rekindled. The solar orb will be replaced by a small, apologetic virgin moon. The natives will grow discouraged. Their caravans will frown on their competitor, the noisy, lurching metal monster. People will pray to God in all the languages of the land. Meanwhile, Ilg and Chefneux, the project's Swiss designers, will rejoice. It will move forward. Paris will look on with a covetous eye. People will be surprised by the duration of the lull. Pacification will have taught the outlaws a lesson. Nomads who cooperate will be given sacks full of dates.

It will cross the land of reality.
It will cross the land of dreams.

It marked space. It pared away the earth. It branded men. It stamped their tongues. Small towns flourished along its path as if greeting it ceremoniously.

The white man's interpreter said:

"Venerable assembly, the white man wishes you no harm. He wants only a corridor through your territory, just wide enough to lay down two iron rails."

The assembly said nothing. The interpreter spread his legs and said:

"The white man wants only this narrow space between my legs."

The assembly was plunged into confusion. Half of them acknowledged the insignificance of the request. The other half remained suspicious, ready to take up arms.

The value of the promise was dwarfed by the engine's speed. Spores of doubt found receptive hearts in the surrounding countryside. The rapacious realism of the railway company triumphed. Distress among the elderly natives increased as the years went by:

It crossed the sun-bronzed land.
It crossed the haggard land.

It will advance steadily. It will leave the tiny French colony on the shores of the Red Sea. The dynamite used to blast tunnels will trigger earthquakes: the earth will resist in the land of the Rift. The Meharis will ridicule the multi-jointed monster. It will advance steadily. It will stall in the little plain of Galilee. It will leave Aicha. It will encounter blazing emptiness at the entry to the great plain of Hadagalla. It will emerge near nests of termites.

The few remaining adversaries had yet to speak their final word. Men crawling on their stomachs and clenching daggers in their teeth attacked the camps. White engineers met with death by cold steel. Menilik, emperor of Ethiopia, was displeased. His punitive expeditions showed no mercy. The corruption of decadence was in the air, as if the world were about to end. Thus . . .

> It crossed the sun-bronzed land.
> It crossed the haggard land.

It will leave the desert. It will leave the savanna. The landscape will exchange its ochres for a palette of greens. It will build the greatest city of the region: Dire Diwa in the narrow pass between two mountains. The sky will darken. Thick clouds will shroud it in shadow. Rain will fall as usual: a tropical rain, short and violent. It will pause to catch its breath, to regain its strength. The workers will stock up on fresh supplies.

It trembled at the sight of the first river: the Awash. It labored near the town of Awash; the soil is volcanic basalt, the population Afar, Issa, or Orgabo. It suffered martyrdom. People sabotaged its wheels. The sun sniggered by day, and hyenas threatened after nightfall. It was looted. They almost finished it off.

> It crossed the burning land.
> It crossed the hemmed-in land.

Drumrolls: it will reach the aptly named city of Nazareth. It will plow through the sinuous flanks of the mountains of the Shoa. Menilik will rejoice. Paris will sigh. Addis Ababa, the new flower of the ever-conquering Abyssinian Empire, will smile upon it. Addis Ababa, the gleaming capital, will allow the workers' sweat to flow freely. A small white moon will open the festivities. A day without parallel: champagne, palm wine, Abyssinian mead, soda for the austere Muslims. Cannon fire from the garrison at Entoto. The line will open on June 2, 1917. Long live the Franco-Ethiopian Railway Company!

It transformed the notion of time and space, the meaning of history. It imposed itself on the natives. They called it *firhoun* and *Ibliss*.* Unable to ignore it, they adopted it—with words of their own:

* Names of the devil.

The moving steel (the train);
The supporting iron (the rails);
And what goes with them (the telegraph poles):
What are these metals
That invade the land?
It spits, it moans, and it stinks.
But with it you burn up miles.
Here in the morning, far away by night,
Encamped with your clan at milking time,
To share with them the still frothy milk.*

* This Bedouin song, as well as the foundation for this tale, is taken from reports by Djiboutian journalist Ali Moussa Iye, "Le djibouto-éthiopien ou l'épopée du Far East," *Autrement* 21, January 1987.

Translated from the French by Arthur Goldhammer

The title "Conte de fer," literally "Tale of Iron" in English, evokes two alternate phrases: "conte de fées" (fairy tale) and "conte de faire" (story of the "making" of the railroad).

MARJETICA POTRČ

NORTH AMERICANS LIKE TO THINK OF THEIR HOMES IN GREEN ARCADIA: IT IS OPEN AND SHARED WITH OTHERS

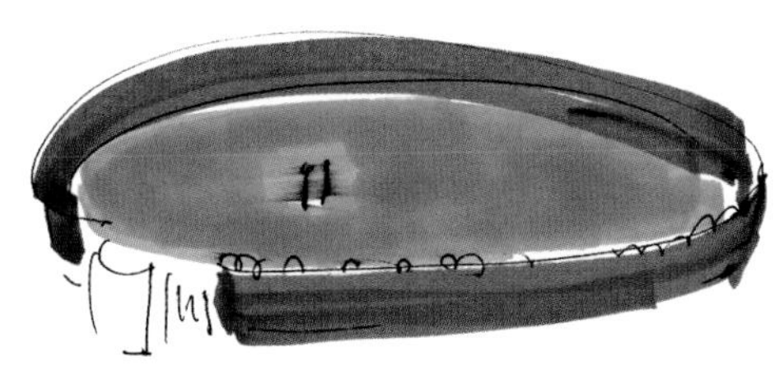

SOUTH AMERICANS LIKE TO ENCIRCLE THEIR TERRITORY FIRST

THE WALLED CITIES OF CARACAS

BARRIO: HAVING ONLY A FEW ENTRIES TO A BARRIO HELPS CONTROL THE TERRITORY

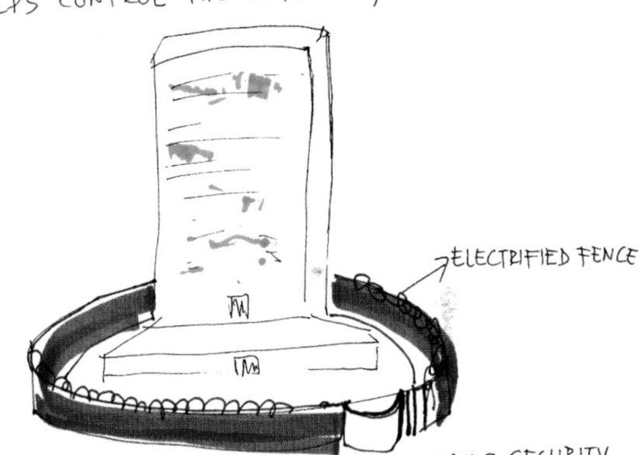

GATED COMMUNITIES OFFER THE MOST PRIVACY & SECURITY. THEY MAKE SURE THAT PRIVATE AND PUBLIC SPHERES ARE CLEARLY DIVIDED.

THE DIVIDED CITY BREEDS INVASIONS

HALF OF CARACAS' POPULATION LIVES IN BARRIOS, THE OTHER HALF IN THE FORMAL CITY. THE VERY EXISTENCE OF THE POPULATION AND ARCHITECTURE IN BOTH HALVES IS THREATENED BY VARIOUS INVASIONS.

CARACAS INVASION No 1:
BARRIOS ⟶ FORMAL CITY

ATTACK OF THE BARRIO INVADERS

CARACAS INVASION No 2:
RURAL ⟶ URBAN

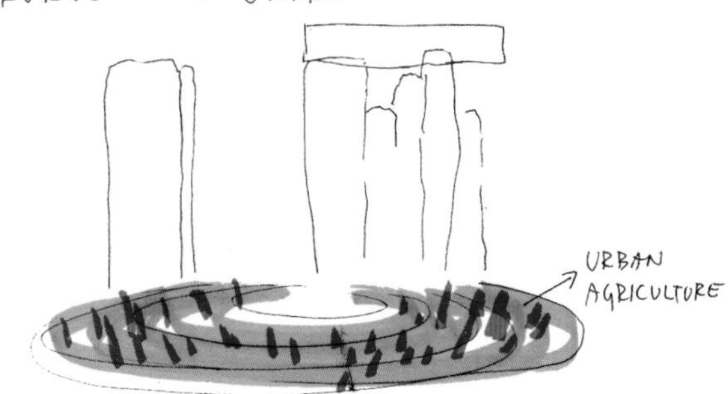

LETTUCE AND RED PEPPERS ARE PLANTED IN A PUBLIC PARK IN THE CITY CENTER.

WORKSHOPS ARE ORGANIZED TO TEACH RESIDENTS TO USE HYDROPONIC TECHNOLOGY TO GROW SMALL SCALE VEGETABLE GARDENS.

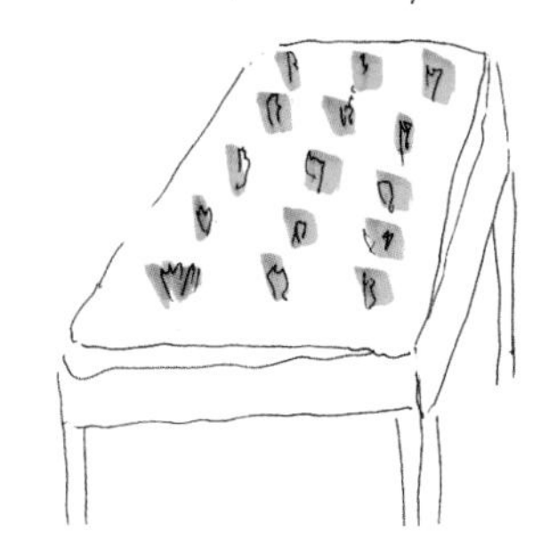

CARACAS INVASION No 3 = INVASIONS OF THE LAND

THE BARRIOS ARE OFTEN IN PHYSICAL DANGER FROM LAND INVADERS, SETTLERS WHO BUILD NEW STRUCTURES UP THE SLOPE AND DESTABILIZE ALREADY EXISTING STRUCTURES.

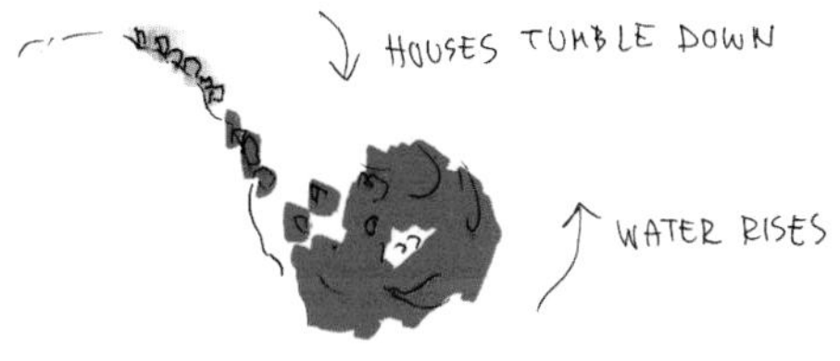

CONSTANT EXPANSION AND CONSTANT EROSION

URBAN NEGOTIATION IS CRUCIAL IN CARACAS, A CITY IN CONSTANT CRISIS AND WITHOUT MUCH HISTORY, WHERE THE SOCIAL STATE HAS NEVER REALLY MATERIALIZED.

IT SOUNDS LIKE A PERFECT CASE STUDY FOR TODAY'S METROPOLIS,
INSTABILITY MAKES YOU RELEVANT.

THE WEST BANK = NEGOTIATED TERRITORY

ZONES A, B, C

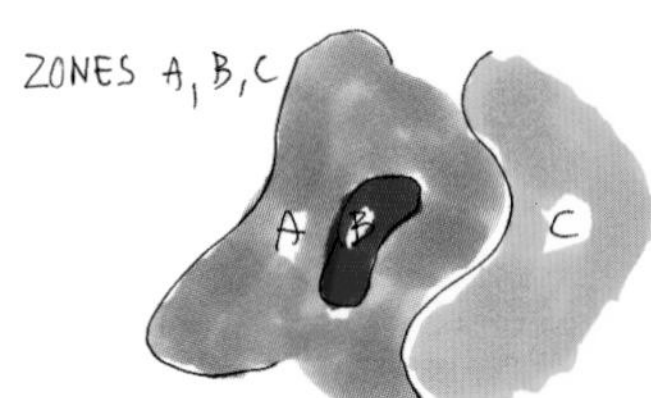

CONTROLLED BY
A - ISRAELIS WITH SOME PALESTINIAN PARTICIPATION
B - HALF·HALF
C - PALESTINIANS WITH SOME ISRAELI PARTICIPATION

ZONES CHANGE SHAPE ALL THE TIME

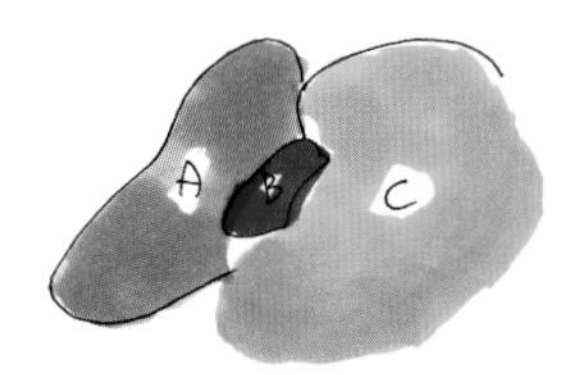

SPACE IS IN CONSTANT FLUX IN THE WEST BANK, SIMILAR TO WHAT ONE FEELS IN THE FAST GROWING CITIES OF LATIN AMERICA.

DIVISIONS BREED NEW FRAMES OF MIND

IN THE WEST BANK, YOU HAVE TWO ROAD SYSTEMS THAT RARELY INTERSECT
- ONE CONNECTING JEWISH SETTLEMENTS
- THE OTHER ONE CONNECTING PALESTINIAN TOWNS AND VILLAGES

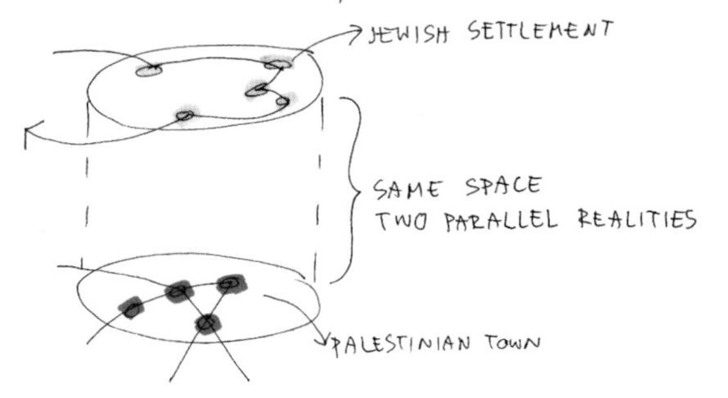

CARACAS' WALLS AND BORDERS ARE WITHIN US.

Marjetica Potrč

Slovenian artist Marjetica Potrč's medium is architecture—or perhaps more specifically, the sculptural representation of architecture as it relates to city planning. Much as Robert Smithson discovered found "monuments" in the industrial wastelands of his native New Jersey (leading to one of postmodernity's defining documents, his 1966 essay "Entropy and the New Monuments"), Potrč has located a model for contemporary urban survival by visiting the poorest neighborhoods ringing the world's city centers—the *favelas*, or slums, of Rio, for instance, and the townships of Johannesburg. While others see blight within these global growths of metastasizing shanties, Potrč finds creative potential. The artist is not a romantic, however; these neighborhoods do not signify some kind of post-apocalyptic Eden for her. Rather, she is a clear-eyed pragmatist who sees in the spontaneous generation of favela architecture the expressions of both sustainable environment and political self-determination.

These ideas are perhaps most evident in Potrč's "core building" pieces, like the one for which the Guggenheim Museum awarded her the 2000 Hugo Boss Prize. In these simple prototypes for contemporary dwellings, the most basic amenities—a roof over one's head, a line for water and another for waste—provide the infrastructure around which the favela or township inhabitant can improvise his or her own idea of home. It is interesting that Potrč includes a satellite dish as a core amenity, an acknowledgment, perhaps, that the unfixed and ever-changing nature of favela neighborhoods is itself a reflection of the nomadic streamings of the information age. In the works shown here, which debuted at the 2003 Venice Biennale, Potrč explores the parallels among various types of informal cities, from shantytowns in Caracas to gated communities in Houston, finding unexpected common ground between the architectures of poverty and exclusivity.

HOWARD HALLE

C70

Looting and Empire

CHARLES MEREWETHER

CASUALTIES OF WAR

The act of looting represents the unleashing of an anarchic energy that appears to defy all principles of civil order and rule of law, a spectacle of crowds mobilized into action. By the time the Allied forces had reached Baghdad this spring, everything appeared to be up for grabs, as if the advent of external invasion had unplugged a hitherto repressed desire for material and symbolic wealth. The U.S.-led invasion brought about a situation in which food, household appliances, and whatever objets d'art could be carried out from the vast palaces, state museums, and unprotected archaeological sites were all fair game. The only form of discrimination was an item's immediate value: was it an object of daily use or an investment to be traded in the marketplace? The impression given by the Western media was that, however illegal, the looting was evidence of the impoverishment and oppression of the Iraqi people.

Offices, hospitals, universities, and stores were all plundered, but it was the theft of art and antiquities that caused the most anxiety in the West: among the sites looted were the National Museum in Baghdad, the National Library and Archives, and the Awqaf Library, with large holdings of Islamic books and manuscripts, at the Ministry of Religious Affairs. There were doubtless other collections that we learned about too late. Robert Fisk reported in *The Independent* on April 15, 2003, that he had witnessed the vestiges of Iraq's written history, including the Ottoman records of the caliphate, in flames.

> Amid the ashes of Iraqi history, I found a file blowing in the wind outside: Pages of handwritten letters between the court of Sharif Hussein of Mecca, who started the Arab revolt against the Turks for Lawrence of Arabia, and the Ottoman rulers of Baghdad.

Stories and images recording these actions—which soon rivaled war coverage in the Western media—provoked an outcry from the art and archaeological community, for whom the looting represented both a failure on the part of the Allied powers to protect museums as well as they protected oil fields and a recurring pattern of destruction of cultural heritage by a booming illicit trade in antiquities. The identity of the looters was a source of debate: some accused an international trade ring that was poised to strike during civil disorder, while others pointed a finger at locals whose impoverishment had driven them to the extreme measure of plunder. And the extent of the looting itself came under question. At first the damage seemed immeasurable, but reports in later weeks suggested that the initial accounts of looting had been exaggerated and that much of the supposedly destroyed or stolen art had been safely stored away before the conflict reached Baghdad, presumably to be brought out again when order was restored. It was as if the specter of looting had overshadowed its actuality, enabling the West to view Iraqis as reduced to the basest of instincts with little regard for cultural property or moral values and therefore potentially in need of protection from both Saddam Hussein and from themselves.

This story is far from new. The spectacle of looting is a recurrent motif in narratives of empires and invasion, calling to mind Walter Benjamin's remark that the histories of civilization are also those of barbarism. A common reaction to such events is to suggest that someone step in to protect a nation's "heritage" from those who do not appreciate its unique value and history even though it may be their own. But to make that attempt is to raise a number of questions underlying the very idea of a national heritage, and the extent to which it can be represented by objects. It may be that the scene of looting is also the site of a struggle between different ethnic communities over what has been and has not been valued in the creation of national mythologies. In Iraq, for example, the dominant Ba'th Party has worked to shape a historical identity for the nation that reduces a multiethnic society of Arab and Islamic descent to a unified pan-Arab culture that nevertheless excludes minority groups such as the Kurds. The motivations for looting cannot be limited to criminal intent or economic gain. In fact, to offer only those motives would be to misread the issue as purely socio-economic as opposed to political and historical.

One of the underlying assumptions about Iraqi sites and antiquities has been that they represent the "birthplace" or "cradle" of Western civilization, and, as repositories of culture from the first great cities—Nineveh, Babylon, Ur—they hold special meaning for the West. The struggle over what matters as heritage in Iraq intensified during its colonial period, when the British began to conduct excavations and assemble collections that privileged a certain picture of Mesopotamian culture in the service of Britain's own narrative of progress. While this policy facilitated the acquisition of museums' worth of Mesopotamian antiquities outside of Iraq, it also contributed, not surprisingly, to the rise of a reactive nationalism within Iraq. Words like "cradle" or "birthplace" evoke abstract notions of a universal origin, but concepts of heritage and cultural property also relate to particular, lived experiences. These dual interests are perhaps most difficult to reconcile precisely when cultural property is introduced into the marketplace.

While a civilization may be measured by its acts of preservation, universal values should recognize the idea of cultural property. As the 1954 Hague Convention for the Protection of Cultural Property in the Event of Armed Conflict states, "damage to cultural property belonging to any people whatsoever means damage to the cultural heritage of all mankind." Yet as archaeologists and art historians weigh in as custodians of civilization, curiously, the fate of contemporary Iraqis recedes from view as if their lives bear little relation to this ancient world and its relics, with which they coexist. It is difficult to avoid the impression that the preserving of antiquities takes some priority over the protecting of human lives, precisely because those antiquities represent traces of our civilization that have been subsequently diverted or lost to us. When the future of these sites is in jeopardy, how important is it to maintain the geographical setting of the objects they bear? If they were to be removed, the result could be a deracination not only of cultural patrimony but equally of cultural memory that, embedded in those objects, may be vital to a society's well-being—especially one on the point of being rebuilt.

CLAIMING HERITAGE

In the past fifty years, the question of looting has been framed primarily within legal terms of property and heritage claims. This has taken the form of a series of international, national, and state conventions established to outlaw looting and regulate the trade of stolen property, including the Hague Convention of 1954 and the 1970 UNESCO Convention on the Means of Prohibiting and Preventing the Illicit Import, Export and Transfer of Ownership of Cultural Property, to name two of the most significant.[1] At the same time, a host of organizations emerged to monitor and implement these treaties. Their achievements, however, are shadowed by the dismal picture they provide of the extent of illicit trade worldwide. The Art Loss Register, for example, currently lists more than one hundred thousand missing or stolen artworks, including both "spoils of war" removed from museums or other cultural repositories and items that have been looted from sites. While this subject has received most attention in relation to cultural property displaced during World War II, it has also led to a more general inquiry into museum acquisition practices and the need for a paper trail of provenance to show evidence of legal ownership. The implications have been staggering for the museum world, in terms of reviewing the history of their collections and assessing their current collecting practices.

The 1970 UNESCO Convention states that countries should itemize their national treasures to ensure that they will be protected if stolen. It also provides mechanisms for states to recover stolen cultural property. However, the convention does not secure the rights of cultural institutions to have property restored to them, rights which the Unidroit Convention of 1995 subsequently recognized. But sustained enforcement of these laws is nearly impossible, particularly in light of individual nations' unwillingness to comply; the United States, for instance, adopted only portions of the UNESCO Convention in its 1983 Convention on Cultural Property Implementation Act. In principle, the idea of national sovereignty seems right, but one complication involves the potentially conflicting claims of ownership by an object's country of origin and the country where its finder resides. Moreover, today's nation-states are not

1. Other noteworthy agreements include the ICOMOS Charter for the Protection and Management of the Archaeological Heritage (1990); the International Workshop on the Protection of Artistic and Cultural Patrimony (1992); and the Unidroit Convention on Stolen or Illegally Exported Cultural Objects (1995).

TOP: Felice Beato, Imperial Summer Palace, before the Burning, Yuen Ming Yuen, Pekin. Between October 6 and 18, 1860.

BOTTOM: Felice Beato, View of the Imperial Summer Palace, Yuen Ming Yuen, after the Burning, Taken from the Lake, Pekin. After October 20, 1860.

necessarily the direct inheritors of those cultures in which the antiquities were produced. They may claim rightful ownership through lines of descent, by rewriting history, or by inventing traditions, but the basis for such claims can effectively exclude the interests of marginalized ethnic or minority groups. Equally likely is the possibility that an object was produced during a period of empire, and therefore belongs to a much larger economy of imperial and mercantile trade, eclipsing the sovereignty of any one nation-state altogether.

EMPIRE AND LOOT

The history of loot reveals its entanglement with both trade and expeditionary military force. Looting is an illicit economy that symbolizes defeat and humiliation: in many cases a necessary, if temporary, transgression of law that precedes the imposition of a new order. The word loot derives from the Hindi word lut, meaning valuables pillaged in time of war. It appears to have entered into English usage through accounts of colonial-era British campaigns conducted in India and later in China. In short, the history of the word loot can be seen as synonymous with the history of European intervention and empire building in Asia. However, while we may define looting as illicit trade, these military incursions also relate to the establishing of trade treaties, in particular by the East India Company, to facilitate Western access to primary resources and markets. The British had been waging war against the Chinese empire in part to open their ports to opium from India. The first intervention, later known as the First Opium War (1839–42), resulted in the opening of five treaty ports to British trade and the ceding of Hong Kong to Britain.

In 1858, British and French forces began a second incursion to ratify the Treaty of Tientsin, which would open additional ports to trade. Among the British officers was the Earl of Elgin, son of the Lord Elgin (Thomas Bruce) who in 1802 began to ship home to London sculptures from the Parthenon in Athens. The Elgin marbles, as they became known, are now one of the main attractions at the British Museum—and a perennial flashpoint for arguments about imperial booty. The younger Lord Elgin had seen active service in India before going on to China. By June 1858, the British and French had occupied Canton and imposed trading concessions on the Chinese. Fighting resumed when China failed to comply, and on October 6, 1860, English and French troops under the command of General Hope Grant and French military leader General Montauban advanced separately on the capital, Peking. The French entered the city first and shortly thereafter occupied the emperor's summer palace, Yuanmingyuan (Garden of Perfect Brightness), on the northwestern outskirts of Peking. The vast estate, built in the early eighteenth century by the Emperor Kangxi, was one of three summer parks belonging to the Qing dynasty (1644–1911). It occupied sixty-five square miles and incorporated traditional and Western-style buildings, as well as a scientific workshop and ateliers of artists and craftsmen drawn from the ranks of the Jesuit Order.

The looting began the day after troops entered the palace precincts. In his *Narrative of the North China Campaign of 1860*, Robert Swinhoe, staff interpreter for General Hope Grant, observes that the "scene afforded a very good proof of the innate evil in man's nature when unrestrained by the force of law or public opinion. Licensed theft soon displays the love of greed natural to every heart; and its concomitant vices, jealousy and dissension, speedily follow." Three days later, the general issued an order that looted objects be handed over to a prize committee. The objects were put on display and auctioned off, mostly to officers, over three days, with the proceeds apportioned out to the troops according to rank. Many of the objects stolen from Yuanmingyuan entered the collections of the French and English courts; some found their way into Peking markets. Still others appeared in the auction markets of London the following year and in public displays at the Paris Tuileries and the International Exhibition in London. Perhaps the most famous souvenir, though, was not an object of art but a Pekinese dog, which Captain Hart Dunne of the Wiltshire Regiment christened "Lootie" and presented to Queen Victoria.

The ostensible reason for the auction was to curtail the potentially unregulated behavior of the lower ranks within the armed forces. But its effect was to sanction the act of plunder and humiliate the Chinese emperor. Swinhoe writes: "Fancy the sale of an emperor's effects beneath the walls of the capital of his empire, and this by a people he despised as weak barbarians and talked of driving into the sea!" Accounts of the proceedings show the British and French blaming one another for the looting—or better still, the rapacious locals. In 1861, Victor Hugo wrote the following words in an open letter condemning the actions in China: "We call ourselves civilized, and them barbarians; here is what Civilization has done to Barbarity."

In the days that followed the looting, the Qing dynasty's Manchu rulers refused to negotiate a peaceful settlement. A delegation of about forty Westerners had been detained by the Chinese military and imprisoned in Yuanmingyuan. Threatened by the advance of the allied forces, the Chinese military tortured the prisoners and twenty of them died. The day after their bodies were returned, Lord Elgin ordered that Yuanmingyuan be destroyed in retaliation. The palace was burned to the ground on October 18, 1860. A week later the emperor's younger brother signed treaties with the English and French forces, and the Second Opium War came to an end.

Many narrative accounts exist of these tumultuous days, but there are comparatively few visual records. Felice Beato, an Italian war photographer, was following the British military forces and reached Canton in April 1860. One of the photographs he took on that trip is *Nine-Storied Pagoda and Tartar Street, Canton*, an odd shot in which the pagoda is partially obscured by buildings along the street. There were better vantage points from which to photograph the pagoda, as is evident from other pictures of it; Beato's choice indicates that he was intent on capturing a different aspect of the scene. The street itself is small, more like an alley, distinguished neither by its vista nor by its architectural facades. The pagoda appears in stark contrast to the ramshackle buildings in the foreground. A foreign officer stands in the middle ground, and in front of him at least two discernible figures sit on porch steps while another leans against a doorway. Beato's careful composition suggests that the upright, watchful eye of the foreign law has assumed authority over the local people.

When the Anglo-French forces moved north toward Peking, Beato followed, recording the confrontation. But although Beato was clearly in the vicinity of Yuanmingyuan during the looting and burning, none of his photographs show it. They simply document the view before and after. His record of Yuanmingyuan is thus one of relentless decay, as if symbolizing the condition of the empire itself. He is remembered, in other words, as a witness not to a violent episode in history but to a glorious past at the moment of its disappearance.

TRADING THE PAST

In April 2000 the Hong Kong offices of two prominent auction companies, Sotheby's and Christie's, announced forthcoming sales of Chinese antiquities. As one of China's first centers of trade, Hong Kong has remained a semi-colonial enclave and clearing-house for Chinese commodities, even after its 1997 handover from Britain back to the People's Republic. Christie's auction, held on April 30, 2000, was titled "The Imperial Sale: Yuanmingyuan," which seemed sure to provoke even the most disinterested government. Among the many items for sale at the two auctions were four precious cultural relics: a hexagonal ceramic vase commissioned by Qing dynasty Emperor Qianlong in 1743 and three bronze animal heads—tiger, monkey, and ox. In both cases the auction houses provided the connoisseur and potential buyer with notes on the iconographic significance and value of the objects but little information as to their provenance. However, any student of Chinese antiquities would recognize that what he or she was gazing on were treasures belonging to a crucial chapter of exchange between China and the West. In 1747, Emperor Qianlong asked the Italian Jesuit artist Giuseppe Castiglione if he knew of a missionary capable of designing a fountain similar to ones he had seen in European paintings. Astronomer and mathematician Father Michel Benoist was chosen to build the fountain, and on seeing the model the Emperor commissioned Castiglione to design a palace behind the fountain to show off the waterworks. The result was a small enclosure of European palaces, Xiyanglou, built between 1747 and 1759 (further additions were made in 1783, seventeen years after Castiglione's death). The three bronze pieces on sale at Christie's and Sotheby's were part of a water clock and fountain in the imperial garden that featured the heads of the twelve animals of the Chinese zodiac.

The announcement of the two auctions in Hong Kong sparked a fierce debate with the Chinese State Bureau of Cultural Relics. Stating that the looted relics belonged to China, the bureau asked the auction houses to cancel the sales and, according to a report in the *People's Daily* on May 1, 2000, commented: "We wish that all the cultural relics lost in the wars could be returned to their motherland." But the auction houses' sales technically did not violate any laws in Hong Kong, which still maintained a distinct legal system although it was now part of China. However, Chinese relics experts, citing international laws stating that looted relics belong to their home countries, held that China should have the right to take them back. As reported in the *China Daily*, the bureau went on to argue that the auction houses showed "no respect to Chinese laws or international treaties," referring to the 1970 UNESCO treaty (to which China is a signatory)

Bronze heads of a monkey, an ox, and a tiger,
Qing dynasty, mid-eighteenth century.

which states that any cultural relics looted or lost in wars should be returned home. Despite government requests and protests from Hong Kong residents chanting slogans—"Stop Auction! Return Chinese relics to motherland"—the auctions took place as planned. On May 3, Leung Chun-ying, convener of the Special Administrative Region's Executive Council, criticized the two companies for engaging in commercial activities damaging to the collective Chinese psyche. "After all," Leung told the *People's Daily*, "the auction items were national treasures looted by foreign troops during the most humiliating invasion of China."

All four of the contested objects at Christie's and Sotheby's were in fact returned to China through the sale. China Poly Group, a Beijing-based state-owned corporation, paid approximately $4 million for the three bronzes. The company, once known as an arms dealer, was originally owned by the People's Liberation Army; it is ironic to say the least that a former arms dealer should buy back loot carried off by Anglo-French forces. In addition to holding a wide variety of commercial interests from futures trading to photography studios, Poly Group now also supports an art museum in Beijing, and the three relics join a collection of rare Chinese antiques bought by the company outside of China—chiefly in Hong Kong and Taiwan—during the past few years. The ceramic vase was bought by Beijing Cultural Relics Company, presumably bound for the capital as well.

Meanwhile, the antiquities market in China is thriving, and the capital is becoming one of Asia's most active auction centers. According to a 2002 report published by *China Today*, Beijing's market, with annual sales exceeding 1.1 billion yuan (more than $100 million), employs over four thousand people and supports more than twenty auction houses that are run or supervised by the government. Still, the transfer of stolen relics through China's borders persists, exacerbated by decades of inadequate administration and record-keeping. As is the case in many nations, a thorough inventory of China's many relics collections does not yet exist, so it can take years to notice a theft, let alone identify and litigate against those trading in stolen objects. *China Today* states that in the seven months between August 2001 and February 2002, the Cultural Relics Bureau organized four market inspections, confiscating more than five hundred items from fossils to pottery to parts of ancient buildings.

In fall 2002, Christie's Hong Kong published a full-color catalogue for an auction on October 28 of that year: "Imperial Devotions: Buddhist Treasures for the Qianlong Court," comprising forty-nine lots. Anthony Lin, chairman of the Asian region for Christie's Hong Kong, introduces the catalogue with a text titled "Tibetan Buddhism at Court–A Short History." On the facing page is a photograph of the monastery complex at Chengde, a UNESCO World Heritage site. Situated about one hundred miles northeast of Beijing, Chengde holds a rare collection of imperial Chinese relics and antiquities passed down from the era when the Qing dynasty court spent part of every year there. Lin's preface outlines the history of the Qing dynasty, especially the period of Emperor Qianlong (1736–1795), and its devotion to Tibetan Buddhism. The concluding paragraph begins: "It is rare indeed to find such a group of objects related to a little known but highly complex aspect of Imperial life and history," a sentiment enhanced by the fact that there is no indication of ownership in the catalogue entries. The cover is adorned with a jade Amitayus figure and the first item is a stunning eighteenth-century enamel statue Amitayus, or Buddha of Infinite Life, from the Qianlong period, estimated at between $260,000 and $380,000.

In May 2003, however, the *Washington Post* reported allegations by Chinese officials in Beijing that the relics set to be auctioned at Christie's were in fact stolen from the temples in Chengde. A month later, China's official news agency, Xinhua, and the *Daily Telegraph* of London revealed that just weeks before the auction the Chinese government had launched an inquiry into the relics, after a Beijing art historian and former Palace Museum employee who was visiting Hong Kong noticed that some of the items for sale bore the museum's identifying stickers. In his May 28 article in the *Washington Post*, "China Uncovers Looted Buddhas," John Pomfret cites Chinese sources claiming that Li Chunping, a wealthy Chinese American antique collector, had been purchasing stolen relics from Chengde since 1995. The article states that Li Chunping and an official at the Chengde monastery complex had been detained along with several others in the investigation in December 2002, but that Chinese officials had kept the suspects' identities secret for five months to avoid causing embarrassment to prominent figures. (Li Chunping, the *Post* reported, is vice president of the Beijing Charity Society and has donated hundreds of thousands of dollars to fight crime and the SARS outbreak in China.) Allegedly, after posting a $1.46 million bond he offered to buy back the items and return them to Chengde in order to avoid prosecution. Xinhua does not implicate Li Chunping but instead notes that the investigation in China was focused on Li Haitao, the Chengde Palace Museum's security director, at whose home authorities discovered seventy stolen relics from Chengde, and who they suspect had been stealing objects from the museum for twelve years. Responding to the allegations, a spokeswoman for Christie's told the *Washington Post* that the auction house denied any wrongdoing, adding that Christie's was "cooperating with the Hong Kong police." The Hong Kong government has reportedly complied with the Chinese government and has requested that buyers of the auctioned lots keep them in Hong Kong.

The ramifications of this story of looting, still unfolding after one and a half centuries, are inestimable. The cultural legacy inherited by a nation became part of the global commodity market, in which its historical significance was subordinated to its perceived worth. Chengde has been closed and its Palace Museum drained of some of its most precious objects. Yuanmingyuan was not rebuilt after the fire, but construction on a new complex began in 1886 under Xianfeng's widow, Empress Dowager Cixi, using monies (estimated at over one thousand tons of silver) that had been intended for the building of China's modern navy. Located in a part of the former Summer Palace (Wanshoushan or Hill of Longevity), the new retreat was named Yiheyuan, Garden of Peace and Harmony in Old Age. It was rebuilt yet again, beginning in 1902, after its destruction by allied forces from eight nations (Britain, France, and Russia, among others) during the Boxer Rebellion.

Present-day view of the Summer Palace in Beijing.

Visiting the site now is a strange experience. What is on display is not the palace where the emperors once lived, which has been lost to decay and to decades of looting that followed the initial vandalism and destruction. Rather, one visits the refurbished sector named Yuanmingyuan Yizhi Gongyuan (Yuanmingyuan Ruins Park). Packed with foreign and local tourists, it has become a place to pass a Sunday afternoon wandering by the lake or through the gardens, buying souvenir replicas or posing for the camera. The experience of Yuanmingyuan is paradoxically one of both desolation and pride: the billboards at each entrance speak of the nineteenth-century looting and fire at the hands of the West, while the reconstructed buildings evoke the accomplishments of another era. The Qing dynasty itself had represented the imposition of a foreign regime (Manchus from the North), but its subjugation by the allied forces became, and remains, a justification for Chinese nationalism. Yuanmingyuan can be seen as a theme park where the future of the nation is built on the ruins of empire. As historian Geremie Barmé points out in his 1996 article "The Garden of Perfect Brightness, a Life in Ruins," the continuing incidence of petty looting from the Summer Palace quite literally provided some of the building blocks of a new Beijing.

What virtually disappeared with the destruction of Yuanmingyuan was evidence of a high cultural watermark achieved in China, a watermark that also reflected a fruitful intellectual and aesthetic exchange with the West. But was the loss of its treasures also a loss to the people of China and therefore to the well-being of a collective cultural memory? Perhaps not. The art and architecture of the Summer Palace represented imperial wealth, bringing prestige to China's leaders but at the expense of the general population. From a contemporary perspective, it may seem natural to value these treasures as contributing to a nationally shared cultural heritage. But this is a relatively modern inclination, which posits the nation, not its people, as the organizing principle of culture.

An inquiry into the history of looting uncovers the spectral trail of civilizations at a time when empires, though they may operate under different guises, still exercise control over what is and is not valued. It also warns one of the difficulty of attempting to differentiate between civilization and barbarism at such moments in history. The examples of Yuanmingyuan and Chengde and the still unfolding story of looting in Iraq reveal that the looting of cultural treasures is deeply intertwined with struggles for sovereignty, whether between nations or within them. To the extent that these treasures can represent a people's culture, past or present, their meaning will remain contested even after the actual fighting is over.

EMILY JACIR

WHERE WE COME FROM

If I could do anything for you, anywhere in Palestine, what would it be?

إذا قدرت اسوي اي اشي الك في اي محل في فلسطين شو بكون؟

Water a tree in my village of Dayr Rafat.

I am forbidden entry into the 1948 areas.

أروي شجرة في قريتي دير رافات.

إنني ممنوع من الدخول إلى مناطق ال ١٩٤٨.

IYAD

Born and lives in Dheisheh refugee camp, Bethlehem

Palestinian passport and West Bank I.D.

Father and mother from Dayr Rafat

(exiled in 1948)

إياد

من مواليد وسكان مخيم الدهيشة للاجئين في بيت لحم

جواز سفر فلسطيني و هوية ضفة غربية

الأب والأم من دير رفات

(نفيا عام ١٩٤٨)

Visit my mother, hug and kiss her and tell her that these are from her son. Visit the sea at sunset and smell it for me and walk a little bit . . . enough. Am I greedy?

I have a Gazan I.D. so I should be in Gaza. I left Gaza for Ramallah in 1995 and cannot go back. I also cannot move to any place in the West Bank because of Israeli restrictions. The Israelis refused to give me a West Bank I.D. for "security reasons," they claim!

JIHAD
Born in Shati refugee camp, Gaza City
Living in Ramallah
Gazan I.D. card
Father and mother from Asdud
(both exiled in 1948)

Notes: We sat together and drank coffee and tea while she asked all about Jihad, his wife and kids. We also talked about the intifada and its effect on everyone. When I was leaving, she put two handfuls of sweets in my handbag to bring back to Jihad.

زوري أمي و عانقيها و قبليها، و أخبريها
أن كل هذا من إبنها، وزوري البحر وقت
الغروب و تنشقي رائحته نيابة عني
و تمشي قليلا... وكفى. هل أنا طماع؟

هويتي غزاوية ولذلك يتوجب عليّ أن أكون
في غزة، لقد غادرت غزة إلى رام‌الله عام ١٩٩٥
ولا أستطيع العودة، كما لا أستطيع الانتقال إلى
أي مكان آخر في الضفة الغربية بسبب القيود
الإسرائيلية. لقد رفض الإسرائيليون منحي
هوية الضفة الغربية بحجة أسباب أمنية!

جهاد
من مواليد مخيم الشاطىء للاجئين، مدينة غزة
يعيش في رام الله
هوية غزة
الأب والام من أسدود
(نفيا عام ١٩٤٨)

ملاحظات: لقد جلسنا و شربنا القهوة والشاي معا فيما كانت أمه تسأل عن احوال جهاد وزوجته و أولاده. وقد تحدثنا عن الانتفاضة و أثرها على الجميع. و حينما كنت أستعد للمغادرة و ضعت حفنتين من الحلوى في حقيبتي لكي أعطيهما لجهاد.

nd bring me a photo of my family,
er's kids.

g at Birzeit University for the past
ave not been allowed to go to Gaza
I have no permission to be in the
an, so I am confined to Birzeit until

هيا وأحضري لي صورا
ولاد أخي.

يرزيت منذ ثلاث سنوات. ولم
إلى غزة لزيارة عائلتي،
زيا فليس لدي تصريح
غربية، وعليه فأنا محاصر
لإنتهاء من دراستي.

iving in Birzeit
and Gazan I.D. card

و يعيش في بير زيت
و هوية غزة

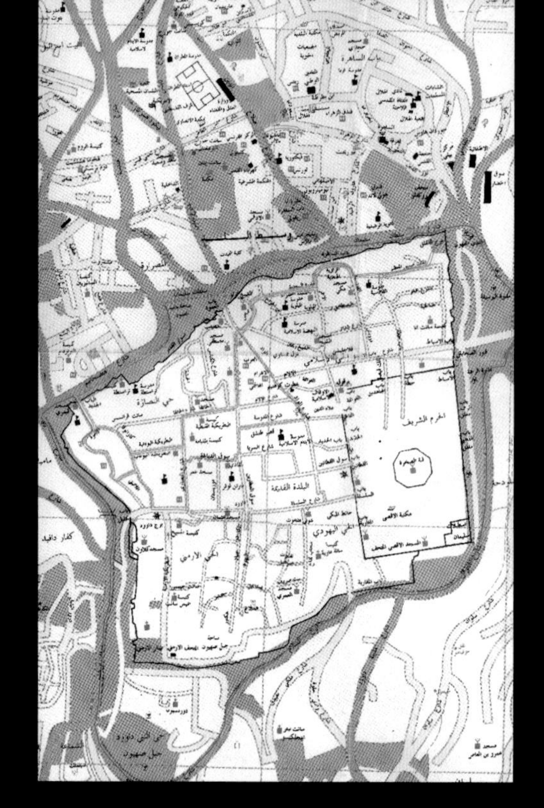

Spend a day enjoying Jerusalem freely. I always wanted to go there without any fear, without feeling that I might be stopped and asked for my I.D. . . . just enjoy Jerusalem as much as you can.

I need special permission to go to Jerusalem, and if I go without permission I will be fined and imprisoned.

OSAMA

Born in Beit Jalla, living in Delaware
Palestinian passport and West Bank I.D.
Father and mother from Beit Jalla

مضي يوماً بحرية وتمتع بالقدس.
حلمت دائما بالذهاب إلى هناك دون أي
خوف، و بدون الشعور بأنني قد أوقف
و تطلب مني هويتي...فقط إستمتعي
بالقدس، بقدر ما تستطيعين.

إنني أحتاج إلى تصريح خاص للذهاب إلى
القدس، و اذا ذهبت دون تصريح سوف أغرَّم
و أسجن.

أسامة

من مواليد بيت جالا، و يعيش في ديلاوير

Go to the Israeli post office in Jerusalem and pay my phone bill.

I live in Area C, which is under full Israeli control, so my phone service is Israeli. In order to pay my phone bill, I must go to an Israeli post office, which does not exist in my Area C. I am forbidden from going to Jerusalem, so I am always looking for someone to pay my phone bill.

MAHMOUD
Born in Fowar refugee camp, Hebron
Living in Kufar Aqab
Palestinian passport with West Bank I.D.
Father and mother from Iraq al-Manshiya
(both exiled in 1948)

إذهبي إلى مكتب البريد الإسرائيلي في القدس و ادفعي فاتورة هاتفي.

إنني أعيش في منطقة (ج)، و هي تحت السيطرة الإسرائيلية الكاملة، و عليه فإن خدمات الهاتف التي أتلقاها إسرائيلية. وحتى أتمكن من دفع فاتورة الهاتف يتوجب عليّ الذهاب إلى مكتب البريد الإسرائيلي، و هذا غير متوفر في منطقة (ج) و بما أني ممنوع من الذهاب إلى القدس، فإنني دائما ابحث عن شخص ما يستطيع الذهاب لدفع فاتورة الهاتف نيابة عني.

محمود
من مواليد مخيم الفوار في الخليل
ويعيش في كفر عقب
جواز سفر فلسطيني و هوية ضفة غربية
الأب والأم من عراق المنشية
(نفيا عام ١٩٤٨)

Go to my mother's grave in Jerusalem on her birthday and put flowers there and pray.

I need permission to go to Jerusalem. On the occasion of my mother's birthday, I was denied an entry permit.

MUNIR
Born in Jerusalem, living in Bethlehem
Palestinian passport and West Bank I.D.
Father and mother from Jerusalem
(both exiled in 1948)

Notes: When I reached the grave of his mother, I was surprised to see a circle of tourists surrounding a grave nearby. It was the grave of Oskar Schindler . . . buried next to a woman whose son living a few kilometers away is forbidden to pay his respects without a permit. There were many graves with smashed crosses and sculptures of the Virgin Mary that had been destroyed. The caretaker of the cemetery told me that Jewish extremists had raided it and desecrated many of the graves. He showed me the ones he had fixed.

زوري قبر والدتي يوم عيد ميلادها وضعي الورود على قبرها وصلي.

كنت بحاجة إلى تصريح للذهاب إلى القدس في يوم عيد ميلاد والدتي، ولكن تم رفض منحي التصريح.

منير
من مواليد بيت لحم، و يعيش في بيت لحم
جواز سفر فلسطيني/هوية ضفة غربية
الأب و الأم من القدس
(نفيا عام ١٩٤٨)

ملاحظات:عندما وصلت قبر والدته فوجئت برؤية مجموعة من السياح يحيطون بقبر قريب. كان ذلك قبر أو سكارشندلر، الذي يرقد الان بجوار السيدة التي لايستطيع ولدها المجيء لزيارتها بدون الحصول على تصريح. و الذي يقيم بضعة كيلو مترات فقط. لقد وجد العديد من الصلبان و تماثيل السيدة مريم العذراء محطمة. قال لي حارس المقبرة إن مجموعة من اليهودالمتعصبين هاجموا المقبرة والحقوا الدمار بالعديد من القبور. لقد أراني الحارس الصلبان والتماثيل التي أعادها إلى مواضعها.

Pick oranges from the family grove in Jericho and eat them right there.

Because of the closures and the current situation, my family has not gone to our grove in two years. To me, Jericho was always part of my life in Palestine. As a child we used to spend winters there and commute to school in Ramallah every day.

RIYAD

Born in Ramallah, living in Ramallah
Palestinian passport and West Bank I.D.
Father and mother from Ramallah

Notes: Due to current closures, Jericho has been completely sealed off making it impossible for me to enter. It's March 20th now, and the trees in Jericho have no oranges on them. The season is over.

أقطفي البرتقال من بيارتنا في أريحا وكليهم
هناك في البيارة نفسها.

بسبب الإغلاقات والوضع الحالي، فإن عائلتي
لم تتمكن منالذهاب إلى بيارتنا خلال عامين.
بالنسبة لي، فإن أريحا كانت
دائما جزء من حياتي في فلسطين. عندما
كنت طفلا، كنا نمضي الشتاء هناك ونذهب
إلى المدرسة في رام الله كل يوم.

رياض

من مواليد و سكان رام الله
جواز سفر فلسطيني / هوية ضفة غربية
الأب والأم من رام الله

ملاحظات: ان منطقة أريحا مغلقة بالكامل، ولا يمكنني
الدخول إطلاقاً.اليوم العشرين من آذار و موسم البرتقال
قد إنتها. لا يوجد برتقال على الشجر.

Emily Jacir

For most people the question "Where are you from?" can be answered in a word. Paris, Delhi, Tokyo, Kiev. For a Palestinian, there are several ways of responding, all of them complicated, leading back to a place that is beyond reach or that no longer exists as an Arab town. Lydda today is Lod, home to Tel Aviv airport, but it was an Arab town along with Ramleh, whose 60,000 citizens were evacuated by Israeli forces in 1948. Fifty-plus years later, how can a young man born in Kuwait and now living in Detroit still say that he comes from Lydda? The point is, of course, that he does.

"Palestine" has become a worldwide metaphor for trouble, unrest, violence: for Palestinians, that combination of words evoking fact, memory, and aspiration and the images associated with them stands in for citizenship or passport. In fact, this document simply establishes a person's freedom to move from one place to another. Impersonal text and a photograph together can do the job, but the less fortunate refugee who is prohibited from movement remains paralyzed. Someone and something else have to stand in.

Palestinians are frequently under curfew, and, as stateless refugees, they are often forbidden to work or travel. They are besieged, their houses demolished; they are made homeless for the third or fourth time. Surrounded by restrictions devised by the modern bureaucratic mentality—laws and scraps of paper that either permit you to go somewhere or prevent you from going—the Palestinian has to resort to improvisation or persistent stubbornness to overcome these obstacles. For the most part, Palestinians wait: wait to get a permit, wait to get their papers stamped, wait to cross a line, wait to get a visa. Eons of wasted time, gone without a trace.

Emily Jacir's series "Where We Come From" cuts through all that, reducing an intractably untidy mess to the simple, humane question "What can I do for you in Palestine, where you can't go but I can?" Having done what was asked of her, she further reduces the answer to a creative juxtaposition of wish, wish fulfillment, and wish embodied in picture and text: writing and image elegantly brought together with a clarity that most Palestinians cannot experience in the present. Her compositions slip through the nets of bureaucracies and nonnegotiable borders, time and space, in search not of grandiose dreams or clotted fantasies but rather of humdrum objects and simple gestures like visits, hugs, watering a tree, eating a meal—the kinds of things that maybe all Palestinians will be able to do someday, when they can trace their way home, peacefully and without restriction.

EDWARD W. SAID

Reenactment, Gettysburg

JOANNE DIAZ

Late summer. Bloodred clouds. The sky
a cave of hot stars, white with distance.
Outside, the sandy road takes the shape
of a long animal curled in sleep.
Fruit bats swing, lisp in the branches.
I can almost count them from our bed.

Tonight I think of the reenactment,
of the heat that haloed each soldier,
of the cannon's long tremble
against the parched grass. At Pickett's Charge,
I found myself almost wanting
the clots of blood to rise and glisten
on the men's woolen uniforms, to stick
in the folds of their necks. Only the smell
of apples in your hair kept me
from fainting in the sun, that spinning wheel.

How can you live with these smells
in our room—sour bleach on the motel towels,
dust on the dimpled sheets? I watch you twitch
and breathe until the venetian blinds
cut the young, brindled sun.

Sven Hedin, view of the ruins at Loulan, 1901.

Buying a Fishing Rod for My Grandfather

GAO XINGJIAN

I walk past a new shop that sells fishing equipment. The different fishing rods on display make me think of my grandfather, and I want to buy him one. There's a ten-piece fiberglass rod labeled "imported," though it's not clear if it's the whole rod that's imported or just the fiberglass, nor is it clear how being imported makes any of it better. All ten pieces overlap and probably retract into the last black tube, at the end of which is a handle like a pistol's and a reel. It looks like an elongated revolver, like one of those Mausers that used to be in fashion. My grandfather certainly never saw a Mauser, and he never saw a fishing rod like this even in his dreams. His rods were bamboo, and he definitely wouldn't have bought one. He'd find a length of bamboo and straighten it over a fire, cooking the sweat on his hands as he turned the bamboo brown with the smoke. It ended up looking like an old rod that had caught fish over many generations.

My grandfather also made nets. A small net had about ten thousand knots, and day and night he would tie them nonstop. He'd move his lips while he knotted, as if counting or praying. This was hard work, much harder than the knitting my mother did. I don't recall his ever having caught a decent-sized fish in a net; at most they were an inch long and only worth feeding to the cat.

I remember being a child, things that happened when I was a child. I remember that if my grandfather heard someone was going to the provincial capital, he would be sure to ask the person to bring back fishing hooks for him, as if fish could only be caught with hooks bought in the big city. I also remember his mumbling that the rods sold in the city had reels. After casting the line, you could relax and have a smoke as you waited for the bell on the rod to tinkle. He wanted one of those so he'd have his hands free to roll his cigarettes. My grandfather didn't smoke ready-rolled cigarettes. He ridiculed them as paper smokes and said they were more grass than tobacco, that they hardly tasted of tobacco. I would watch his gnarled fingers rub a dried tobacco leaf into shreds. Then all he had to do was tear off a piece of newspaper, roll the tobacco in it, and give it a lick. He called it rolling a cannon. That tobacco was really powerful, so powerful it made my grandfather cough, but that didn't keep him from rolling it. The cigarettes people gave him as presents he would give to my grandmother.

I remember that I broke my grandfather's favorite fishing rod when I fell. He was going fishing, and I had volunteered to carry the rod. I had it on my shoulder as I ran on ahead. I wasn't careful, and when I fell, the rod caught in the window of a house. My grandfather almost wept as he stroked the broken fishing rod. It was just like when my grandmother stroked her cracked bamboo mat. That mat of finely woven bamboo had been slept on for many years in our home and was a dark red color, like the fishing rod. Although she slept on it, she wouldn't let me sleep on it, and said if I did, I'd get diarrhea. She said the mat could be folded, so in secret I folded it, but as soon as I did, it cracked. I didn't dare tell her, of course, I only said I didn't believe it could be folded. But she insisted that it was made of black bamboo and that black bamboo mats could be folded. I didn't want to argue because she was getting old and I felt sorry for her. If she said it could be folded, then it could, but where I folded it, it cracked. Every summer the crack grew longer, and she kept waiting for a mat mender to come; she waited many years, but no mender came. I told her people didn't do this sort of work anymore and that she'd had the mat so long, she might as well buy a new one, but my grandmother didn't see it that way and always said the older, the better. It was like herself: the older she got, the kinder she became and the more she had to say, by repeating herself. My grandfather wasn't like that: the older he got, the less he had to say and the thinner he became, until he was like a shadow coming and going without a sound. But at night he coughed, and once he started, he couldn't stop, and I was afraid that one day he wouldn't be able to catch his breath. Still, he kept on smoking until his face and fingernails were the color of his tobacco, and he himself was like a dried tobacco leaf, thin and brittle, and it worried me that if he wasn't careful and bumped into something, he might break into little pieces.

My grandfather didn't just fish; he also loved to hunt. He once owned a well-greased shotgun made out of steel tubing. To make the shotgun was a lot to ask of anyone, and it took him half a year to find someone who would do it. I don't recall his bringing home anything except for a rabbit. He came in and threw a huge brown rabbit onto the kitchen floor. Then he took off his shoes, asked my grandmother to fetch hot water so he could soak his feet, and immediately started rubbing some tobacco he'd taken from his pouch. Wild with excitement, I hovered around the dead rabbit with our watchdog, Blackie. Unexpectedly my mother came in and started yelling. *Why didn't you get rid of that rabbit like I told you to? Why did you have to buy yourself that shotgun?* My grandfather muttered something, and my mother started yelling again. *If you must eat rabbit, ask the butcher to skin it before you bring it into the house!* My grandfather seemed very old then. After my mother left, he said German steel was good, as if with a shotgun made of German steel he could shoot something more than rabbits.

In the hills not far from the city, he told me, there used to be wolves, especially when the grass started to grow in the spring. Crazed with hunger after starving all winter, the wolves came into the villages and stole piglets, attacked cows, and even ate young cowherd girls. Once they ate a girl and left only her pigtails. If only he'd had a German shotgun then. But he wasn't able to keep even the shotgun he'd had made locally from steel tubing. In the book-burning era of the Cultural Revolution they called it a lethal weapon and confiscated it. He sat on a little wooden stool just staring ahead without saying a word. Whenever I thought about this, I felt sorry for the old man and dearly wanted to buy him a genuine German-made shotgun. I didn't, but I once saw a double-barreled shotgun in a sporting goods store. They told me I would need a letter of introduction from the highest-level sports committee in the province as well as a certificate from the public security office before they could sell it. So it was clear that I would be able to buy my grandfather only a fishing rod. Of course I also know that even with this imported ten-piece fiberglass fishing rod he won't catch anything, because our old home turned into a sandy hollow many years ago.

There used to be a lake not far from our home on Nanhu Road. When I attended primary school, I often passed the lake, but by the time I started junior secondary school, it had turned into a foul pond that only produced mosquitoes. Later, there was a health campaign and the pond was filled in. Our village also had a river. As I recall, it was in an area far from town, and when I was a child, I went there only a couple of times. Once when my grandfather came to visit, he told me that the river had dried up when a dam was built upriver. Even so, I want to buy him a fishing rod. It's hard to explain, and I'm not going to try. It's simply something that I want to do. For me, the fishing rod is my grandfather and my grandfather is the fishing rod.

I step into the street shouldering a black fishing rod with all its fiberglass pieces fully extended. I can feel everyone looking at me and I don't like it. I'd like to get on a bus, where I won't be noticed as much, but I can't get the rod to retract. I hate it when people stare at me. Shy since childhood, I am uncomfortable in new clothes, and being dressed up is like standing in a display window; but it's worse carrying this long, swaying, shiny fishing rod. If I walk fast the rod sways more, so I go slow, parading down the street with the rod on my shoulder, feeling as if I've split my trousers or I can't zip up my fly.

Of course I know that people in the city who go fishing are not after fish. The men who buy tickets to fish in the parks are out for leisure and freedom. It's an excuse to escape from home, to get away from the wife and children, and to get a little peace. Fishing is now regarded as a sport, and there are competitions with divisions according to the type of rod used; the evening newspapers rate the sport highly and carry the results. Fishing spots and party venues are designated, but there are no signs of any fish. No wonder skeptics say that the night before the competitions, people from the fishing committee come to put fish into nets, and that's what the sportsmen catch. As I am carrying a brand-new rod on my shoulder, people must think I'm one of those fishing enthusiasts. But I know what it will mean to my old grandfather. I can already see him: so hunched over that he can't straighten his back, carrying his little bucket of worms. It is riddled with rust and bits of dirt fall out. I should visit my old home to get over my homesickness.

But first I must find a safe place to put the rod. If that young son of mine sees it, he'll wreck it. I hear my wife shouting at me, *Why did you have to buy that? It's cramped enough in here already. Where will you put the thing?* I put it above the toilet tank in the bathroom, the only place my son can't reach, unless he climbs onto a stool. No matter what, I must go back to the village to get rid of my homesickness, which once triggered is impossible to shake. I hear a loud crash and think it's my wife using the meat cleaver in the kitchen. You hear her yelling, *Go and have a look!* You then hear that son of mine crying in the bathroom and know that calamity has befallen the fishing rod. You've made up your mind. You're taking the fishing rod back to your old home.

But the village has changed so much you can't recognize it. The dirt roads are now asphalt, and there are pre-fab buildings, all new and exactly the same. On the streets women of all ages are wearing bras, and they wear flimsy shirts to show them off—just as each rooftop must have an aerial to show there's a television in the house. A house without an aerial stands out and is regarded as defective. And of course everyone watches the same programs. From 7:00 to 7:30 it's the national news, from 7:30 to 8:00 the international, then short TV films, commercials, weather forecasts, sports, more commercials, then variety shows, and from 10:00 to 11:00 old movies. The movies aren't aired every day: on Mondays, Wednesdays, and Fridays, it's TV series instead. On the weekends, programs on cultural life are shown through the night. Anyway, the aerials are magnificent. It's as if the rooftops had grown small forests but a cold wind came and blew off all the leaves so that only bare branches remain. You are lost in these barren forests and can't find your old home.

I remember that every day on my way to school I had to pass a stone bridge, and the lake was right next to it. Even when there was no wind, there were waves lapping all the time, and I used to think they were the backs of swimming fish. I never imagined that the fish would all die, that the sparkling lake would turn into a foul pond, that the foul pond would then be filled in, and that I would not be able to find the way to my old home.

I ask where Nanhu Road is. But people look at you with surprise, as if they can't understand what you are saying. I still speak the village dialect, and anyone who does will always have a village accent. In our village, the word for "grandfather" is *laoye*. However, the word for "I," "me," or "my" is *wo*, produced between the back palate and the throat, and sounds like *e*, which means "goose." So *wo laoye* to a nonlocal sounds like "goose grandfather." And "goose" asking for directions using the back palate and throat fails to kindle any of that village friendliness in people. When I stop two young women and ask them, they just laugh. "Goose" doesn't understand why they're laughing. They laugh so hard, they can't answer, and their faces look like two pieces of red cloth. Their faces aren't red because they, too, are wearing bras, but because when I say "Nanhu Road" I also say *nan* between the back palate and throat, and it sounds funny to them. Later, I find an older man and ask him where the lake used to be. If I know where the lake was, it will be easy to find the stone bridge, and when I find the stone bridge it will be easy to find Nanhu Road, and when I find Nanhu Road I'll be able to feel the way to my old home.

The lake? Which lake? The lake that was filled in. Oh, that lake, the lake that was filled in is right here. He points with his foot. This used to be the lake. So we're standing on the bottom. Was there once a stone bridge nearby? Can't you see that there are asphalt roads everywhere? The stone bridges were all demolished and the new ones use reinforced concrete. You understand. You understand that what used to be no longer exists. It is futile to ask about a street and street number that used to exist; you will have to rely on your memory.

My childhood home had an elegant, old-style courtyard. The gate-screen had a relief mural inlaid with carved stone images depicting Good Fortune, Prosperity, Longevity, and Happiness. Old Man Longevity, who had half of his head missing, held a dragon-head staff. The dragon's head had worn away, but we children were absolutely sure that Old Man Longevity's staff was in the shape of a dragon's head. The gate-screen also had a spotted deer carved in it. The spots, of course, were those faint indentations on the deer's back. Whenever we went in or out we always touched the antlers, so they became very shiny. The courtyard had two entrances, one in front and one in the back. The bankrupt owner of the house lived in the back courtyard. There was a little girl in that family called Zaowa. She used to stare at me wide-eyed; it was funny but somehow sweet.

That courtyard definitely existed, as did the date trees growing there that my grandfather had planted. And the cages hanging in the eaves held my grandfather's birds. He kept a thrush there and once even a mynah. My mother complained about the mynah being noisy, so my grandfather sold it and brought home a red-faced tit. But the tit died soon afterward; these birds are temperamental and shouldn't be caged. When my grandfather said that it was the tit's red face that made him fall in love with it, my grandmother scolded him for being shameless. I remember all this. The courtyard was No. 10 Nanhu Road. Even if they'd changed the name of the road and the number, they wouldn't have filled in this perfectly good courtyard, as they had that pond of foul water. But I ask everywhere and search street after street and lane after lane. I feel as if I'm rummaging through my pockets; I've taken out everything, but still can't find what I want. In despair I drag along my weary legs, uncertain whether they still belong to me.

Suddenly I have a brainstorm and remember Guandi Temple. It was in the opposite direction from the way I went to school, in the direction of the movie theater. When my mother took me to see a film we had to pass a lane called Guandi Temple. If I can find Guandi Temple, it won't be hard to work out the location of my home. So I start asking people how to find Guandi Temple.

Oh, so you're looking for Guandi Temple? What number? This confirms that Guandi Temple still exists. The person I encounter is so earnest and keen to help that he asks for the house number. Unable to think of a number right away, I mumble that I was wondering if the address still existed. If there's an address, of course it exists. Who are you looking for? What family do you want? He wants more details. Probably he thinks I'm back from overseas searching for my roots, or that I'm some drifter who abandoned his village. I explain that my family used to rent the house, and that it didn't belong to my grandfather. What was the name of the landlord? All I know is that the landlord had a daughter called Zaowa, but I can't tell him that. As I continue mumbling, a scowl appears on the man's face and his eyes turn cold. He looks me up and down as if he's considering whether to report me to the police.

If you're looking for No. 1, go straight, then take the first lane on the right, it's on the south side of the road. If you're looking for No. 37, go that way, after about a hundred paces take the second lane, go to the very end, and it's on the north side, on the left. I thank him repeatedly, but when I go, I can feel his eyes boring into my back.

I see the first lane on the right, but before turning I see the brand-new blue road sign beside the red sign of the men's public lavatory. Written on it clearly and unmistakably is Guandi Temple, but this is not the impression I had of it as a child. I turn into the lane to show that I really did come to see my old home and am not up to any mischief. There is no need for me to look from No. 1 to No. 37; at a glance I can see to the end of the lane: it is not as long and winding as I remembered. I don't know whether or not a temple was there then. No tall buildings are on either side of the lane; rising above the old-style buildings there is only one three-story red-brick building, an economy structure that seems less permanent than these old courtyards. Suddenly I remember that Guandi Temple burned down after being struck by lightning, but that was before I was capable of remembering anything. My grandfather told me about it. He said that the spot attracted lightning because the *qi* energies underground were in disharmony, so they built the temple to drive away the demons and evil spirits. Still it ended up being struck by lightning, proving that the site was not suited to human habitation. Anyway, my home was not in Guandi Temple, it was somewhere not too far away from it. I must retrace the way my mother took me when I was a child. Having a child myself won't make it any easier, but I know that it's futile to keep asking people. I have gone in circles on the lake, beyond the lake, in the middle of the lake, around the lake, but if the sea can turn into mulberry trees, so too can this little lake. I suspect that my old home is hidden deep in the little forest of aerials in that stretch of old buildings, new buildings, and economy buildings that are neither old nor new, right in front of me. But no matter how much you keep going around them you can't see it. So you can only imagine it from your memories. It might be beyond that wall, converted into family dormitories by some urban environmental-protection authority. Or a plastic button factory might have turned it into a warehouse with iron doors and a guard, so unless you can state your business, don't even think about going in to nose around. Just tell yourself that people couldn't be so cruel as to demolish the gate-screen with the carvings. But past and present sages and philosophers in China and the West believe that humans have a propensity for evil, and that evil is more deeply rooted than good in human nature. You like to believe in the goodness of people. People just wouldn't be so mean as to deliberately trample the memories of your childhood, because they too have a childhood worth remembering. This is as clear as one plus one cannot equal three. One plus one may change in quantity and substance, change into something grotesque, but it will never become three. To abolish such thoughts you must get away from these asphalt roads that all look alike, and away from these new buildings and old buildings, these block upon block upon block of half-new, half-old economy apartment blocks under their forests of television aerials, bare branches devoid of leaves, as far as the eye can see.

I must go to the country, to the river where my grandfather took me fishing. He took me to the river, and although I can't remember if we caught any fish, I know I did have a grandfather and a childhood. I remember feeling awful when my mother made me take off all my clothes in the courtyard for a bath. I have also searched for the other houses I have lived in as a child. I remember getting up in the middle of the night to go hunting, but it was not with my grandfather. After a whole day, we killed a feral cat we thought was a fox. And I remember my poem in which I've strapped rattling hunting knives all over myself. I am a tailless dragonfly flitting over a plain, but the critic has barbed thorns growing in his eyes and a wide chin. I want to write a novel so profound that it would suffocate a fly.

I see my grandfather sitting on a small wooden stool, his back hunched, sputtering on his pipe. *Grandfather!* I call out to him, but he doesn't hear. I go right up to him and call again, *Grandfather!* He turns around but is no longer holding his pipe. Tears stream from his ancient eyes, which seem bloodshot from smoke. In winter, to get warm, he always liked to squat by the stove and burn wood. *Why are you crying, Grandfather?* I ask. He wipes the snivel with his hand. Sighing, he wipes his hand on his shoe but it doesn't leave a stain. He is wearing old cloth shoes with thick padded soles that my grandmother made for him. Without saying a word, he looks at me with his bloodshot eyes. *I've bought you a fishing rod with a hand reel,* I tell him. He grunts deep in his throat but without any enthusiasm.

I come to the riverbank. The sand underfoot crunches and sounds like my grandmother sighing. She is fond of chattering endlessly, although no one understands her. If you ask, *Grandmother, what did you say?* she will look up absentmindedly and, after a while, reply, *Oh, you're back from school? Or, Are you hungry? There are sweet potatoes in the bamboo steamer.* When she chatters it's best not to interrupt, she is talking about when she was a young woman, but if you eavesdrop from behind her chair, she seems to be saying, *It's hidden, it's hidden, everything is hidden, everything. . . .* All these memories are making noises in the sand under your feet.

This is a dried-up river, flowing with nothing but rocks. You are walking on rocks that have been rounded and smoothed by the river, and, jumping from rock to rock, you can almost see its clear flowing water. But when the mountain floods came, an expanse of muddy water spread into the city. To get across the road people had to roll their trousers up, and they kept falling in the brown slush where worn-out shoes and rotting paper floated. When the water receded, the bottom part of all the walls was covered with a sludge that, after a few days in the sun, dried into a shell and flaked off like fish scales. This is the river where my grandfather once took me, but now there is no water even in the gaps between the rocks. In the riverbed there are only unmoving big round rocks like a flock of dumb sheep huddled close to one another, afraid that people will drive them away.

You come to a sand dune with sinewy willow roots in it. The willows were cut, stolen, made into furniture, and then not a blade of grass would grow here. As you stand, you begin sinking, and suddenly the sand is up to your ankles. You must get away quickly or you will sink to the calves, knees, and thighs and be buried in this dune, which resembles a big grave. The sand murmurs that it wants to swallow everything. It has swallowed the riverbank and now wants to swallow the city along with your childhood memories and mine. It clearly does not have good intentions, and I can't understand why my grandfather is just squatting there, not fleeing. I decide to make a hasty getaway, but a dune suddenly looms before me. Under the hot sun appears a naked child: it is myself as a child. My grandfather, in his baggy trousers, has risen to his feet. The lines on his face are no longer as deep and he is holding the child's hand. The naked child, who is me, hops and skips at his side.

Are there any wild rabbits?

Mm.

Is Blackie coming with us?

Mm.

Does Blackie know how to catch rabbits?

Mm.

Blackie was our dog, but he disappeared. Some time later someone told my grandfather he saw Blackie's fur drying in a courtyard. My grandfather went there, and the people claimed that Blackie had killed their chicken. It was lies. Our Blackie was very obedient, and only once was he rough with our rooster and pulled out a few feathers. He was punished with a broomstick by my grandmother until he lay whining, front paws flat on the ground, begging for forgiveness. My grandfather was miserable, as if he had been beaten with the broomstick. The rooster was my grandmother's pet, and the dog went everywhere with my grandfather. From that time on, Blackie never bothered chickens, just as a good man never fights with a woman.

Are we going to run into wolves?

Mm.

Are we going to run into black bears?

Mm.

Grandfather, have you ever killed a black bear?

Grandfather grunts loudly but you can't tell whether it's a yes or no. I worshipped my grandfather because he had a shotgun, and it was exciting when he filled his empty cartridges with gunpowder for it; I would pester him nonstop until he got cross. He seldom lost his temper, but once he did. He stamped his feet and yelled at me in a loud voice, Go *away*! Go *away*! I went inside, then heard a sudden explosion. I was frightened and almost crawled under the bed, but finally peeked out the door and saw that one of my grandfather's hands was covered with blood; his other hand was frantically wiping his face, which was all black. He was hurt, but he didn't cry.

Grandfather, are you also going to shoot a tiger?

Stop talking so much!

It was only after I grew up that I learned that real hunters don't talk much. My grandfather's hunting friends probably talked all the time, and that's why they didn't ever shoot anything; they also kept my grandfather, who didn't talk much, from shooting anything. When my grandfather was young, he came upon a tiger; it was in the mountains and not in a zoo. This happened in his old home, which was also my father's old home, so it was my old home, too. Back then, there were thick forests, but one time I passed my old home in a bus while on a work assignment. There were only bare brown slopes, and even the mountains had been turned into terraced fields. Those fields were once forests. The tiger looked at my grandfather and walked away. On television they say that in south China tigers have been extinct for more than ten years, except for those in zoos. Not only has no one ever shot a tiger in the wild, no one has even seen one. In the northeast there are still tigers: the experts estimate there are at most a hundred of them. It's not known where they've hidden, and hunters would count themselves lucky if they saw one.

Grandfather, when you saw the tiger were you scared?

Bad people scare me, not tigers.

Grandfather, have you ever run into bad people?

There aren't many tigers but lots of bad people, only you can't shoot people.

But they're bad!

You can't tell right away whether they're good or bad.

What about when you can tell, can you shoot them then?

You would be breaking the law.

But aren't bad people breaking the law?

The law can't control bad people, because bad people are bad in their hearts.

But they do bad things!

You can't always be sure.

Grandfather, do we have far to go?

Mm.

Grandfather, I can't walk anymore.

Just grit your teeth and keep walking.

Grandfather, my teeth are falling out.

You bad boy, stand up!

Grandfather gets down on his haunches and the naked child climbs onto his back. With the boy on his back, he totters a step at a time in the sand, his feet turned outward. The boy whoops with joy and kicks his little feet, as if spurring on an old horse. You watch your grandfather's back gradually recede into the distance and sink behind a dune. Then there is only you and the wind.

Voller has three of his team protecting him. Their solid bodies form a barrier, and it won't be easy to take the ball from him. At the edge of the sand, a line of yellow smoke rises, and like an invisible hand it brushes the big dune into a roll of unfurling silk. You are in a desert. It is a dry sea to the horizon, burning red, still as death. You seem to be flying in a plane over the great Taklamakan Desert. The towering mountain range looks like the skeleton of a fish. The vast mountains will certainly be swallowed up in this burning dry sea, yet in March the Taklamakan can be extremely cold. Those few blue circles are probably frozen lakes and the white edges are shallow beaches. The dark green spots that look like the eyes of dead fish are where the water is deep. In the second half of the match everyone can see that West Germany has stepped up its attack and is in the lead. Argentina will have to strengthen its defense; everything depends on how they counterattack and take advantage of gaps in the other side. Good kick! Valdano has the ball and he scores! There is no wind, just the gentle rocking of the motor. Outside the cabin window, there seems to be no horizon. The Taklamakan looms up diagonally in so straight a line that it could only be replicated on a blueprint; it divides the window into two. Following the line of vision and direction of flight, it moves clockwise from 0.50 to 1.20 or 1.30 degrees. At the end of the needle is a dead city. Is it the ancient city of Loulan? The ruins are right below and you can see the collapsed walls. The palaces have all lost their domes: here the ancient cultures of Persia and China once fused, then sank into the desert. Look, everyone! Argentina is making a rapid counterattack and the other side can't keep up. Argentina scores a goal. In 51 matches in the series 127 goals were scored, and if you count the penalties in extra time, 148. In today's match, there were 2 more goals. Not counting the penalties in extra time, the 128th and 129th goals have been kicked. Now Maradona has the ball. Shifting sands and the ball. With a loud howl yellow shifting sand slowly forms a mound, then trickles down in waves—waves that rise, fall, and ripple outward, like breathing, like singing. Who is singing with a kind of sobbing under the shifting sands? You want desperately to dig it out, the sound that is right below your feet. You want to make a hole to let out this sound tinged with sadness, but as soon as you touch it, it twists and bores downward, refusing to come up. It's like an eel, and you catch only what seems to be a slimy tail that you can't hold on to. You dig furiously with both hands into the sand. On the riverbank you had to dig only a foot deep and water would percolate up—cool, pure, sparkling river water—but now there is just cold grit. You put your hand into it and feel a tingling sensation, then touch something sharp and cut your finger, although it doesn't bleed. You are determined to find out what it is. You dig and scrape and finally pull up a dead fish. The head was pointing down, and it's the tail that cut you. Stiff and hard, the fish is as dry as the river: mouth clamped shut, eyeballs shriveled. You prod it, squeeze it, step on it, throw it, but it doesn't make a sound. It is the sand that makes a noise, not the fish, and it whispers to mock you. The dead fish, stiff in the blazing sun, sticks up its tail. You look away, but its round eye continues to stare at you. You walk off, hoping that the wind and sand will bury it again. You won't dig it up again. Let it never see the daylight and stay buried in the sand. Burruchaga is offside, loses a great opportunity, and the defense kicks the ball out. In the second half Argentina gets a third corner but West Germany takes it, goes for a goal, and scores! At the twenty-seventh minute Rummenigge kicks it right at Maradona. The score is 1-2, and everyone sees Maradona taking his team toward the goal—

Grandfather, can you kick a soccer ball?

It's the soccer ball that's kicking your grandfather.

Who are you talking with?

You're talking with yourself, with the child you once were.

That boy without clothes?

That naked soul.

Do you have a soul?

I hope so. Otherwise this world would be too lonely.

Are you lonely?

In this world, yes.

What other world is there?

That inner world of yours that others can't see.

Do you have an inner world?

I hope so. It's only there that you can really be yourself.

Maradona is taking the ball past everyone. There's a goal! Whose is it? The score is 2-2, a draw for the first time. Doves of peace soar in the stadium. Seventeen minutes to the end of the match: time enough to have a dream. They say it only takes an instant to have a dream; a dream can be compressed into hardtack. I've eaten hardtack, dried fish in a plastic bag—without scales, eyes, or pointy tails that can cut your fingers. In this lifetime you can't go exploring in Loulan, you can only sit in a plane and hover in the air above the ancient city, drinking beer served by the stewardess. The sound in your ears is music, eight channels on the armrest. Screeching rock and roll or a husky mezzo-soprano purring like a cat. Looking down at the ruins of Loulan, you find yourself lying on a beach; the fine sand flowing through your fingers forms a dune. At the bottom of the dune lies the dead fish that cut your finger without drawing blood. Fish blood and human blood have an odor, but dried fish can't bleed. Ignoring the pain in your finger, you dig hard and uncover a collapsed wall. It's the wall of the courtyard of your childhood. Behind it was a date tree, and once you sneaked off with your grandfather's fishing rod to knock down dates that you shared with her.

She walks out of the ruins and you follow, wanting to be sure that it is the girl with whom you shared the dates. You can only see her back. Excited, you pursue her. She walks like a light gust of wind, but you can never catch up. Maradona is looking for a path, a path where none exists, and the other team watches him closely. He takes a fall but charges on. Now they're trying for a goal. It's in! You give a loud yell, and she turns around. It's the face of a woman you don't want to recognize. There are wrinkles on her cheeks, eyes, and forehead: a flabby old face without any color. You find it painful to keep looking. Should you smile? A smile might mock her, so you grimace, and of course it's not a pleasant sight.

Alone in the middle of the ruins of Loulan, you look around. You make out the brick room in the courtyard with the gate-screen depicting Good Fortune, Prosperity, Longevity, and Happiness. It is where Blackie used to sleep and where my grandfather kept his little iron bucket for the worms: it is my grandfather's room. Before the wall collapsed, my grandfather's shotgun hung on it. That should be the passageway leading to the back courtyard, to Zaowa's home. Staring at me without blinking is a wolf crouched in the window frame of the collapsed wall of the back courtyard. This does not come as a surprise. I know that in the wilderness there is often little sign of human settlement, only wolves. But these crumbling walls around me are crawling with wolves. They have taken over the ruins. Don't look back, my grandfather once told me. A person attacked from behind in the wilderness must never look around. If he does, Zhang the Third will tear out his jugular.

I am scared stiff: these crouching Zhang the Thirds, treacherous bastards that attack from behind, are going to pounce, but I mustn't show that I'm frightened. The cunning animal at the window frame stands up like a person, resting its head on its right forepaw and watching me out of the corner of its left eye. All around, the wolves loudly smack their long tongues; they are losing patience. I recall how it was when my grandfather, as a young man, came face to face with a tiger in the paddy fields of his old home. Had he started to run, the tiger would have pounced and made a meal of him. However, I can neither retreat nor go forward, and can only bend quietly to feel in the earth with my hand. I find my grandfather's shotgun. Without hesitation, I raise the shotgun and slowly level it at the wolf before me. I must be like an experienced marksman, must not give them reason to think otherwise, must shoot them dead one at a time, not allowing my feet to get confused. I will start by shooting the wolf at the window, then turn left in a circle. Between each shot, I must work everything out in my mind. I can't hesitate or be careless. There were 132 goals in the 13th World Cup competition. The match is over; Argentina has beaten West Germany 3-2 and is the winner of the World Cup. I pull the trigger, and just as with the cornstalk shotgun my grandfather made for me when I was a child, the trigger breaks. The wolves roar with laughter, hooting and guffawing. Joyful shouts crash like waves at the Azteca Stadium in Mexico City, each wave higher. I am embarrassed, but I know that the danger has passed. These Zhang the Thirds are only people dressed as wolves, playacting. Look, the players have been surrounded like heroes and are being lifted over everyone's heads. They're protecting Maradona, and he is saying, "Let me kiss all the children of the world." I hear my wife talking, and her aunt and uncle, who have come from far away. The soccer match, broadcast from early morning, is finished. I should get up to see if that ten-piece fiberglass fishing rod that I bought for my grandfather, who died long ago, is still on top of the toilet tank.

Beijing, July 18, 1986

Translated from the Chinese by Mabel Lee

Black Map

BEI DAO

Translated from the Chinese
by Eliot Weinberger

in the end, cold crows piece together
the night: a black map
I've come home—the way back
longer than the wrong road
long as a life

bring the heart of winter
when spring water and horse pills
become the words of night
when memory barks
a rainbow haunts the black market

my father's life-spark small as a pea
I am his echo
turning the corner of encounters
the former lover hides in a wind
swirling with letters

Beijing, let me
toast your lamplights
let my white hair lead
the way through the black map
as though a storm were taking you to fly

I wait in line until the small window
shuts: O the bright moon
I go home—goodbyes
are less than reunion
only one less

Ramallah

in Ramallah
the ancients play chess in the starry sky
the endgame flickers
a bird locked in a clock
jumps out to tell the time

in Ramallah
the sun climbs over the wall like an old man
and goes through the market
throwing mirror light on
a rusted copper plate

in Ramallah
gods drink water from earthen jars
a bow asks a string for directions
a boy sets out to inherit the ocean
from the edge of the sky

in Ramallah
seeds sown along the high noon
death blossoms outside my window
resisting, the tree takes on a hurricane's
violent original shape

DOROTHEA TANNING

The Artist as a Dog, 1967.

ABOVE: *Untitled*, 1971.

RIGHT: *Ouvre-toi* (*Open sesame*), 1970.

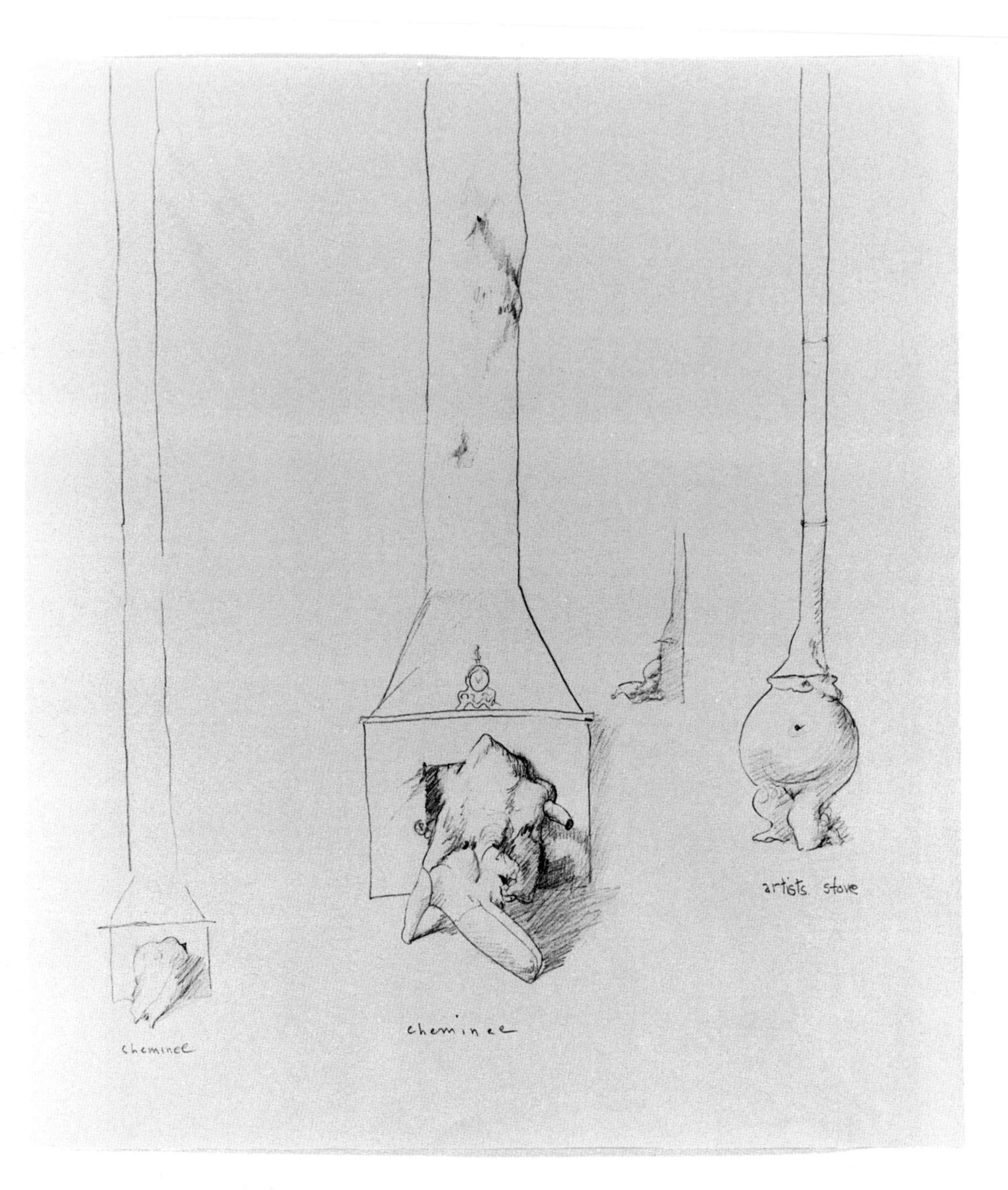

Studies for Hôtel du Pavot, Chambre 202, 1970–71.

Hôtel du Pavot, Chambre 202, 1970–73.
Installation at the Centre National d'Art
Contemporain, Paris, 1974.

ABOVE: Wall figures from *Hôtel du Pavot, Chambre 202*, 1970–73.

RIGHT: *Révélation ou la fin du mois* (Revelation or The end of the month), 1970. From *Hôtel du Pavot, Chambre 202*, 1970–73.

Family, 1976.

Nue couchée (Reclining nude), 1969–70.

Pelote d'épingles pouvant servir de fétiche
(Pincushion to serve as fetish), 1965.

Dorothea Tanning

In the late 1960s, Dorothea Tanning set aside her paintbrushes and took up scissors and her sewing machine. The scissors were heavy shears, sharp enough to penetrate the luxurious tweeds she favored. The sewing machine was a portable Singer that had accompanied her from Galesburg, Illinois, to Manhattan, to Sedona, Arizona, and across the Atlantic to France. For the seamstress, the machine made stylish dress affordable. For the sculptor, it offered not convenience but a challenge: stitched inside out, like dresses, the final forms were apparent to the artist only after they left the machine.

Tanning's fabrics were acquired on expeditions to the Marché Saint-Pierre, an emporium near the Sacré-Cœur in Paris. Along with the tweed came pink cottons, white wools, and even fake fur—all carried back to Seillans, the hilltop village in the south of France to which Tanning and her husband, Max Ernst, had moved in 1964. Nearby were flocks of sheep, which obligingly produced plenty of wool for shearing each spring. Tanning's next-door neighbor carded the wool in the backyard, providing her with an ongoing supply of stuffing. Beyond that there were simple things: Ping-Pong balls (the vertebrae of *Reclining Nude*), a plastic funnel (*Pincushion to Serve as Fetish*), a pocket handkerchief (*Xmas*). A friend contributed a loveseat and chair, which were summarily swallowed into tweed (*Rainy Day Canapé*; *Revelation or The End of the Month*). One day the paneled kitchen door was sacrificed to art (*Ouvre-toi*).

An epiphany had announced the onset of the sculptures. Attending a concert in 1969 at the Maison de la Radio in Paris, Tanning heard Karlheinz Stockhausen conduct his own composition *Hymnen*. In her autobiography, Tanning writes, "Spinning among the unearthly sounds of *Hymnen* were the earthy, even organic shapes that I would make, had to make, out of cloth and wood; I saw them so clearly, living materials becoming living sculptures, their life span something like ours."

In an intensive response to this vision, Tanning made almost twenty individual fabric figures—soft, strong creatures whose ambiguous anatomies and faceless heads somehow add to their life force. Full of an eroticism that can be read as both pleasure and pain, they tumble and sprawl, linger and twist, oblivious to past or future events. In the ensemble titled *Hôtel du Pavot, Chambre 202*, created for Tanning's 1974 retrospective at the Centre National d'Art Contemporain in Paris, a shabby room with dated wallpaper and wainscoting is peopled by tweed figures burgeoning out of the fireplace and furniture. Above

LEFT: Untitled, 1963.

RIGHT: Xmas, 1969.

them, two pink bodies, one embraced by a furry arm and leg, tear through the wallpaper. Was it an orgy? A crime scene? The mood is far from innocent, but not clearly sinister.

Tanning's sculptures, primarily made between 1969 and 1974, are three-dimensional matches for the effulgent figures found in her paintings and drawings from the previous decade. By 1975, Tanning returned to her easel, and the bodies once again took form in luminous oil on canvas.

ANN TEMKIN

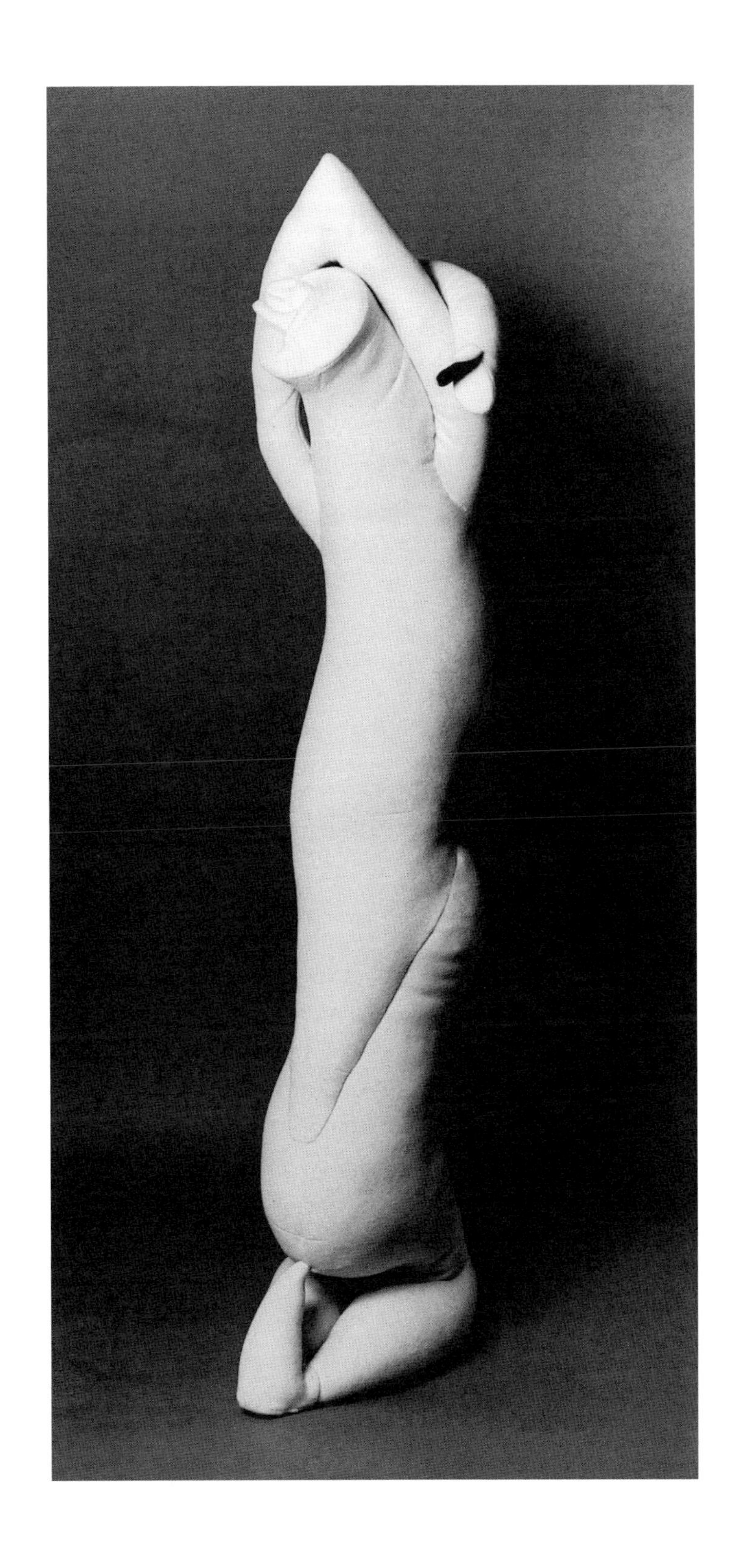

Watersteps

INGER CHRISTENSEN

Translated from the Danish
by Susanna Nied

I

1 The fountain in Piazza Nicosia was built in 1572. Jacopo della Porta was the architect in vogue at the time.

Piazza Nicosia isn't actually a plaza. It's part of Via di Monte Brianzo, widening in a northwesterly direction.

I sit at a table with covers and glasses. They don't start serving until 1:00.

A red Jaguar drives into the square. It vanishes down Via Leccosa.

The sun shines. The water reflects the light. The paint of the red Jaguar reflected the light as it drove past.

2 The fountain in Piazza Colonna was sculpted from marble by Rosso dei Rosso in 1575. He came from Florence.

Piazza Colonna is dominated by a column (42 meters) with a twining relief that tells of Marcus Aurelius's victory procession.

I sit at a table with a hot cappuccino a glass and a pitcher of water.

A red Jaguar has stopped in the crosswalk. The light changes from Alt to *Avanti*. People look irritated.

The sun shines. The paint of the red Jaguar reflects the light. Cars block the view of the water.

3 The fountain in Piazza Campitelli could have been built by Jacopo della Porta in 1589. But it's not certain.

Piazza Campitelli stretches along Santa Maria in Campitelli. Alongside a nice restaurant.

I stand on the opposite corner between two ordinary houses that belong to the municipality of Rome.

A red Jaguar zooms across the square. It comes from Via Campitelli and vanishes around the corner down Via Delfino.

The sun shines. The water reflects the light. The paint of the red Jaguar reflected the light as it drove past.

4 The fountain on Via del Progresso was built during Jacopo della Porta's second period in 1591.

Via del Progresso connects Via Santa Maria del Pianto with Lungotevere dei Cenci.

I sit on the steps of Santa Maria del Pianto. It's the only place you can sit.

A red Jaguar is parked at an angle outside the Palazzo Cenci.

The sun shines. The water reflects the light. The paint of the red Jaguar reflects the light.

5 The fountain in Piazza Farnese could have been built by Girolamo Rainaldi in 1628. But it's not certain.

Piazza Farnese is where it is because the Palazzo Farnese was where it was. There are actually two fountains. They're identical.

I walk around in the square.

A red Jaguar drives searchingly past the houses.

The sun shines. The water and the paint of the red Jaguar reflect the light.

II

1 There are three steps up to the fountain in Piazza Nicosia. The fountain is octagonal and the upper basins rest on four dolphins.

Piazza Nicosia is not famous. There's a post office there.

I study a menu. *Pomodori ripieni*, stuffed tomatoes, something to start with, maybe seasoned with basil and mint.

While the red Jaguar starts up and quickly drives away from Via del Progresso.

While the sun shines and the water falls from the upper basins and splashes into the pool.

2 There is a railing around the fountain in Piazza Colonna. The pool is elliptical, broken by four concave curves. The dolphins are arranged on seashells. Two and two.

Piazza Colonna is famous. On the facade of Il Tempo hangs the newspaper case. You can read there about the postal strike (*sciopero*).

My coffee is cold. The water glass drips. The sugar packet is wet.

While the red Jaguar drives into Piazza Campitelli for the third time in a row.

While the sun shines and the water falls and hangs like a veil from the basin in the middle of the pool. It's water that splashes. You can't see it for the cars. Nor can you hear it for the cars.

3 There is a lower railing around the fountain in Piazza Campitelli. It's made of three kinds of marble: the bottom pool grayish, the top basin pink, between them the white balusters.

Piazza Campitelli is neither famous nor unknown. It's well preserved.

In the corner between the houses you look down into a narrow space with ruins and cats.

While the red Jaguar probably vanishes from Piazza Nicosia.

While the sun shines and the water falls from the pink basin into the gray pool and from the gray pool through the masks out into a drain channel in the edged platform. There are no dolphins. It's water that splashes.

4 There are two steps up to the fountain on Via del Progresso. It is made of marble that they say was taken from Nero's grave. There are masks but no dolphins.

Via del Progresso is not famous at this time. At this time it's fairly unimpressive.

I light a cigarette.

While the red Jaguar drives on because the light has turned green on Piazza Colonna.

While the sun shines and the water falls from the upper basin and splashes into the pool.

5 There is a wrought-iron fence with gates that don't close around the fountain in Piazza Farnese. It is made of Egyptian granite originally used in Caracalla's baths. There are no dolphins but there are masks and lions. The lions sit on an extra pool. It is shaped like a bathtub.

Piazza Farnese is famous because the Palazzo Farnese is famous.

I look at the famous facade of the Palazzo Farnese.

While the red Jaguar drives away from Piazza Nicosia down Via Leccosa or away from Piazza Campitelli down Via Delfino or away from somewhere else in the city.

While the sun shines and the water falls from the upper basin through masks bathtub and lions to the big pool which is bowed as well as edged. It's water that splashes.

III

1 The four dolphins do not move in the fountain in Piazza Nicosia.

Because of the strike the post office is closed.

While I wait for strawberries with sugar and white wine.

While someone or other gets out of a red Jaguar in Piazza del Popolo.

Reporting that the sun shines the water falls and the paint on the red Jaguar reflects the light.

2 The four dolphins do not move in the fountain in Piazza Colonna.

Because of the strike you can read about the strike on the facade of Il Tempo.

While I wait to drink a little water from the dripping glass without having it drip.

While someone or other gets out of a red Jaguar in Piazza del Popolo/Piazza di Spagna.

Reporting that the sun shines the water and the paint fall and reflect the light.

3 The four masks do not move on the fountain in Piazza Campitelli.

Because of the strike you can find a letter among the cats down in the narrow space.

While I wait for some municipal employee or other to come out of the houses that belong to the municipality of Rome.

While someone or other gets out of a red Jaguar in Piazza del Popolo/Piazza di Spagna/Piazza Barberini.

Reporting that the sun shines the water and the paint and the light fall and are reflected.

4 The four masks do not move on the fountain on Via del Progresso.

Because of the strike at this time no one is hearing of Via del Progresso at this time.

While I wait for the next cigarette.

While someone or other gets out of a red Jaguar in Piazza del Popolo / Piazza di Spagna / Piazza Barberini / Piazza Venezia.

Reporting that the sun and the water and the paint and the light shine and fall and are reflected.

5 The two times four masks and the two times two lions do not move on the two fountains in Piazza Farnese.

Because of the strike the Palazzo Farnese can be read like a letter.

While I wait for a letter from someone or other.

While someone or other gets out of a red Jaguar in Piazza del Popolo / Piazza di Spagna / Piazza Barberini / Piazza Venezia / Piazza della Repubblica.

Reporting that the sun and the water and the paint and the light shine and fall and splash and are reflected.

IV

1 The four dolphins begin to move.

While the letters smell of white wine and sugar.

While I think of Jacopo della Porta's many fountains.

Reporting del Popolo Over Nicosia The red Jaguar.

Reporting that the water is overflowing.

2 The four dolphins begin to move.

While the letters drip water and the writing flows out.

While I think of Rosso dei Rosso's memories of Florence.

Reporting di Spagna Over Colonna The red Jaguar.

Reporting that the sun is overflowing.

3 The four masks begin to move.

While the letters belong to the municipality of Rome where the writing flows out.

While I think of the many fountains that Jacopo della Porta did not get to build.

Reporting Barberini Over Campitelli The red Jaguar.

Reporting that the light is overflowing and melting.

4 The four masks begin to move.

While the letters tell of writing that flows out.

While I think of Jacopo della Porta's opinion of Rosso's fountains.

Reporting Venezia Over del Progresso The red Jaguar.

Reporting that the paint is overflowing and melting.

5 The masks and the lions all begin to move.

While the Palazzo Farnese is read like a letter that flows out.

While I think of Rainaldi's opinion of Jacopo della Porta and Rosso.

Reporting Repubblica Over Farnese The red Jaguar.

Reporting melting.

V

1 While the dolphins dance all over Nicosia.

While the letters are opened and drunk like white wine.

Reporting Jacopo della Porta in The red Jaguar.

Reporting del Popolo Melting Nicosia

Over.

2 While the dolphins leap with the flood all over Colonna.

While the letters' flowing writing is drunk up and acts like white wine.

Reporting Rosso dei Rosso in the red Jaguar Over Jacopo della Porta in the red Jaguar

Reporting di Spagna melting Colonna.

Over.

3 While the masks murmuring flow in the waters all over Campitelli.

While the letters' flowing writing is drunk up and acts like white wine.

Reporting della Porta Over dei Rosso Reporting della Porta 17 years later in the same Jaguar.

Reporting Barberini Melting Campitelli.

Over.

4 While the masks sing in the swirling bodies of water down to del Progresso.

While the writing moves into the blood

Reporting della Porta Over dei Rosso Reporting della Porta Over della Porta 19 years later in the same Jaguar.

Reporting Venezia Melting del Progresso

Over

5 While the masks and lions dance and sing and leap in a waterfall all over Farnese.

While the blood does the same

Reporting della Porta dei Rosso Over della Porta della Porta
reporting Girolamo Rainaldi in the same Jaguar.

Reporting Repubblica Melting Farnese.

Over

VI

1 While the dolphins dance in place and all Nicosia vanishes

Reporting that the letters tell of del Popolo's fountains

Reporting della Porta

Melting Nicosia del Popolo

Over

2 While the dolphins leap from fountain to fountain and all
Colonna vanishes.

Reporting that the letters tell of di Spagna's fountains.

Reporting dei Rosso Melting della Porta

Melting Colonna di Spagna

Over

3 While the masks murmur of the dolphins' freedom and all
Campitelli vanishes

Reporting that the letters tell of Barberini's fountains

Reporting dei Rosso Melting Jaguar della Porta

Melting Campitelli Barberini

Over

4 While the masks sing of the masks' freedom and all del Progresso vanishes.

Reporting that the letters tell of Venezia fountains.

Reporting della Porta Melting dei Rosso della Porta Jaguar

Melting del Progresso Venezia

Over.

5 While the masks and lions merge with the dolphins and all Farnese vanishes.

Reporting that the letters tell of Repubblica's fountains

Reporting della Porta Jaguar Melting dei Rosso della Porta Rainaldi

Melting Farnese Repubblica

Over

VII

1 Reporting that the dolphins sit at a table drinking water:
della Porta Nicosia del Popolo

2 Reporting that the dolphins drive a red Jaguar:
dei Rosso Colonna di Spagna

3 Reporting that the masks smell of sugar and white wine:
Jaguar Campitelli Barberini

4 Reporting that the masks drive a red Jaguar:
del Progresso Venezia

5 Reporting that the lions read the red Jaguar like a letter:
Rainaldi Farnese Repubblica

VIII

1 Dolphins masks and lions of marble

2 Smells sugar and white wine of marble

3 Red Jaguars of marble

4 Letters of marble

5 Water of marble

A Stranding

PAUL FARLEY

We make a big noise, audible down bandwidths
past every thunderstorm girdling the planet
to where the big cetaceans talk in vast
engine room cycles, across open ocean.

Their spouts are even seen in estuaries
so shallow that St. Paul's could hold its dome
above the waves, the Whispering Gallery
attuned to the tinnitus of the deep.

We form a human chain and hand down buckets
to drench the warm skin. Fire engines, stretchers,
carrier bags like giant sticking plasters . . .
a beached whale has some claim upon the soul:

we are bending over backward at the local
level, grafting selflessly as neighbors
bonded by a house fire in their street,
who don't look up or care for the cathedral.

A God

The god who checks you've turned the oven off
in some unnumbered radio galaxy
never sleeps or swerves from His one duty.
You never know: in the middle of the night
you could be up putting a pizza in,
and what does He care? It's the Middle Ages

where He lives. Watching over your stove
beats anything closer to hand: in two places
at once, He'd rather listen to the ticks
of the oven preheating than sit through jousts
or another spit roast. He enjoys the rings
glowing concentrically in your dark kitchen;

planetary, He thinks. Music of the spheres.
Hell, in His pianoless world, what He'd give
to stand before it like an instrument
and set its greasy dials for the hearts of suns,
careful not to raise the number of the beast
on its console—that would be a mistake—

but play all night bathed in its infrareds;
electric music (the god of hearth
is banging from His sealed-up chimney breast),
ammonia, wire wool, black residue
on the brain pan, the upright honky-tonk
of metals cooling down when morning comes.

A Wooden Sky

After Ikea, a wooden sky
glowered, freshly planed, all the way home.
Winding the window down brought turpentine
and wood sap smells, while a black sun shone
low in the west all the way to our exit sign,
a knot in pine, trapped in its own jet stream.

We followed the evening's grain, keeping the sun
to our left. Resinous crosswinds shook the car.
I don't mean a church roof or vaulted barn:
I mean a wooden sky. You could sand it down
and get the blue back: sawdust like pink snow
out of a wooden sunset, covering the roads.

Someone in the back asked, What's been gained
by cutting down our woods, building a navy,
losing an empire, and moving indoors?
and I had to say, There's no answer to that
except look at this wooden sky we've got.
The craftsmanship of it. Those wood-turned clouds.

Edge of the West

DIETER M. GRÄF

Translated from the German
by Andrew Shields

the polishing, with each step, of the sub
lime uneven marble threshold: shoeshine boy
beauties resembling—papered over!—the ad
jacent wooden shed on the thousand
and first night. The *conversation* ver
ging on the carpet-hawker
words ("friendship," for example) streaming
in from the side: friendly voices take
turns, collect small green fruit, the
embryos of the trees;

ate, too, from
the pear "*armut*," so gigantic: the hills
of garbage covered with cats; syphilitic sandals,
metal locker; the longing for the jeans
body on the edge of the West. Wrench
peddlers, traces of the Middle Ages, shells
of buildings with what is veiled in the rubble;
our parchment skin:

ants, building
Pergamos again. Soldiers (?)
bearing blades of grass . . . well: *very* hot
here! The sun goes down. The air goes out
of the Southern balloon, and they (men) are all
sitting on the street, in the rack
et, dusty, shabby, friendly, inhaling their
diesel fuel—

Detail from the Edge of the West

in it (here, too, it is an uneven, omni
present cloak-and-dagger-light
poverty):
pink cotton candy, bell bangs of kiosk
boys in this headscarf idyll of slower
motions:
a rivulet of people runs back
through the needle's eye at the cash
register. Past another (everywhere else
confusion) stand quaking individuals in
front of illuminated relics, the foot
print, the hair of the prophet;
from
his, back to the real green of a rainy
morning in G—

WANGECHI MUTU

Riding Death in My Sleep, 2002.

I've moved and moved so much, I'm back where I began
I can BUILD MY HOME WITH A LITTLE PIECE OF TWINE FROM MY

Spider, 2003.

Intertwined, 2003.

Untitled, 2003.

Wangechi Mutu

"The people who have 'disappeared' (and are still disappearing) because of the Central African Holocaust have reemerged and are being redistributed amongst the living," wrote Kenyan artist Wangechi Mutu in 1997. Mutu was speaking literally, referring to victims of genocide in Rwanda in the mid-'90s; many of their bodies, floating down the River Kagera into Lake Victoria, were said to be eaten by fish that were in turn consumed by people living in neighboring countries. But her words could also apply to the women in her recent works on paper, composites of pop-cultural images reborn into figures of monstrous beauty.

At the time, Mutu was making fetish objects by juxtaposing, for example, the head of a black doll with the body of a figurine of the Virgin Mary. While her keen sense of the morbid and fantastical was already evident in those early sculptures, it is in collage that she has found the ideal form for transforming quotidian materials into creatures of myth and metaphor. Influenced as much by master collagist Romare Bearden as by the Dadaist Hannah Höch, Mutu's mixed-media works on paper share common ground with the work of other young women artists who use the body as a site to explore themes of exploitation and resistance. Combining delicate watercolor-and-ink drawings with body parts cut out of fashion glossies and images culled from wildlife magazines, travel brochures, and coffee-table books on tribal Africa, Mutu creates hybrid figures that are simultaneously abject and flamboyant, seductive and repulsive. Her works tell a story of trauma and regeneration too often left out of our edited versions of cultural history.

FRANKLIN SIRMANS

from Flash

HERBERTO HELDER

Translated from the Portuguese
by Alexis Levitin

VIII

Sudden adolescents, they don't know, just the torment of whirling
excess. With their zoological heads.
Rings on their paws.
A dancing burst of light weighs heavy on them.
Their outer self.
The blindness of horns they lift
like an enormous star
released. Their swiftness searches for the weight
of stone. And the weight they have
of pure light without weight, the sinister movement
along the ground,
the terror, a
violent richness—they search for someone to touch them.
On the mouth.

So they may turn transparent, moving round and round.
And when turquoises cross from one hand to another, leaving them
on fire,
one sees that they are angels touched by vipers, angels,
anatomical and barbarous.
Exposed to the moon like animals. Darkness
on their shoulder blades.
They lay waste to the world just by staring at it.
The sleep that attacks them shows them
filled with arteries. And then their delicacy weighs them down
like death. Just touch them on the face and they turn
white. Pierce them with the venous blood of
sleeplessness, the matter that we are.

And then their flesh becomes a sweat-soaked star.

Myotis, Pipistrelle

TAYLOR GRAHAM

The dead have splattered their mistakes all over
this mortal world, and moved on. No, these
are our own mistakes, that we blame on the dead
of whom no one speaks ill, who walk among us
with gentle hazel eyes and enigmatic smiles
and disappear an instant before
we glimpse them. Do they have a grip
on daylight? It slips down the screened
upstairs window, as bats under the eaves begin
their evening chirping humming purring
shaking of wings, before they pour out in waves
darker than a night sky. I say, look
at the bats. You name them, *pipistrelle,*
myotis. Fliers of our sleep, sleepers
of our day. By midnight they'll be zig-
zagging invisible to come again at dawn,
you say, and hang upside down
under our rafters. Is it the bats
we mean?

Hands in Pockets

SARAH EMILY MIANO

On a quiet evening in January 2002 I set off from Norwich to look for the grave of my late professor, W. G. Sebald, at St. Andrews churchyard in Framingham Earl, a journey that would take me southeast through the Norfolk countryside. Settled behind the wheel of my rented Fiat I headed for the open road, but darkness fell suddenly, as if it had been stealthily waiting for me, and my hopes of getting there while it was still light—or getting there at all—fell along with it. Indeed, I had traveled only a few miles along the vacant, winding roads lined with hedges, and the monstrous oak and beech trees beyond, when my ignorance of the area and inability to navigate English motorways led me to believe I would become completely lost.

There wasn't anyone to ask for directions, but I found a sign for the A146 and, following its curves, remembered that at one time my professor had driven this same road, though on the other side and in the opposite direction. My thoughts meandered through the previous months that added up to years behind me. There are many reasons I should not be making this journey, I thought, and the foremost reason is that while he was alive I never really knew him. But this is why I *should* be making this journey—because now that he is gone, it's time to get to know him, to reach into my pockets for anything that could make sense of who he was: *that word, that look, that gesture*, all trapped in images coming at me in a mismatched fashion.

Writing is obsessive work, so you often seem to others as if you are staring into the same hole. . . . You are the black sheep of the family until you appear on television.

Although he used his initials W. G. as a pen name, Winfried Georg Maximilian Sebald was adamant about never being called Winfried (which he hated as a child and which was later mistaken for a female name when he moved to England) or Georg (the name of his father, with whom he was never very close) and preferred to be called "Max," because he associated it with eighteenth- and nineteenth-century German tradition. He was everything people say he was: melancholic, solitary, lugubrious. He never revealed himself too much, concealed more than he disclosed, and when one thought to have figured him out, he did or said something out of the ordinary—or simply disappeared from view. Max was transient, as if from another age and world. Anyone desiring to know him bumped up against his belief that you shouldn't inquire into another person's life unless invited. Having known him for a short time I had seldom been invited, but it occurred to me that being American was to my advantage, as I was not dissuaded by Max's rare invitations. I forged ahead and asked many questions and, when he retreated, I only inquired more.

Remembering is a completely random process. . . . Physicists now say there is no such thing as time. Chronology is the unnatural thing; everything coexists inside our heads like furniture in a room.

I gripped the wheel and stayed to the left side of the double lines. The beaming headlights on the black road grew increasingly hypnotic. As I reached Framingham Pigot, my senses began to play tricks on me and I witnessed, this January night, the event of only weeks earlier: a man driving his little gray Peugeot on the motorway to Norwich, two hands on the wheel (cautious as he was), in one mysterious moment losing focus as the green lorry plowed toward him, and the sudden panic causing him to freeze, then the eventual crossing of white lines. I heard the screech of tires and the honk of the Erf tanker like a foghorn in the mist. I heard the loud crash, the quiet whirring of his car afterward, and then: silence. I pulled to the side of the road and sat there, trembling, looking to regain my composure. Resting my head on the seat I tried to understand this recent, relived tragedy, and was led to recall other moments that I did witness but that did not shine as clearly.

Be consistent: "sitting back down heavily" does not jell with the slender American woman. If you have a limping character, limp judiciously.

During the last four months of Max's life, as his student, I saw a side of him that most never got to see, the one that taught me writing. Considering his eccentricity and otherworldliness, I found it surprising that he remembered each of his pupils' names from day one and, in addition, the names of our fictional characters as if he knew them personally. While he seldom prepared or rehearsed lectures, and never carried notes, his relaxed spontaneity made him an excellent teacher. His instruction was littered with anecdotes, jokes, wanderings, and staggering insights, so most of us sat pen in hand, jotting the words down as he said them.

I can still see him, seated in front of the classroom, and us, his students, forming a half circle around him. He is talking in a pleasant monotone, casually leaning back in his chair, running a hand through his soft white hair. He is commenting on one of our stories. "There's something very odd about this," he says, or "I like this because it does not sound right." He stops mid-sentence to stand up and scribble something on the chalkboard, the name of a German book or writer: Koestler, Stifter, Walser.

One day, early on, Max asked us to bring in some passages from our favorite novels and proceeded to point out their fundamental problems, discrediting and demystifying them to emphasize that rhythmical prose, after a while, "gets tedious" and "every sentence has to stand for itself." We learned that lesson quickly. Other comments, equally amusing and valuable, would not reach their full impact until later, or much later, when I sat alone at my desk, getting down to business.

Sometimes, during our breaks, Max accompanied us to the café and crammed into a booth with six, seven, or eight of us, and we felt close to him, sharing our cigarettes, drinking coffee, munching flapjacks. At other times he shrank from the crowd and disappeared down the elevator shaft. With a glimpse of him ambling away, I suspected that many years of walking had tired him, because he did not take the stairs down, just two flights to his office. There the door was closed, and he often did not answer when you knocked, though he insisted we come for personal advice—and if you made an appointment, you were sure to get in.

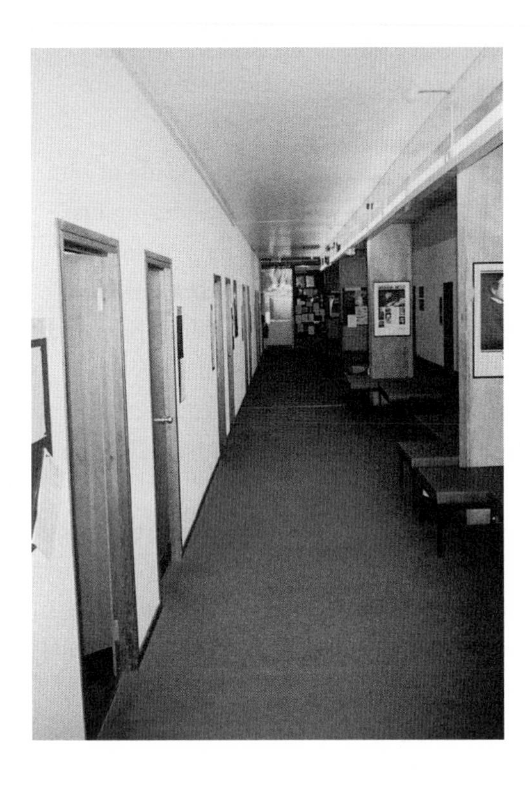

Meteorology is not superfluous to the story. Don't have an aversion to noticing the weather. . . . There is nothing trivial attached to the notion of snow.

I decided to abandon my vehicle and, pulling my scarf tighter around my neck, walked down the long stretch of road leading to Framingham Earl. The vault of the sky was mostly clear and the stars had come out, but I was surrounded by a limitless darkness. Currents of air were pouring through what was left of the leaves on the trees, depositing snowflakes on their branches. When I gazed out across the fields, my eyes could make out an enormous ash, its mostly barren limbs outstretched, swaying and bending and covered with snow. Except for the slight sounds of the wind, everything was calm, and, although seized with apprehension, I continued on.

Characters need details that will anchor themselves in your mind. . . . You need acute, merciless observation. Is the radio on quietly in the kitchen all day long?

Max opened the door, stepped back, and, with a slight gesture, offered me a seat. His office was small and tidier than I expected. Sitting down, I noticed that his desk was uncluttered and his shelves were not overstocked with books as one might think: along with a dusty selection of European literature, the wooden planks held interesting tidbits like a collection of seashells from the Norfolk coast and a tiny wooden house made for him by an Italian reader. I wondered if his secrets were locked up in the row of filing cabinets along the back wall, or if they weren't there at all, but tucked in a rucksack somewhere.

He extracted a squared pack from the pocket of his navy wool vest and offered me a cigarette. After I accepted one he lit it for me, and I asked if Players was his usual brand. I'll smoke anything, he said, but you should know better—with a slight emphasis on *you*. This statement led to a brief but amusing conversation on the American's obsession with good health.

Alongside a few stacks of papers and an ashtray was a telephone, which rang after we had been speaking for a quarter of an hour. He waited for a long while, as if he were undecided about answering, then apologized, picked up the receiver, and conducted his business in a gruff, rushed manner. Something about technology made him obviously uneasy. He was probably the only faculty member not to have an e-mail address, or a computer for that matter. When I asked him why, he said, Computer? It sounds like something we eat at Christmas, probably because in German the word for turkey is *Puten*.

Get off the main thoroughfares. You'll see nothing there. For example, Kant's Kritik *is a yawn but his incidental writings are fascinating.*

I ventured through the stubbled fields and, little by little, took comfort in the silent world of creatures that kept vigil. I was contemplating whether I should complete the rest of my journey when I called to mind how, even while lacking in consolation, my professor could be strangely gregarious and funny: a man who smoked at his desk while everyone else went outside; who complained about the bad coffee in the university cafeteria but drank it anyway; who consistently matched his socks to his shirt; who wore two wristwatches, one on each wrist and facing in opposite directions; who told what seemed like random stories but in actuality was sharing ones he thought might appeal to you; who again and again caught you off guard with his comic timing (a dark humor that was sometimes wry, sometimes sarcastic); who could even play the zither.

You need to set things very thoroughly in time and place. . . . Young authors are often too worried about getting things moving on the rails, and not worried enough about what is on either side of the tracks.

On a blue-sky, early September afternoon I made my way toward the lake to a more peaceful part of the University of East Anglia campus, which was, at the beginning of the semester, abuzz with the chatter of new students. As I settled on the grass outside the art center, I thought there was no better place to be,

and sat there quietly in the warmth of the sun, with the cool wind coming off the lake. Suddenly, a shadow came over the postcard I was writing to a friend back home. I was surprised to see a pair of brown suede shoes in the grass beside me and, when I looked up, two legs in honey corduroy trousers. Shielding my eyes, I saw a handsome man with carefully trimmed hair, ruddy cheeks, a slim physique, and buttery, stylish clothes towering over me, hands in his pockets. He wore round spectacles and his lids were lowered over his eyes, but this could hardly conceal their hazel color: Max.

Hello, he said. Hello, I replied. He must have recognized me from the initial meeting of our group, although he didn't say so, and was seemingly drawn to the image on the card. What do we have here? he asked in a slight German accent, pointing. I held up the card and showed it to him: a Degas dancer. I like it, he said, as the breeze rustled his white hair. You're my professor. He nodded. And you are not from around here. No, I'm from New York. Raising a hand to his face, he smoothed down his thick mustache. I am going there soon, he said. Where are you from? I asked, as if I did not know. I am from Germany originally. Oh! I tried to act surprised. So what are you doing here? Teaching, I suppose. No, I mean *right now*. He glanced over the green and said he was going to move his car from where he'd illegally parked it on the grass that morning. One can't imagine how difficult it is to find somewhere decent to leave your vehicle in this place, he said, scowling. There's something very odd about this. What kind of car do you drive? I asked. Oh, it's a French machine of some sort. I laughed. Well, you'd better hurry up before they come and get you.

Looking out the window usually symbolizes some sort of regret, loss.

With a stiff breeze at my back and the light crunch of frozen ground beneath my feet, I returned to the country road, remembering an occasion when I'd tried to convince him he needed another person in his life with whom to share his discoveries. No, he replied, shaking his head, having two sets of eyes on a journey is a sort of blindness, which makes it nearly impossible to travel properly unless one is alone. How can you find your way, turn off where and when you wish, or stuff things in your pockets, if there is another person to worry about? Furthermore, he said, looking out the window, most people like the sight of my back to the door. Don't you get lonely? I asked too quietly, and by that time he had retreated somewhere in his mind.

It is good to have undeclared, unrecognized pathologies and mental illnesses in your stories.

A week before his death, Max came to my house for dinner and brought a bottle of white wine, although he didn't drink alcohol. He had warned me ahead of time that he wouldn't eat much; nevertheless, he cleaned his plate. (The following day I discovered that the advance notice had been an "out" for him, in case I was a bad cook.) While we ate we chatted and, when another guest told a joke that merited only token laughs, he leaned back in his chair and said, Yes, it is difficult to tell a good joke—a genuine observation that tickled us all into genuine laughter.

After dinner we moved into the sitting room where we smoked cigarettes and Max told stories about disastrous dinner parties he'd attended: one host decided his gathering should end promptly at ten o'clock, so he left his guests in the living room at precisely this time, went upstairs and returned in his full pajama regalia, then washed the dishes and turned off the lights, ignoring his guests, who sat in silence. Another time, a host tried to entertain his friends with music, but nodded off during Schumann—or was it Bach?—falling forward completely in his chair so his hands and head were touching the floor (and relating this story, Max did the same). A long while later, after the movement ended, the host realized what he had done and, in embarrassment, retreated upstairs to his bedroom. Even when his guests, including Max, knocked on his door and asked him to come out, he refused.

These stories continued as we drank espresso and ate tiramisu, and we were glad Max had stayed so late, though we knew he would get only a few hours of sleep before he awoke at 4 A.M., his usual time, when he did such things as "sit in the potting shed" and "potter about."

There is more to love than boy meets girl.

From the Bungay Road I turned left at the roundabout, left again at the T-junction, and on another four hundred yards until I reached St. Andrews graveyard on the right and entered through the iron gate. There, lurking in the shadows of yew trees on the low end of the cemetery, was the freshly laid grave. It was strewn with white lilies from his mother and draped with a banner that read, in German: *We are infinitely sad.* In the moonlight my eyes made out a wooden cross poking up from the ground. Bending down, I extracted a lighter from my pocket to read its inscription, tracing my fingers over each letter slowly.

Include precise, uncomfortable attractions in your stories.

The last time I saw him—either months ago or a century, I don't recall—I gave him a little box wrapped in crinkled cream paper. Why do you buy me things? he asked, with a grimace. His lackluster reply stung me, so I moved toward the door. Tell me, his voice softened, how are you doing?—meaning, *Come back.* I looked over my shoulder at him opening the box and pulling out the surprise: a brass compass. It's for your travels, I said, to keep you from getting lost. How did you know? he asked, feeling the weight of the instrument in his palm. I didn't know, I said. I just wanted to thank you. I'm glad you like it, I added. He ran a thumb over its face, grinning as much as I'd ever

seen and remaining quiet for a long while. It's perfect, he said finally. What else do I say? Then he turned and looked out the window at the chestnut tree outside, which had attained some height. I placed my cold hand on his cheek.

Spirit presence is always a good idea.

Sitting on the soft snow near the grave, I was lulled by the solemn hush of the churchyard until I heard a rustling sound coming from the shadows near the round tower. Startled, I looked up, but saw only the empty pathway and the tree clumps in moonlight. I rose to my feet and listened intently, holding my breath. There was a stillness everywhere: no breeze stirred the air, not a twig moved. The night was asleep and stale with cold. After several minutes, I turned to leave. Then I saw him. He was standing under a Lebanese cedar, wearing a beige overcoat, hands in pockets. At his side, his black Labrador retriever, tail wagging, held a stuffed white bear in its teeth. I stepped toward him. In a reassuring gesture he stretched out his hand, and I took it. He was holding my compass in his other hand. Eyebrows raised, he looked at me over the top of his spectacles. It's about time, he said.

The Traveling Medium

JOHN KINSELLA

She'd turn up on a whim or the sniff
   of a rumor, some said
death notices in a local paper.
   She never appeared Sundays;
   and so rarely at night.
She had a way about her—invited
inside without the usual mutterings

or glances over the shoulder,
   there was something calming
and soothing about her manner: the
   elderly were her stock-
   in-trade, though more than a few
young widower-farmers took up her
offers to take them back to those days

of love; her hand on theirs brought back
   that moment when the fields
called for work and it wasn't habit.
   First contact made, she would
   efficiently arrange
to return after dark when the owl
cast its light; the cool of the night set

floorboards contracting, and stone walls
   shivering; her fee was
never mentioned, and they paid without
   asking. The smell of her
   body was what they would
remember: a hint of the bush
on a slightly damp morning. After

that, memories crowded all else out;
    even the young men who'd lost
wives couldn't recall if she was
    a great beauty. In her
    lips the voice of their love
spoke somnolently across acres,
fired blood, summoned ectoplasm

in spurts through fabric, with the calm
    that follows. "Do you mind
if I smoke?" some would ask. She never
    objected and, snapping out of it,
    would ask about crops and the state
of livestock. She'd say, "I'm going to travel
a long way out, out where the dead gather

when no one's left to call them back; out
    where they cluster like
flecks of moisture. Imagine breathing
    on a window in the
    middle of winter: the
breath appears like it was *always* water . . .
That's where I'll go, where business takes me."

Breakout

WILLIAM T. VOLLMANN

Continued from Grand Street 71.

19

Let's say for the sake of argument (although it's really not credible) that even then Lieutenant-General Vlasov didn't know about the bloody-beaten boys wrist-tied together in pairs for easier shooting, the bandaged girls led off to be shot against a wall, the schoolteachers clambering obediently up onto barrels while the noose was tied, the families noosed and then thrown off their own balconies, the young men lined up against the wall for the double-rowed firing squad. —We'll bypass that for now, as Strik-Strikfeldt would say. No, he knew; he groaned in his sleep; awaking once and twice, he'd drink away his pangs, struggling through the logic (which he stubbornly defended) of *Stalin is worse* to overtake his ideal, his love, his Eastern objective; and from a sufficiently distant aerial perspective he comes to resemble the German soldiers straining eight on a side to move a truck through kilometer after kilometer of knee-deep mud whose shining puddles proclaim their ever so beautiful reflections of birch trees. On the night table beside the almost empty bottle of schnapps there stood upended, now tarnished green from much finger-oil, a certain cartridge, Geco 7.65 millimeter. (Call it his defensive front.) But to claim on Vlasov's part more *knowledge* than that (and without knowledge it may well be that there's no responsibility) would be as simplistic and old-fashioned as Stalin's cordon strategy of defense. Strik-Strikfeldt insists in his own postwar memoirs that it wasn't until he was a prisoner and an American sergeant assaulted him with photographs of Dachau that he learned that *in German concentration camps there had been bestialities such as in no other camps in the world.* The sergeant, he indignantly writes, refused to pay credence to his cries of ignorance. But then, after all, *the world still does not believe that these thugs managed to conceal their crimes from a great part of the German people. The Western world refused to believe it—just as we, at that time, refused to believe in the betrayal of freedom by free America.* There you have it, and from a figure who always spoke as openly as his oath of service permitted him.

20

Vlasov's integrity, then, or, if you will, his wife, had shielded herself from him behind a wall of curving steel plates; through the little bulletproof window he could see her smiling lovingly and mercifully; she was ready to talk to him; she would do whatever she could to help him; but she would never embrace him again—she who had been so weak, she who had sobbingly clung to him, seeking to prolong if only by a few moments their time together in the dark and gentle room; he'd caressed her lovingly, wondering how soon without hurting her he could rise and pull on his boots. How laughable, to think that he couldn't hurt her! All she wanted was to stay with him forever. But he had things to do. Let's say that there was a war on. Or let's say that he was, like so many of us, "creative," or "married," "drafted," "politically involved," "uncommitted," "busy," "distracted," or otherwise engaged and compromised. For one reason or another, he'd made the war his war. She implored him not to go, and maybe he even had to go (let's say that a certain Adolf Hitler had invaded the country), but no, let's say—let's say nothing for a line or two except that, of course, we wouldn't want to "trivialize" World War II by extruding its gruesomeness through the star-shaped cookie-dough gun of some allegory or other—but integrity is love, and love of two entities, faithfulness to them both, may comprise betrayal of them both. (If only the pain in her eyes had killed me!) He had to go. It was like that every time until he expected it and began to manage it; it was like that every time; perhaps it even flattered him, once he became accustomed to what originally afflicted him with dread and guilt; every time it was like that, with this real and intelligent woman who loved him, I mean this allegory, mythic goddess of moral rectitude, no, I mean someone who wasn't perfect but who loved him, someone who was better than he was, someone who said to him: Andrei, can you really live like that? He had to leave her, and hated to do it, but he promised to be right back. *It is well known*, explains the Great Soviet Encyclopedia, *that the structure of emotional life changes from one historical epoch to another. Consequently, the feeling of love also changes, since it is influenced by class relationships, by changes in the personality and by changes in value orientations.* Changes in value orientations, that's it! Her eyes, her big brown eyes so often swollen from weeping, launched reproaches his way, sometimes scared ones, often angry ones; sometimes she wasn't quite fair, but she was his integrity. She warned him: I don't know how long I can do this; and then: I don't think I can do this, because he was, let's say, fighting on the side of someone who'd murdered so many millions. After his actions in that world, he kept coming back to her. His integrity said: I don't think I can do this right now. I feel as if I need to get to know you again first. —His integrity said: Is your mouth clean? You don't taste clean. —She said: You know I'm very delicate down there. I'm just not up for it right now. She said: Please don't go. She said: That feels so *perfect*. She said: Oh, sweetheart. —She was crying when she said: Don't go. Next time he saw her, she was crying, and she said: I can't do this anymore. —After that she stopped crying. She became very calm and gentle.

When the one I loved finally left me, it didn't hurt too much at first, but then my own heart, not yet killed, began to sicken with drop after drop of her poisonous absence. Then all my friends seemed to fall away, which simply means that they didn't seem like friends anymore, being no substitute for her; and with each moment that I could no longer expect to see her, my heart grew a little more inflamed with grief. As yet it was still strong, for our love had been strong (at least I thought so); therefore the death-agony must expand, elongate, and wriggle endlessly like a parasitic worm. A strong organism can't die. And so Vlasov still clung to the time when he'd been intimate with his integrity. (She'd said to him: We can lie down together for a minute if you need to, as long as it's not too intimate. I can't do that anymore, or I'll get confused. . . .)

She was a statue now, safe from him behind that thick glass. She wanted to be his friend. Merciful and distant, she pitied him. He was free now. He must make his own way in life.

21

They sent him on a tour of the occupied territories to drum up support. On 28 February 1943 he arrived in Smolensk, where he spoke to the helots to great acclaim. (This man led the Fourth Mechanized against us at Lvov! Strik-Strikfeldt was explaining to everybody in a reverential voice.) —Russia must be independent, Vlasov kept saying. Standing on a scorched and icy plinth that had once been burdened by a marble titan, he gazed down at his audience: shivering old men unfit for labor service, displaced peasant women in dark head-scarves, hungry office workers who'd been given Vlasov in lieu of a more expensive treat. To these people, who even now hadn't entirely abandoned their hope that the Germans might bring something good, his speech was electrifying. That one of their own—a famous general, no less—would be permitted to say anything at all, much less shout out a call for a Russo-German alliance against Stalin, while Wehrmacht officers stood around smiling indulgently, was a sign that some middle path, however provisional and solitary, to the salvation that most of them after more than two decades of reeducation continued to cast in religious terms, might be more than a tragic figment. (We told you so! the old men whispered. What with the partisans, and Stalingrad, and that breakout at Leningrad, Adolf can't be so arrogant anymore. . . .) Vlasov's right arm rose high in salute to forthcoming Russian victories. Then he was photographed again, at attention in a file of Fascist officers each of whom was wearing shiny knee-high boots. He toured the newly reopened cathedral: Hitler the Liberator was bringing back religion! (But wily Stalin had begun reopening churches, too.) That night, Vlasov addressed a full house at the state theater, standing room only. As yet, his sponsors dared not permit him to broadcast on the radio. He propagandized here and there for three weeks, calling for volunteers. The first Vlasov Men already stood on parade for his inspection. (Let's assume that he didn't know about the Russian prisoners of war who were being gassed at Auschwitz, shot at Dachau and Buchenwald. At Smolensk alone the death rate was hundreds per day.) Insisting that he was no puppet, he quoted the old peasant proverb: *A foreign coat never fits a Russian.* (The uniform they'd fashioned for him was brown like a storm trooper's.) To hostile questioners he replied: The Germans have begun to acknowledge their mistakes. And, after all, it's just not realistic to hope to enslave almost two hundred million people. . . .

(*You can't hang all hundred and ninety million of us,* Zoya had said.)

His erstwhile captor General Lindemann came to congratulate him, and they clinked glasses.

I must say, that was a riveting speech! These people believe in you, there's no doubt about it. . . .

Frankly, I'm in despair, said Vlasov, for he'd just learned that the formations of Russian volunteers had all been broken up and distributed among German units.

Upon my word, what kind of thing is that for a military man to say? Just be patient a little longer, and Berlin will come around, I promise you!

You see, it's not just the war crimes, it's the *absurdity*. How can your leadership fail to understand that by alienating the masses, they're obstructing their own purpose?

The German general sighed and said: Never mind, my dear fellow. The East and the West are two worlds, and they cannot understand each other.

On his return to Berlin, the spring mud of the Reich now mouse-green like Hitler's field jacket, he sent another memorandum admonishing the Reich government: *The mass of the Russian population now look upon this conflict as a German war of conquest.* (His colleague Zykov lost at solitaire and recited another stanza from Pushkin.) He advised his masters that even now it might still be possible to regain good relations with the people, so terribly had they suffered under Communism, but it was essential to make immediate changes in occupation policy.

Olenka the typist had disappeared, but her replacement, a Latvian brunette named Masha, was an even more fun-loving girl.* One morning he awoke at the Russian Court Hotel with her still sleeping in his arms. Gazing into this gentle face, he seemed to see the closed eyes of his broken wife. (And I myself, I see the big brown eyes of the woman who finally left me, the one who would have stayed with me forever if I'd only made a certain promise. She was my integrity.)

* Here we might note that in several accounts Vlasov is said to have fallen into German hands in the company of a certain Maria Voronova, whose husband was being reeducated at the expense of the state, in a certain unknown location in Siberia. To make ends meet, she cooked for the Vlasovs. At Vlasov's wife's behest, she supposedly made her way to the Volkhov pocket to care for Vlasov. In a photograph commemorating their capture, the pair sit in a military vehicle whose machine guns face the sky. Vlasov's taut, exhausted face can be seen only in near-profile. His glasses have slipped halfway down his nose. In his hand he clutches a tapering object that might well be a German cartridge, Geco 7.65 millimeter. Maria Voronova, if indeed this pallid, kerchiefed young woman is she, has managed to retain some of her attractiveness. She sits at his side, almost smiling.

22

I repeat: Thus far, the assault on Vlasov's character had accomplished only a limited tactical breakthrough. The attackers did not know how to achieve operational shock. As Strik-Strikfeldt so wisely aphorized: *Too much propaganda is merely propaganda.*

And so he found himself back at work. Coolish and warmish Berlin spring days, cloud-sogged skies and linden-shade, these exudations transfused themselves most pleasantly into his bones. He sat wondering what to do. Zykov had not yet gone missing. One wall of his shabby little office was stacked up with bales of a colleague's literary production: *And this underworld of the Untermensch found its leader: the eternal Jew!*

He received a warning from the Gestapo that the U.S.S.R. had sent a certain Major S. N. Kapustin to infiltrate his army and assassinate him. He didn't care. Drunkenly he told a bored file clerk of the female gender: I remember when I counterattacked at Nemirov. Tank fighting for four days—

Just as a shattered concentration of troops tends to polarize around the towns or command posts it knows, which is why the attacking enemy will tend to close lethal circles around those very points, so Vlasov couldn't help but be obsessed by that Geco cartridge of his, which he turned around and around between his fingers, trying to steel himself against the next offensive. Zykov laughed at him. Masha once stole his toy, just for fun, but he became very angry until she begged his pardon and blushingly dropped it back into his hand. There always seemed to be so much schnapps on hand that he stopped writing manifestos. Indeed, he soon became so listless that he scarcely bothered to chat with the man from the Office for the Germanization of Eastern Nations. A. A. Vlasov might as well have been one of Berlin's time-smoked building-stones crowned by winged figures or figures with crucifixes or figures with lances, all time-blackened into their own silhouettes. The Germans grew concerned about his health. Moreover, another proclamation of his phantom army had just come out and they didn't want to make him into too much of a one-man show. Why not let him disappear for a bit? So, with Strik-Strikfeldt as chaperon, they sent him on a rest cure. Oh, yes; they permitted him to tour the Rhine, whose coils sometimes nearly complete a circle, their aquatic thumbs and forefingers squeezing various peninsulas of forest and slate-roofed houses into almost-islandness, while summery leaves strain outward. He visited Köln, Frankfurt, Vienna. . . .

What a sight they are! cried his best friend, merrily squinting his eyes. Look quickly, my dear Vlasov! No, no, over there! Why, they practically take my breath away. . . .

In a park, rows of German girls stood with outstretched arms and breasts, mimicking their stiff wax-doll *Lehrerin* who stood above them on the monument's steps, calling out: *One—two—three—four! All together!*

Vlasov continued to drink. After considerable efforts (none of which his ward seemed to appreciate), Strik-Strikfeldt obtained permission to take him to a convalescent home for SS men in Ruhpolding, Bavaria. It was there that Vlasov met his German wife.

23

If you have ever happened to see Adolf Ziegler's *The Four Elements*, which hangs over the fireplace of our Führerhaus in München, you may remember, in the middle panel of that triptych, a slender, small-breasted blond who sits nestling against her darker-haired sister, staring modestly at the checkerboard floor while her elbow guards the junction of her chastely clenched thighs. There is something absurd (or, as Vlasov would say, unrealistic) about the poses of the other three nudes, especially the dark-haired one who daintily pulls a bit of drapery across her lap while clasping a harvest sheaf in her right hand. The blond's compact, withdrawn posture appears at least natural and comfortable. The relentless tidiness of the room in which that painting dwells, the drollness of the little round table between sofa and hearth, the fresh-scrubbed bricks of the hearth, and, above all, the insistently allegorical quality of Ziegler's work, all come together to sugarcoat its lewdness into a veritable pill of propriety. And the ridiculous gestures of those Aryan goddesses double-coat the pill. Nobody would ever hold her arms so, or tilt her head so, unless perhaps a machine-gun blast had caused that effect when it tumbled her into the mass grave! But the seated blond (if we disregard the empty bowl that Ziegler directed her to hold) could almost be a figure out of "real life."

Have you guessed that Heidi Bielenberg was an athlete? She'd been one of those blonds with braids; those blue-eyed blonds who, screaming with crowd-happiness, stretch their white-sleeved arms in salute behind a protective wall of expressionless SS men whose helmets are adorned with swastikas within red shields; so that everything everywhere grows white, black, gray, red, and blond. We first see her in a wall of German girls in tight-fitting undergarments, raising globes above their heads: *One—two—three—four! All together!* Heidi's instructor told her that she might be capable of excellence, if she worked hard and governed herself *with inflexible harshness*. She became a crack shot with a revolver and got licensed to keep a pistol (I think a 7.65 millimeter Walther). Her pretty face, which specialists had measured with calipers from nose-bridge to chin, and her hair, matched against various reference-rectangles of tinted glass, both passed muster, scientifically validating her as Aryan. At a regional competition, she stood atop a rolling hoop, stretching out a swastika flag in each arm. Then they'd invited her to take part in the Nürnberg Rally, where she shared a tent with two other girls and got to see the Führer with her own eyes! (She'd kept in touch with her tent-mates. One had already given birth to a pair of Aryan twins at a Lebensborn facility. The other was now making eighty-eight-millimeter shell fuses to do her part for total war.) Shortly after the Röhm purge, Heidi won the Reich Sports Medal, possession of which is required by any girl who aspires to wed an SS man. Himmler himself, who knew perfection when he saw it, had already entered her into the topmost classification in the card indexes of the SS Head Office for Race and Settlement.

She met her first husband at the 1938 Yuletide bonfire. Everything about him felt right to her, from his agility when he danced to the strangely tender gaze of his skull emblem's baby eyes. Everything happened in a rush. Holding his arm, clutching the bouquet in the crook of her elbow, she passed beneath the arch of saluting hands as the wedding guests chanted: *Sieg Heil! Sieg Heil!* Germany was already at war then, so she'd hardly seen Otto after the honeymoon. Two years later (it was by one of those swinging-door coincidences the time of Vlasov's capture: one husband out, the next one in), Heidi received and immediately framed the regimental telegram, which proclaimed *our proud sorrow*. His commanding officer also wrote her a letter, assuring her that it had been both heroic and instantaneous. Heidi framed that, too. She retained an almost virginal conviction that since she had suffered and borne the suffering in brave German fashion, fate was unlikely to require any further sacrifices from her. It was only at the vigil over his swastika-draped coffin, with her mother clasping her hand and so many of his comrades at attention, holding wax torches, that Heidi realized the seriousness of this struggle against Jewish bandits. Slowly she commenced to understand certain remarks and silences that she had hitherto dismissed as fruitlessly enigmatic or even defeatist. Her mother, who continued to trust in a good resolution of everything, did her best to draw Heidi back up into the mirror-pure realm of faith, and succeeded even more rapidly than she had anticipated; for the widow needed, in the spirit of the times, to give herself unendingly and show that she could be strong unto death. Every day she went to pistol practice. She told herself (but not her mother, whom such resolutions frightened a little) that she must become harder in every respect. In spite of maternity, she continued to possess the streamlined body and frank appetites of a *Sportfraulein*. She loved hiking, skiing, and other exercises in keeping with that wise Nazi adage: *The javelin and the springboard are more useful than lipstick for the promotion of health.* To Vlasov it was an immense pleasure merely to see her eat: white German bread slathered with sweet butter (not even apparatchiks could dine like that in Russia), great draughts of German pilsner, half a roast chicken at a go. At those times her face shone with such utter engrossment in her own enjoyment that Vlasov could hardly help being carried out of his gloom. If his admiration of what he thought of as her innocence might have had a patronizing quality, well, patronization is kin to the voyeurism of an old man, who wants to do what he no longer can. The sad pale face of his own immaculateness had withdrawn forever behind the blackout curtain. He was tainted now; he was mature. Why not look with pleasure upon the antics of somebody who was still fortunate to be in her moral childhood? Moreover, Heidi had a stunning chest.

I don't know whether I love you or not, he told her with his accustomed frankness. But after all this time I—I have very strong sexual feelings. . . .

Smiling, the young widow recited: *The healthy is a heroic commandment.*

24

She felt dreary most of the time. Oh, yes, she was dead, desolate, cut off; what she loved was far away beneath the Russian earth. (No name on the grave, they said—only his helmet.) As long as she could remember, she'd hated to be alone. Sometimes there was nothing to do except flip through *Signal* magazine. What she admired most about this General Vlasov was that he owned a dream for which he was willing to fight fanatically to the end. (This fellow led the main attack on our Army Group Center during the Battle of Moscow! crowed Strik-Strikfeldt with loving exaggeration.) She had heard so much about his qualities—his unshakable will, his charisma with subordinates, his intelligence, and above all (for we Germans believe that strength forms its own justification) his prowess on the battlefield. She knew about his Order of the Red Banner and the medal he'd received in China. (You really admire him, too, don't you, Herr Strik?) She even knew about the wife in Moscow. It was said that he hadn't yet cooperated with Germany one hundred percent. Who can blame Heidi for hoping to smash his defensive front?

Andrei, you're a biologically valuable man, she said, crossing her muscular thighs. You're a fighter, a son of the soil. You *deserve* to have two wives. The Führer needs your children. . . .

Vlasov laughed in embarrassment. —The Führer doesn't know he needs me—

Well, then he hasn't been informed. But didn't he approve your Smolensk Declaration?

He needs to act on it, or the Ostfront cannot be held! I'm getting worried about that. Moreover, the number of tank battalions in each Panzer division must be increased. Fortunately, Guderian's been appointed Inspector-General of Armored Troops—

Heidi rose and touched his hand. —I think you're a real Nazi and you don't even know it. Tell me this: What's your heart's desire?

To fight for the liberation of Russia.

That's exactly what my husband said. Do you find me beautiful?

Scarcely knowing what he was saying, Vlasov muttered: Heidi, when I look at you my heart beats fast. . . .

Since you're ready to die for the Führer, I'm ready to give you what you want.

25

Of course she couldn't believe that in this Slav's arms she'd be able to breed an *Übermensch*, but at the beginning it wasn't even about breeding. (Vlasov is said to have played a guitar when he wooed her. He was always sweet with her little daughter, Frauke.) The blond, blue-eyed SS men who came here to recover and then went back to the Ostfront to die, she'd had as many of them as she liked. Perhaps she wanted a change from bread and butter.

A little later, with what Himmler used to condemn in Heydrich as "cold, rational criticism," she began to brood on the lesson of Stalingrad. Her convalescents (the lucky few who'd been airlifted out of that so-called fortress) couldn't help telling her how it had really been, especially when they lay weeping in her arms. Nearly everyone except General Vlasov was getting cold feet now! —They promised our general full supply by air, so he wasn't permitted to break out even when the Panzers still had enough fuel. So we kept starving, and the Russians kept shooting and tightening the ring. . . . (What else did her charges mention? Probably not the German prison cages, nor the Russian epidemics cured with flamethrowers.) And so Heidi unrolled the map, and her pet Slav, whom they jokingly called the *democratic people's Jew*, held down the furling corners like a good doggie. Below Leningrad crouched the flag comprising four squares, two white, two black: 18. Bolshevo; then clung Korück 583 below that, Span. Legion to the west of it, SS Nordlund in between, all of them seemingly sheltered by that black frontline that ran east along the gulf shore below Leningrad, then curved by fits southeast and southwest, down toward Moscow. But her soldier-boys had whispered to her that the Russians were beginning to introduce homogenous tank armies, hundreds and then thousands of those terrible T-34s. They could break through anywhere, at any time. What if the war were really lost? Maybe even then Heidi could be First Lady of the new Russia if she married General Vlasov and he . . . —Like everybody associated with the SS, she'd grown accustomed to dreaming magnificent dreams. Besides, her mother insisted on marriage to legitimize the relationship.

Andrei darling, what do you think of what I just said?

Looking at the map, not at her, he replied with a sad little grin: Oh, well, in Moscow I had to haul everything on sleds attached to tanks. The struggle for life—

She flung her arms around him. She said: I understand you with all my heart.

The hostility of her friends, and especially of her mother, who could hardly have imagined her to be capable of committing racial disgrace with a Slav, was painful, to be sure, but not unexpected. Moreover, there comes a moment in almost everyone's life when fate (as our Führer would call it) summons us to cross the gulf of change and reestablish ourselves in an antipodal world. At such a time, even the most earnest protestations of those who love us dwindle into the merest formalities of departure.

And perhaps it enhanced Heidi's self-confidence that in every true German sense she was better than the man she'd agreed to marry. Oh, she could admit that without pity toward herself! (Allegations that Strik-Strikfeldt, whom everyone considered to be sunnily indispensable, had lent her a copy of Vlasov's Gestapo file, need not be entirely ruled out.)

He was stroking her hair. He seemed constrained or worried about something.

She murmured: Andrei, darling, I know you will always be grateful to me, and give me whatever I wish. . . .

26

Wilfried Karlovich, whatever happened to Masha?

My dear fellow, I don't have enough gray cells to remember every skirt you've—

She was a typist at Viktoriastrasse.

A typist, you say? Probably an illegal element. Here, have a look for yourself; there's nobody by that name on the roster. Come, come, why are you glaring at me in that way? Do you really think that here in the Reich people simply disappear without cause? In Stalinist Russia, now, that's a different matter—

She—

Our faithful advocate of the *Wlassow-Aktion* raised a finger for silence. Far away, they both could hear the short blasts of the early warning siren. Then he shrugged and said to Vlasov: I fear that certain assumptions are obstructing you again. Think about it. Would it be rational to harm anybody who can contribute to the war effort?

No. Not rational—

Did you really care for her all that much? If so, perhaps I can—

She was the merest flirtation, replied Vlasov in his flat way. But I'm concerned for her as a human being.

Most likely she's working in an armament factory. Meanwhile, how do you feel about Heidi? I want you to know that in recognition of your hard work, certain regulations have been waived. Your union with Heidi has been sanctioned *at the highest level*. Or is there some obstacle? By the way, what are you playing with in your pocket? Oh, I see, it's that stupid cartridge of yours. . . .

27

On 22 March 1943, we find Vlasov presiding over the graduation of the first officers' class at Dabendorf. He was very happy with his Russian Liberation Army cockade, which made use of the same three colors as the French *tricouleur* and the American Stars and Stripes. Gripping the lectern, which barely came above his waist, he continued the commencement speech: I expect each of you not only to take a stand, but to be a fanatical fighter for our ideal. What do I mean by fanaticism? Well, let's momentarily consider the logic of this war. Logically speaking, we are incapable of forcing the Bolsheviks, with their incomparably greater forces, to withdraw. Logic compels us to abandon our struggle. Therefore, I call on you to abandon logic. When I led the Fourth Mechanized at Lvov, we attacked Sixth Army—long before Stalingrad, you understand, so they were close to full strength, while we hardly had any tanks (Kroeger, stop filling up my glass!)—and so logically speaking we shouldn't have hoped for any success. But that was when General von Kleist himself paid me a real compliment. He said . . .

Let's hope he can pull this off, one officer muttered to another.

Anyhow, better here than in a camp!

What if he's been tricked?

The Führer says . . .

At her own request, and against the wishes of her mother—who'd warned: *Liebchen*, stay out of politics. It's not healthy for a woman!—Vlasov's fiancée attended the reception. I've read that she was wearing her German National Sports badge, whose interlocking letter-tendrils had been encircled by a wreath whose fruit was a single swastika. A Russian prisoner of war complimented her on it, with what might have been an ironic smile. Heidi said to him: I have to pass a test every year, or they'll take it back.

28

On the morning of 13 April 1943, a few hours before Radio Berlin made a spectacular announcement to the world, launching what Goebbels would call a *one-hundred-percent victory for German propaganda and especially for me personally*, Vlasov was sheltering listlessly in the arms of Heidi Bielenberg, enduring her endearments (the only Russian words she was ever to learn), when the telephone rang. Praying that it be a summons to command, execution, or anything other than more of this, he reached for the receiver. It was Strik-Strikfeldt.

My dear Vlasov, am I disturbing you? Listen, I have some extremely important news. I'll be over in a quarter hour.

Ya tebya lyublyu, his wife was saying.

I love you, too, he said mechanically. Rising, he began to dress.

Andrei, be prepared for everything. Be ready; be healthy—

(He was choking within his tightly buttoned collar.)

Andrei, did you hear me?

The buzzer assaulted him. He went downstairs.

Well, well, Vlasov, and have you been keeping busy?

I've been making up a list of words that are considered obscenities in both Germany and the U.S.S.R. Want to hear a few? *Internationalism. Cosmopolitan. Plutocracy. Intellectual. Softness. Weakness. Mercy.*

And what would you expect, my dear fellow? We're at war with each other, so it's natural that both our systems would get a trifle hardened and bunkered down. . . .

That's good, murmured Vlasov, you always show respect. . . .

And how's your pretty wife?

She's pretty, and she's my wife.

I take it she's *en déshabillée*, or you'd have invited me up. . . .

Wilfried Karlovich, I'm the son of peasants. I don't understand French.

Let's take a walk, said his jocular genius, and before Vlasov knew it, they had passed the Zeughaus and were crossing the river by means of the dear old Schlossbrücke whose wrought-iron horses Strik-Strikfeldt rarely failed to caress in a triply echeloned offensive. This time, however, he denied himself the snaky fish, the martial sea horse, and even the cheerfully grotesque merman whose tail transformed itself into horse legs. He was very excited. Beneath a winged Victory who proudly watched them from her pink-granite pillar he paused and said: I wanted to be the first to tell you. . . .

I'm listening.

Although I flatter myself that I've become your friend, of course there are certain aspects to your situation here that . . . well, you haven't always been fairly treated. I admit that, and I'm sorry. But there's one matter very dear to my heart in which you've never quite believed: *the honor of the German soldier*. To get right down to it, Germans really are honorable people. They don't murder women and children. I don't deny that there's been occasional wartime harshness, but not—not what you think.

So? said Vlasov.

Well, the news is going to be broadcast this afternoon. Lieutenant-Colonel Ahrens of our 537th Signal Regiment first made the report last month, but it was classified top secret until the forensic teams had made a complete investigation.

Vlasov stared at him.

It seems that a wolf was nosing around in the forest near Smolensk, and uncovered bones. Some Hiwis on work detail found the pit. They erected a cross. In due time Ahrens was notified.

You love to spin out a story, don't you?

The site is riddled with graves! The largest one is stacked twelve bodies deep. We've uncovered four thousand victims so far, and Ahrens believes there will be ten thousand more. We're already calling it the "Katyn Massacre." Do you want to guess who's buried there?

Jews, I suppose. Maybe Russians—

You joker! No, no, *no*! They're all Polish officers, and from their identity documents we've established that they were murdered between April and May of 1940.

Well, and why not? muttered Vlasov dully. You were already in Poland by then—

My dear fellow, you're really beginning to offend me! We're recording their names, and when the exhumations are completed those names will be given to the world. *Without exception, those officers were in Soviet custody.*

I can't—

It's incontrovertible. Some of them were finished off with bayonets. The German army doesn't use four-cornered ones—

All right, I believe you. So the NKVD murdered fourteen or fifteen thousand prisoners of war. Well, but—

Don't you want to know about the ammunition? his friend demanded triumphantly.

What about it?

Geco, 7.65 millimeter.

Vlasov froze. And his wooer, seeing that deep penetration had been accomplished at last, moved instantly forward to exploit the initial success.

You know very well that the Reich sold many thousands of rounds to Latvia, Estonia, Lithuania, and even the Soviet Union. Apparently your NKVD preferred the reliability of German death, as it were. (That's right; reach into your pocket and take a look.) Now, I beg your pardon if I'm trespassing on some private grief, but whatever it was that you saw in that burned village, wouldn't it be just as well if you could lay your prejudices to rest? Wouldn't you be better off, not to say happier, if you could be fair and logical? With this discovery, your hopes have been *exonerated*. So try to relax and trust in us—

29

They sent him back to the occupied territories in the hope of retaining some sort of ideological bridgehead. Their new slogan: *humane and correct treatment.* He was as pliable now as one of Buchenwald's little "doll boys" who offer themselves to the Kapos in exchange for food. From the train, he thought he heard shooting and screaming. He got drunk then and muttered: Between the breasts of Zoya . . .

Excuse me, my dear friend, laughed Strik-Strikfeldt, but perhaps I shouldn't report that comment to your wife!

In Kiev a man who'd been waiting in the lavatory whispered, in words as evenly spaced as the numbered silver standards of vanquished regiments: General Vlasov, I was a waiter at the big Nazi banquet this March. And I heard what the quartermaster said. He was quoting the Reich Commissioner of the Ukraine. I was so horrified that I memorized every word. General Vlasov, he said, and I swear this: *Some people are disturbed that the population here may not necessarily eat enough. The population cannot ask for that. One merely has to keep in mind what our heroes at Stalingrad were forced to do without. . . .*

Vlasov smilingly clapped the man's shoulder, just as he would have done with any timorous recruit. He replied in a parade-ground voice: But what can we do now? It's too late. We have to go forward and perform our best, don't you see? Because otherwise, everything we believe in would be endangered.

In Riga he saw a German private beating and kicking a Russian artist for being five minutes late to an agitprop meeting of the Vlasov Men. He sat watching; helplessly he rubbed his heavy eyes.

For the May Day celebrations at Pskov (which lies on the former Stalin Line), Vlasov appeared only when they menaced him. He'd been reliably informed that many more White Russians as well as Jews had been shot. He shaved; he cleaned his German boots. A standing ovation! Afterward, approaching the line of SS dignitaries, all of them with their hands in the pockets of their long gray cloaks, he found himself compelled to bow forward in order to grasp the barely extended hand of the SS colonel, who smiled stiffly, his eyes unsmiling, as he tilted backward and away from Vlasov, that tall, tapering statue-self of his. He said: You Russians are not soldiers as that word is usually employed. You are ideological enemies. —Vlasov shrugged. He hardly cared for his own life anymore, or so he supposed, the anguish of his lost love now falling into dormancy, but still viable like a virus, waiting for contact with the host, which was why that host, his integrity, had to smile gently and stay away, waiting patiently for his love for her to die. Off to another factory, to serve the workers hope instead of bread! Then, with true Germanic mobility, he continued back to Riga, the railroad tracks' rank grass failing by a long shot to grapple with the gray summer sky; and here he had to meet with more workers and then with a delegation from the Orthodox Church. Justifying the existence of his still hypothetical Russian Liberation Army, he quoted the proverb *A Russian can bear much which would kill a German*. (Whenever he thought of Russia, unclean feelings afflicted him, like water and blood seeping out of mass graves.) In Luga the crowds broke through the police line as they would almost do years later in Moscow when the American pianist Van Cliburn made his debut.

Do you wish to be German slaves? he dared to shout.

No!

Then fight at my side! Fight for a free Russia on equal terms with the Reich! Show the Germans what we can do!

The SS men smiled in disgust. (Come to think of it, the Germans beside Vlasov in the photographs were always smiling just a shade too broadly.) In the aisle, a Waffen-SS captain and Strik-Strikfeldt were arguing in low voices. The Waffen-SS captain said: If one gave Vlasov's army a flag—

We have!

—and his soldiers honors, one would have to treat them as comrades with natural human and political rights, and the *national Russian idea* would break through. Nothing could be less desirable to us than such a development.

Yes, yes, said Strik-Strikfeldt, smiling straight into the curtainlike, willow-like wings of the eagle on the Waffen-SS man's tank battle badge, but, if you don't mind my saying so, might it not be counterproductive to take absolutely *everything* from the population here?

Captain Strik-Strikfeldt, I'm not sure you appreciate the situation. Aren't you aware that the Führer himself has already decreed that within ten years our eastern territories must be entirely German?

Indeed, my friend, I've been told of that, although I've never seen any—

Then don't get above yourself.

(In enthusiastic corroboration of his thesis that the military situation could still be reversed, Vlasov was earnestly explaining: The problem of developing a tactical breakthrough into an operational breakthrough is only now being solved.)

Please excuse him, for he thinks in Russian. And, after all, from a strictly *rational* point of view—

I've read Vlasov's manifesto. It's a stinkingly *rational* manifesto, to be sure.

The audience was applauding Vlasov now, but afterward the only person who came forward to speak with him was a functionary from the SS Building Inspection Office for Russia. Strik-Strikfeldt, trying to improve his pet orator's morale, said: My dear fellow, you've done for the occupied territories what Shostakovich did for the other side at Leningrad last year! What powerful propaganda!

My intention was not to make mere propaganda.

He seemed satisfied then, for they'd indulged him as they would have a little child, letting him get in the last word; but then they saw him sitting with his head in his hands. Strik-Strikfeldt ran to him: Is something wrong, old fellow?

Just a mild case of operational shock, he said with a broken laugh.

In the prisoner-of-war camps he addressed the senior block leaders, who wore black armbands. (Someone was playing the accordion.) He proposed to them that fighting imperialism might be better than hauling stones up quarry steps until they collapsed and were shot; better than being torn to pieces by SS dogs, or being buried alive by trembling Jews who were then themselves buried alive; better than the experiments in the decompression chamber at Dachau (their blood didn't boil until the altitude equivalent was above seventy thousand feet). Soon he'd raised a million Vlasov Men, a million Russian soldiers fighting for Germany. He said to them: If we can help the Reich resist for another twelve to fifteen months, then we can build ourselves up into a power factor that the West won't be able to forget.

Himmler got a transcript of his speech at Gatchina, the infamous one in which he dared to call the Germans "guests of the Russians." The SS Reichsführer was furious. He reported this treason directly to the Führer's headquarters, in consequence of which the order went out to remand our Slav directly to a concentration camp. Meanwhile, the Vlasov Men were disbanded. Strik-Strikfeldt, who knew how to get around all obstacles in the most refined way, found his protégé a nice little villa on Kiebtzweg in Dahlem, not far from the Russian Liberation Army training camp. —Don't tell him he's actually under house arrest or he might feel a little trapped, he advised Heidi, who'd appeared filled with loving resolution to heal her husband.

Are you sure it's healthy for him to live in a fantasy?

Only if he believes can he make others believe. As soon as the Führer believes, it must come true.

Well, of course, the blond murmured in confusion.

And, you know, my dear girl, sometimes a man needs, how should I put it, a little bolstering up. Especially an exhausted man.

Oh, Herr Strik, you're so right, and so good to us! Do you think we'll be staying here long? If so, these walls must be whitewashed—

Vlasov was at the door. Heidi rushed into his arms, gazing at him adoringly. He kissed her three times, in the Russian manner.

30

Screened by the theatrically leafy camouflage netting over the Charlottenburger Chaussee, sequestered between bright-postered walls and sandbagged museum windows, Vlasov took long walks with his gilded victory angel. As long as she accompanied him (humming Mozart's ever so healthy German melodies), he was permitted to go almost anywhere a German could. For a long time after the woman I loved so much had left me, I kept encountering mutual friends, small gifts from her, abandoned possessions of hers; place names on the map ambushed me with recollections; from the walls, her photographs continued to smile at me so gently; after a while I realized that there was nothing to do but seek out these things whose associations caused me such agony and bury the freshly bloody grief under the dirt of new experience. Vlasov did the same. The thick green foliage of the Tiergarten reminded him of how it had been in the Russian swamps during the last days of his immaculateness; needless to say, he never mentioned anything about this to Heidi.

They both enjoyed visiting Moltke's statue in the Grosser Stern. That old Prussian genius was gazing up into the distance, stern and old and withered, with an eagle on either side of his coat of arms. (Soon there'd be Soviet bullet-holes in his legs.)

Heidi stopped humming and said: What a genius he must have been! Pure Aryan!

He was a brilliant field commander. He showed your generals the way to outflank the French—

But, Andrei, how could you have been allowed to study him in that horrid Soviet zone?

Her husband smiled a little. He said: I can quote him if you like. Here's one of his maxims from 1869: *The stronger our frontal position becomes on account of its success of fire, the more the attacker will focus his attack on our flanks. Deep deployment is appropriate to counter this danger.*

What does that mean exactly?

It means that if a river course gets blocked by a boulder, the river will flow around it.

So how can the boulder keep from being surrounded? I assume that the boulder represents—

By being longer than the river is.

But that's—

Irrational, isn't it?

So what are you saying?

That Moltke's notions are obsolete. Nobody can avoid encirclement in this age of tanks and planes. . . .

When you're encircled, what should you do?

Well, that's the question, isn't it? said he with his pitiful smile. (She was so glad that she'd been able to distract him.) You break out. You give up being a rock, and turn yourself into, let's say, oil. Then you flow around the enemy water, and, if you're strong enough, you encircle it.

But then the enemy can do the same!

Correct, he said flatly. There's no end.

His didactic, lecturing attitude irritated her. But then her mouth softened, and she slipped her arm around his waist. —I'm sorry, she said. I know you're thinking about the Ostfront.

He kept silent.

You're thinking about the Ostfront, aren't you?

Yes. . . .

Darling, you'd feel better if you told me.

Pressure on our Orel salient seems quite dangerous, although I try to reassure myself that the High Command knows more than I do. The enemy can flow right around us. At this rate—

Andrei, how close will they come before we turn them back?

I can easily see them crossing the Dnieper.

When we get home, can you show me on a map?

Yes, I can show you. No doubt Stalin still has many reserves to call on. I remember in my time, when the Siberians—

You said they might cross the Dnieper. But you still haven't said where we'll stop them?

Well, if somebody would only give me the responsibility I could . . .

You do trust in the Führer, don't you?

Ha ha! I'm not a politician; I'm only a . . . Listen. I want to ask you something. You know how hard I've tried to warn the High Command. They won't listen.

I know, I know—

Should I try to reach Himmler directly?

Oh, Andrei! she cried compassionately.

Is there anything you're not telling me?

Now she seemed to him suddenly to possess the same quality of distant gentleness as his lost brown-eyed woman, his integrity. Something terrible had happened. She was gazing at him without weeping or kissing; something was over.

Shall I call Himmler or not?

Hanging her head, Heidi temporized: What does Herr Strik say?

Vlasov stiffened. —It's no good, is it? And you won't even tell me why.

His wife swallowed nervously. She said: Andrei, be brave. You deserve to prevail. Even if the river pours over the rock, the rock can outlast it. You—

Let's go home, he said. I want a drink.

After that, disregarding all warnings, he went out alone when Heidi was in the bath. It's not likely that he was present when the heavy wooden doors of the Zeughaus opened for a show of captured Soviet weapons (and an assassination attempt upon the Führer failed, thanks perhaps to the vigilance of the facade's stone helmets turned everywhere in different directions), because who would have wanted to take responsibility for allowing Vlasov near our Führer? Still, he could have his little promenades; he could breathe the summer breath of linden trees. A girls' corps with their rakes held gun-straight against their shoulders was marching to the harvest. (An old pensioner was saying to his wife: *According to our concentration of strength . . .*) Strik-Strikfeldt, who happened to be standing right around the corner, invited Vlasov to speak to an association of military convalescents, but he declined, wandering listlessly away past a house that had been demolished by an English bomb. His best friend sprinted after him with the enthusiastic ease of a new recruit. —Not that way, dear fellow! Why, there's the Gestapo over there! They'll make mincemeat of you! Don't you remember what happened to Masha? Never mind about that stupid hospital even if they *are* expecting you; here, let me . . .

In short, Vlasov remained mired in Berlin, whose name ironically derives from a Slavic word: *brl*, meaning "marsh." He could not seem to break out of this limbo. From one blacked-out window to the next his tall reflection flicked, as pallid as a flash of lightning. (Drinking schnapps, or sitting on the toilet reading *Signal*, he remembered Vinnitsa, with himself and Strik-Strikfeldt at the rustic table, the pretty stenographer typing everything. How relaxed it had all been!) Although everybody reassured him that his blueprints for action were still being studied at the highest level, on 8 June 1943 the supreme commander himself had said, not without irritation: I don't need this General Vlasov at all in our rear areas.

With all respect, my Führer, if Vlasov helped keep the Slavs quiet until we'd finished the war, we could release many, many soldiers from anti-partisan operations—

No and again no, Hitler interrupted. No German agency must take seriously the bait contained in the Vlasov program.

The Russian Liberation Army—

That's a phantom of the first order.

Like a loyal friend, Strik-Strikfeldt concealed this new disappointment from Vlasov as long as he could. (He did think it best, however, to sit the poor fellow down and show him a report whose correctness had been confirmed by Himmler himself: Vlasov's Russian wife had been arrested and put to death in retribution for his treason. In the interest of that highest good, rationality, it was needful to show Vlasov that there could be no turning back.) At that point it was already July, by which time the Soviets had developed breakthroughs into a scientific operation performed first with tank and mechanical corps, then with tank armies. The front was becoming a sieve. But Germany's slogan continued to be *Cling to every inch!*

31

In September 1943, due to desertions, Vlasov's fledgling Russian formations were all transferred to the Westfront. This defeated their very purpose. (On the Ostfront, the enemy had now taken to calling their trench-lice *Vlasov*

Men.) Vlasov fell despondent—unhealthily so in Heidi's opinion. Towering over the others, he stood cradling his head as he gazed hopefully down at the smiling Germans, his mouth downcurled in readiness to form the shape of disappointment. Himmler, to whom he was *that Russian swine Herr General Wlassov*, had forgiven his Gatchina speech provided that he write a direct order to his men: Forget Russia; go to France. He paced the room, muttering: This is worse than a betrayal. It's an insult. We're not even to fight on our own territory now. . . . But his best friend reminded him that the Germans and the Vlasov Men were all in this together. Anyhow, there wasn't time to complain about it very long; the Red Army had broken through again. . . .

On 6 November 1943, when Kiev fell, he became as pale as Hitler had, Hitler pacing, stabbing his finger at the map, shouting to Zeitzler: We won't be able to save anything! The consequences will be catastrophic in Romania. This is a major position here . . . But Heidi said: Andrei, I have faith in you. Don't give up hope. The unhappiness you feel, it's just your Slavic blood dragging you down! You can overcome this if you fight; let me help you fight. . . .

Meanwhile the Americans had broken through at Normandy, it seemed. (How could it have been otherwise? All our Westfront had left were divisions of an obsolete static character.) In the interim, the Führer and Guderian kept trying to increase the production of Panther tanks. Vlasov sat reading the newspapers and muttering: That's an untenable line. He often quarreled with Heidi, who thought that he should at least exercise. He kept accusing the German people of a lack of generosity, to which she not unreasonably replied that Germans had bestowed upon him his life, his command, and even a new wife. He was getting pale and flabby now. He couldn't stop drinking. Upon her mother's urging, she strove to keep silent. —You married him, Liebchen. Now you have to hold fast. Like it or not, there's no going back.

I know. I'm not even angry with him really. I just wish he could somehow overcome himself. . . .

She approached her husband's desk. (He was upstairs brooding.) Dear Herr Strik's business card lay beside the telephone. She dialed.

I'll talk with him, her kind friend agreed. Just don't tell him that we've had this conversation. And don't worry about a thing; I've studied your Andrushka for quite a while now. . . .

The telephone rang.

Vlasov, said Vlasov.

Do you know Rilke, my dear fellow? Of course not. You're the son of peasants. Well, one of the early poems is often on my mind nowadays. It's called "Herbsttag," and it goes: *Lord, it is time. Summer was very grand* . . . and then in the last stanza there's a line that runs: *Who owns no house now will build no house anymore.* Do you see what he's driving at, Andrei Andreyevich?

The voice turned stern. —I said, do you see the point?

Oh, I can hold on a little longer. Don't worry about me. I'm not—

That's not what I'm getting at. You need to consider Heidi now. Don't build your future without a foundation of loyalty and—

Vlasov hung up the telephone.

The plot to kill the Führer on 20 July 1944 resulted in the execution of several Vlasov supporters. Heidi's husband had been well acquainted with them all. —I don't know them, was the epitaph he uttered. You see, I have been through Stalin's school.

On 25 August 1944, when Paris fell to the Anglo-American Jewish enemy, Vlasov lay down to dream. Heidi wasn't there at that time. All leisure for sunning herself had been overrun, so that her breasts were now as pallid as the very lights of our military positions. Oh, yes, she was going gaunt; she'd lost her color. And now little Frauke was sick. Meanwhile Vlasov's integrity had agreed to see him just one more time to extend or complete their good-bye, and so all the previous day Vlasov found himself in a state of crazy elation because until the end of their forthcoming meeting he could say to himself that she'd taken him back and was really his again; ordinarily they wouldn't have been sexual together at that time and place, so it wasn't as if anything was different; he'd be meeting her just as they used to do (except that this time the meeting would have no sequel). I myself cherish a certain envelope, sealed by me, which lies entombed in my desk drawer; on it I've written GREEN STONE. *She picked this up from the sea on our last trip together, with the date.* She *actually picked up two stones and asked me if* I *wanted one.* I *chose this.* I *wonder if she already knew that she would leave me two Fridays later?* I don't dare open the envelope to disturb the green stone that she touched when she still loved me. And if I were to try to tell you more, all I could do would be to stammer something about her big brown eyes. As for Vlasov, we know that he kept a certain copper cartridge in his pocket! (Just as Guderian said, *these men remain essentially unable to break free of recollections of positional warfare.*) He went to bed drunk on happiness, dreamed of drowning, and awoke after an hour. For the rest of the night he stared at the ceiling weeping.

On 8 September 1944, Himmler, who'd once referred to Vlasov as a "Bolshevistic butcher's apprentice," finally received him and agreed to let him command some troops. The action would be called Operation Skorpion. Vlasov nodded. Himmler put on a solemn, almost gentle look for the camera as he shook the hand of Vlasov, who was smiling earnestly, his confusion as dark as the smoke from an antitank gun. (Please remember to tell me what he's wearing, Heidi had asked him. He came to my first wedding, you know. I thought he looked awfully splendid.)

In that official photograph, Vlasov seems uncomfortable. But even in the old days he always kept his collar more tightly buttoned than the other Soviet generals, who glared or bleared into the camera, with their heads thrown wearily back. Vlasov was a formal scarecrow, drawn in on himself.

We guarantee that at the end of the war you'll be granted the pension of a Russian lieutenant-general. . . .

But I don't—

Look here, fellow, don't you know whom you're interrupting? And in the immediate future, you will continue to have schnapps, cigarettes, and women. The problem, Vlasov, is this. We can only entrust our defense to politically reliable elements. Now, in the present situation, you Slavs, with all due respect, can't exactly be armed and sent off on your own, and until the front gets shortened we just don't have the manpower to stiffen you up with German personnel. . . .

Surely our fate in the event of capture by Soviet troops ought to make for a guarantee!

Ah, we don't know about that. You changed sides once; maybe you'll do it again. The other possibility is simply to convert all you Russians to Buddhism. You see, Buddhists are pacifists, so they don't cause trouble.

Herr Reichsführer, I'm informed that you've already mustered SS brigades of Baltics and even Balkan Muslims—

Quite so, but their blood isn't as alien as yours. One has to calculate frightfully coolly in these matters. You see, in the context of the overall military situation—

What we could do with a hundred Panther tanks! Vlasov burst out.

Himmler fell silent. He was anxious. The Anglo-Americans were about to breach German soil.

Vlasov tried to hearten him: Don't you remember when Guderian broke out from the Meuse and surrounded French and British divisions from the rear? We can still do it even now!

Himmler didn't care. Himmler didn't believe.

Vlasov tried to reason with him then, saying: Everyone says that Germany is preparing secret weapons—flying bombs, V-weapons, rockets, and I don't know what else. So why not build up a few Slav armies?

Shaking his head, the Reichsführer replied: If we lose the war against you Russians, it must be because our blood has been poisoned by the Jewish virus.

Heidi's tanned face hardened when he told her. (Frauke was out with her little comrades, gathering metal for the war effort.) They sat down at the kitchen table and started drinking schnapps. Pretty soon she was sobbing and drooling on his shoulder. They drank themselves quite sober. He muttered: Well, it wasn't as if I expected him to offer me bread and salt. . . .

Is that what they do to welcome guests in your country?

Only for Germans, he replied bitterly. He added: And now not even for them!

They sat in silence, both afraid to say anything, until finally Vlasov, striving to help them withdraw from the isolated position in which they'd found themselves, cleared his throat, traced his forefinger around the rim of the glass, and murmured: Don't worry about anything. If we're fated to die, we'll die. Otherwise we'll survive no matter what.

Fate is everything, his wife agreed solemnly. I'm going to be sick.

I'm still convinced I can counterattack, if I'm deeply echeloned in both wings—

Andrei, I'll come back in a minute and then we can—

But Himmler—

This isn't healthy!

Of course it isn't, he laughed. But how can you expect anything from an *Untermensch*?

Himmler received him again on 16 September 1944. (The rumor that the meeting was arranged by Heidi through the mediation of an SS man she'd once slept with may not be entirely without foundation.) Vlasov requested ten divisions. Himmler had only two to give, and they weren't ready.

In the interest of Reich security, Himmler had already decided to table Operation Skorpion. As he remarked to SS Colonel Gunter d'Alquen: Who compels us to keep the promises we make?

32

Of course in politics one must gild the truth to the most practical (I mean reasonable) sheen, and so in those autumn days of 1944, when even Vlasov could hardly deny the concentration camps, the hostages shot in batches, the ice-grained women's corpses frozen to their hanging ropes (hadn't he once seen the ice on Zoya's eyelids, everything gray on gray?), our reasonable Russian was compelled in his latest manifesto to define the war as *a fight to the finish of opposing political systems: the powers of imperialism, led by the plutocrats of England and the U.S.A., the powers of internationalism, led by the Stalin clique, and freedom-loving nations, who thirst to live their own way of life, determined by their historical and national development.* Who could those freedom-loving nations be? No, some things he couldn't deny. And so, like a troop train occluding all the rearmost station platforms in its coming, one question he had asked and asked again now stopped before his eyes, momentarily blocking any view of Russia's future.

And what about the Jews? he asked for the very last time.

Sorrowfully clapping him on the shoulder, Strik-Strikfeldt replied: All German-held territories are being cleansed of Jews on political rather than economic grounds.

On political grounds? What exactly does that mean?

My dear fellow, you know very well that everybody in the East is anti-Semitic. And these, well, let's call them pogroms, they're a cheap way to win the trusting obedience of your White Russians.

But the Jews—

They're better off, said his friend. After all, they're unreliable elements. Where could we permit them to go? It's better to release them from the situation.

Vlasov gazed at him gently. —How does that make you feel about yourself, Wilfried Karlovich?

Never mind that. No, don't leave just yet. I still have some pretty good cognac here, and now that the Americans control Paris I don't suppose we'll be getting any more, so we might as well—here. I seemed to know that you'd ask that question sometime, but . . .

Yes, said Vlasov breathlessly. I know what you're thinking. You want to know why I didn't ask you a long time before now.

You did.

I did, but I . . .

Well, I thought of that, to be sure. He'll ask me, I thought. And then . . . From the very first I tried to protect you, because I knew that you were decent, and as long as you didn't know too much, you could save yourself, which no matter how one looks at it is a benefit. (Do you think I've saved myself? In fact, I . . .) I mean, if a single Russian prisoner of war is saved, that's a net good, isn't it? Unofficial sources have told me that three or four *million* have already died in captivity—

Don't worry, Vlasov said. You're still my friend. I just . . . But let me ask you something. What you told me about the Katyn massacre, that was—confirmed?

Ha, ha! I can see your fingers moving in your pocket. You must be playing with that Geco shell. Yes, I swear it!

That's all right then, said Vlasov warmly. Then I don't care. We're all murderers. And maybe if I don't surrender to despair I can still do something good. But what about Heidi? Were you—

Forgive me, my dear fellow. I only wanted to bring you security and perhaps divert you a little. Don't you care for her? If not, I can—

The radio was shouting: *To freshen our German blood . . .*—He went away to stroke the fair and silky hair of his Aryan wife.

33

I know, said Heidi. Of course it's difficult to know how to feel. I went through that stage with my first husband. You need to harden yourself, Andrei.

The bombing of Berlin was growing heavier now.

In October 1944, the Russians captured their first German town. Smashing in the heads of babies, nailing naked women to barn doors, they took their joyous revenge. Heidi, who was now wiring ignition systems for Messerschmitt fighter planes, heard on the radio that the men had been made to hold lamps and watch as their womenfolk were raped by hordes of Red Army soldiers. Men who resisted were castrated; women who resisted were disemboweled. When the Germans recaptured the place, they found lines of women and children laid out in a field, with cartridges glittering beside them. So Goebbels made a speech. He warned that we were all going to have to strengthen our wills and harden our hearts. . . .

34

In November 1944, the Nazis sponsored a conference in Prague. (Where were the Jews who'd lived there? —*Gone away*.) At the railroad station, a long line of German soldiers accorded Vlasov their best Nazi salutes. He stared back, scratching vaguely at the general's stripes on his uniform trousers. He'd been almost promised a command over the criminal remnants of the SS Kaminski Brigade (for Kaminski was shot for excessive ruthlessness against the Warsaw rebels). He'd nearly been given authority over a misplaced light-armed detachment; he had a fair chance of becoming Führer of three shattered, demoralized Russian units recalled from the collapsing Westfront. It was up to him to show what he could do. Could he only help the Reich to break out of the Bolshevik trap—why, then, he'd get rewarded exactly as he deserved! Cleaning his glasses, he waited for Kroeger to bring the schnapps. And now, in the citadel, dignitaries gave speeches in commemoration of the new Prague Manifesto, which the SS had prepared over Vlasov's signature. The only part he'd objected to was an anti-Semitic passage. Strik-Strikfeldt, who'd begun to worry about his own postwar career, refused to interpret Vlasov's remarks at the triumphal banquet, but it seemed that this odd tall Russian didn't hold it against him, for just after midnight he staggered over to say: Wilfried Karlovich, Washington and Franklin were traitors in the eyes of the British crown. As for me . . .

You need to lie down, my dear fellow. Go back to your table. Where's your wife? She must be very proud of you. . . .

God give me strength! But you're a god, aren't you, Wilfried Karlovich?

I beg your pardon? (Excuse me, gentlemen. They get like this when they drink, you know. It's a racial characteristic.)

Wilfried Karlovich, you'll escape with the Führer and help him, because you're a god. You're Loki. And one day you'll tell everybody at Valhalla that I wasn't a traitor. . . .

This man led the Fourth Mechanized against us at Lvov! Strik-Strikfeldt said hastily. He also—

I'll explain how we Russians do it, said Vlasov, and as he said *we Russians* he could not restrain his own pride. It's not only rational; it's as smooth as an execution of Jews! First, we break through the enemy's defenses—

That insect is talking about *our* defenses, said an SS man in disgust.

In at least one sector, more if possible. (Kroeger keeps filling up my glass.

I suppose he thinks that's funny.) Second, we launch offensives into the breakthrough areas. Third, we continue these offensives to the enemy flanks. Fourth, we encircle the enemy's units, which have been isolated by the previous measures—

It's true; he really is the Houdini of breakouts, interrupted Strik-Strikfeldt, looking at the ceiling.

And if you want an example of what I'm talking about, continued Vlasov with a defiant smile, I refer you to the Byelorussian operation of this year, whereby the Soviet army successfully—

This is too much!

Shoot that Slav in the back of the head!

But in the end they decided that, "when the time was right," Vlasov would be permitted to fight on Czech soil.

35

Why not now? The front line was approaching like a tidal wave. All our Russian conquests had long since been submerged. As the *Great Soviet Encyclopedia* explains, *in this long and bitter struggle, the U.S.S.R. armed forces proved to be mightier than the mightiest war machine in the capitalist world.* Now the wave curled over the dismembered corpse of Poland. In the former Reichskommissariat Ostland, the former Reichskommissariat Ukraine and even the eastern regions of our General Government, artillery barrages, infantry beachheads, and hordes of T-34 tanks roiled, comprising discrete aspects of a sentient metallic liquid. The defenders fell back. When Vlasov read that the Red Army had recaptured Lvov, he could not forbear to think of his own long-lost battle there, and he remembered something else, too—namely, that on the day before Lvov fell to the Germans, the NKVD had butchered Ukrainian political prisoners by the hundreds, shooting them right there in their cells. And now Russians in their Studebaker trucks came to run over the carcasses of horses in the burned streets, looted the last stale bread from shops, then passed on, vanishing in the smoky air. Warsaw wouldn't detain them long, it seemed. Soon the General Government would be completely un-Germanized. Then they'd drown the last territories of what had once been Poland—Katowice, Zichenau, Reichsgau Wartheland and Reichsgau Danzig–West Prussia—under a sea of steel that would mask itself as Poland renewed. (It wouldn't be Poland at all. It would be a Soviet vassal state.)

Vlasov understood this much better than Himmler, who has been characterized by Guderian as *an inconspicuous man with all the marks of racial inferiority*. Whenever they hid his schnapps, Vlasov sat poring over maps, with sullen destiny circling overhead like an enemy bomber. There he was, condemned to positional warfare again! (Well, even a non-German like you would be eligible for the War Merit Cross, they said, slapping his shoulder encouragingly.)

His men were digging antitank ditches. When he asked them how they were holding up, they said with weary smiles: Never mind, General. It's not much worse than working on the collective farm. . . .

36

On 20 January 1945, the Russians crossed the borders of the Old Reich and entered our heartland. On 25 January, the despairing, raging Führer appointed Himmler to take command of Army Group Vistula. On 27 January, General Guderian (long since in bad odor for having told too many truths about the military situation) was saying at the briefing conference: Vlasov wanted to make some statement.

Vlasov doesn't mean a thing, snapped Hitler.

And the idea is that they should go around in German uniform! Göring put in, as if to himself. That only annoys people. If you want to lay hands on them, you find they're Vlasov's people. . . .

I was always against putting them into our uniform, said Hitler, scratching at the red spots on his cheeks. But who was for it? It was our *beloved* Army, which always has its own ideas—

The very next day, Vlasov was at last given command of two divisions. Once again he found himself on the front line of a lost war, in possession of a low density of artillery and tanks. At best he could achieve some localized breakthrough into death.

37

And now, when it was once again too late for anything, his troops became ever more various, even fabulous: Great Russians, Ukrainians, Mensheviks, monarchists, murderers, martyrs, lunatics, perverts, democrats, escaped slaves from the underground chemical factories, racists, dreamers, patriots, Italians,

Serbian Chetniks, turncoat Partisans who'd realized that Comrade Stalin might not reward them after all, peasants who'd naïvely welcomed the German troops in 1941 and now rightly feared that the returning Communists might remember this against them, dispossessed Tartars, pickpockets from Kiev, brigands from the Caucasus who raped every woman they could catch, militant monks, groping skeletons, Polish Army men whose cousins had been murdered by the NKVD in 1940, NKVD infiltrators recording names in preparation for the postwar reckoning (they themselves would get arrested first), men from Smolensk who'd never read the Smolensk Declaration and accordingly believed that Vlasov was fighting especially for them, men who knew nothing of Vlasov except his name, and used that name as an excuse—a primal horde, in short, gathered concentrically like trembling, distorted ripples around its ostensible leader, breaking outward in expanding, disintegrating circles across the map of war. When the British Thirty-sixth Infantry Brigade entered Forni Avoltri at the Austro-Italian border, they accepted the surrender of a flock of Georgian officers, no less than ten of whom were hereditary princes "in glittering uniforms," or so runs the brigade's war diary. Suddenly pistol shots were heard. The Englishmen suspected ambush, but it turned out to be two of the princes dueling over an affair of honor. The victors' bemusement was increased by the arrival of the commander, a beautiful, high-cheeked lady in buckskin leggings who came galloping up to berate her men for having yielded to the enemy without permission. Leaping from the saddle, she introduced herself as the daughter of the King of Georgia. (Needless to say, no kings remain in our Georgian Soviet Socialist Republic, which happens to be the birthplace of Comrade Stalin.) All these worthies considered themselves to be members in good standing of Vlasov's army. Vlasov, the princess explained, had guaranteed the independence of Georgia. . . .

By now the Red Army had occupied Silesia, the Americans were about to cross the Rhine, and Vlasov stood regarding the horizon with a wrinkled, distorted, staring, twisted old face, heavily burdened by his horn-rimmed spectacles. His Russians nudged each other when they saw him, proudly infecting one another with the hope they craved more than hot soup: *There goes our general! They say he often gets the Führer's ear.* . . . Munitions, maps, impossible orders, devoted counterattackers silhouetted against snowy fields, these wouldn't help him much. No matter what, he'd be compelled to withdraw into a shortened line.

He requested a copy of Guderian's famous Panzer manual, but they told him that they wouldn't be giving him any tanks, so . . . He said to them: Even under Bolshevism I was permitted to keep this book! and they shrugged.

From behind two machine guns implanted in a heap of snowy mud, a Waffen-SS lieutenant wandered up to Vlasov's men and said in hearing of Vlasov himself: Ha ha! Now I'm glad we didn't finish you off! It's an honor, you know, to be permitted to fight for Germany.

On the night of 13 February 1945, the British and the Americans burned thirty-five thousand people, mainly civilians, in an incendiary bombing raid in Dresden. This slightly bettered the Nazi achievement at Babi Yar, where only thirty-three thousand Jews had been machine-gunned. Goebbels proposed shooting one Allied prisoner for each victim. When somebody told Vlasov, he replied: Kroeger keeps filling up my glass and perhaps he thinks that's how to manage me. He's wrong. I can see and hear. . . .

Not long after that he got his marching orders at last and set off, leading his ill-equipped men into the snow, while a tank gun pointed overhead. He'd do what he could. They reminded him of his doomed Siberians in the Volkhov pocket, fighting Fascists with antitank rifles. (He came across two of his hungry men fighting over a rotten potato, and said to them: We can't beat Stalin with open fingers, only with a clenched fist. Stick together, boys!—and they made up at once, gazing at him with awed faces.) Could he repeat his bygone achievement at the Battle of Moscow? Again and again he told the SS handlers how his breakthrough echelon had thrown back the Fascist Army Group Center. They smirked nervously, warming their hands in their pockets; for even they could see that he was addressing the ghost of his integrity, who, pale and brown-eyed, had taught him how to feel.

Another Katyusha rocket illuminated the night with shards of terror, but Vlasov was saying: Once Comrade Stalin himself gave me a division on its last legs. Well, when I got through with it, it won a competition!

(Where was it now? Hands and rags dangled down from the smoking pyre.)

They sent him to a zone of murderous impossibility. If he "used up" all his men, he could only have delayed the enemy for a few hours. He might as well have marched everybody to Auschwitz to get worked to death! From the girls' school that was now his headquarters (Kroeger had already pinned up a poster of HITLER—THE LIBERATOR), he radioed the new commander of Army Group Vistula.

Frankly, Vlasov, I can't understand why you Russians even want to fight. With the front going to hell, how can two divisions make any difference?

With all respect, that's not the issue. We urgently require artillery support to—

The artillery's not available. Why don't you just attack in waves? You Russians are famous for, you know, overrunning positions through sheer—

Herr Colonel-General, the German cadets who tried that were all wiped out yesterday. Moreover, the river's flooded, so our offensive front is limited to a hundred meters. Naturally, the enemy have trained their guns on that spot—

I really have to say that after all we've done for you, a bit more enthusiasm might . . . Do you have any proposal whatsoever?

Air support—

Out of the question. You're living in the past, Vlasov. I order you to neutralize that bridgehead without further delay.

Colonel-General Heinrici, I'm not under your command.

Oho! Now it comes out! You see, I *knew* you were an unreliable element! Don't think I won't report this! So you refuse to acknowledge German authority?

According to the Prague Manifesto, we're your formal allies. Our status is—

Toilet paper! The important thing is, will you do something about that Russian position or not?

No longer caring how this would end, Vlasov demanded: Could you at least supply us with ammunition?

Capture it from the enemy.

Without adequate support the operation is pointless. I request permission to withdraw my men to another front.

I'll be obliged to speak to Himmler about this, Heinrici said curtly.

As you wish. Good day, Herr Colonel-General.

Heil Hitler!

The conversation terminated. Vlasov lit a cigarette. His deputy, Zherebkov, whom he'd already ordered to seek an understanding with the Western Powers, exchanged with him a salvo of knowing bitter smiles.

Well, sir, what else can we expect?

Vlasov frowned. —Send in the regimental commanders. We'll hear their assessment.

You don't mean—

I'm going to telephone Himmler and tell him we'll attack, but under protest. That's the only way to save ourselves. You and Bunyachenko will take command. I'll go to Berlin for a few days. When the attack fails, break it off and tell Himmler you can't act again without my authority.

I understand.

Before the action, instruct the commanders privately to save as many of our men's lives as possible. That can't come from me, because I'm . . .

Yes, sir. And in Berlin will it still be possible to—

Actually, I'm not going to Berlin at all. I'll be in Karlsbad visiting my wife.

On 13 April 1945, the Russians conquered Vienna. Shortly after that, thanks to the convenient contraction of the front, Vlasov was able to see Heidi for the last time. She'd become even thinner, and much more dependent. In honor of his coming, she'd painted her lips as bright a red as the service colors of the Luftwaffe flak division. She and her mother kept praising him, for they believed that he'd performed another miracle of breaking out of Russian encirclement. He sat there stiffly, unwilling to pain them with the true case; fortunately they weren't suspicious at all; they'd never read an untrue line in *Signal* magazine. —Don't worry, her mother was saying. The Führer won't allow the Russians to get us. He'll gas us instead.— They drank schnapps together. Heidi's mother wanted to know whether he had passed through Reichenhall when he came, for that was a very pretty, very *German* little town. When they raised glasses for the toast, Heidi's hand began shaking. Vlasov cried out: Here's to disappointed hopes! and then they drank in silence.

I suppose you lovebirds want to be alone, said his mother-in-law, while Heidi smiled mechanically, plucking at her wasted face. A concussion sounded far away. Vlasov gazed at the blackout curtain. The stuffy, shabby little kitchen constricted him so much that he could hardly breathe.

(Yes exactly—disappointed hopes! Just as the Führer himself, enslaved by positional illusions, had consistently refused to allow the Ostfront to contract under enemy pressure, and thereby permitted the Russians first to break through, then to encircle many of his most crucial units, so Vlasov for his part had withheld from his various hopes the power of mobility. Faith masqueraded as reason; spearheads of circumstance isolated those static hopes of his, and the hopes perished.)

As soon as little Frauke fell asleep, his wife drew him into the bedroom. The love and need in her eyes made him feel ashamed. She'd remained as steadfast as the stars on his collar. Weeping softly, she begged him to impregnate her. She said: This may be my final chance to receive the Honor Cross of the German Mother.

(They heard her mother coughing on the other side of the wall.)

Five days later, Vlasov's scouts found the little house in the Allgaü where his best friend's family lay hiding. Peeking through the almost-curtained window, Frau Strik-Strikfeldt clapped a hand over her open mouth. She had thought them all safe, settled here at the heart of this last isle of German summer, where steep yellow-green meadows were shaded by evergreen forests. For years she'd vainly tried to persuade her husband not to mix himself up with Slavs. And now this. Smiling, our jolly old Balt emerged in the doorway. Fruitlessly he stretched out his hand. He swallowed. With a pettish laugh, he cried: How changeable fortune is! Sometimes a man can hardly catch his breath! Don't think I'm indifferent to all you've suffered. (By the way, you need a shave.) What can we do when—speaking of which, I heard a splendid joke the other day. *Definition of cowardice: Leaving Berlin to volunteer for the Ostfront!* Ha ha, ha ha ha ha!

The tall, pallid puppet seated itself before him on a concrete shard. It plucked a dandelion. Then it drew a tall bottle of schnapps from its rucksack. Resheathing the bottle without sharing it, it rose, and remarked with wooden formality: Germany has collapsed sooner than I expected.

But, my dear fellow, the Führer has promised that our "Wonder Weapons" will soon be ready. . . .

Forgive me, Wilfried Karlovich, but I . . . Anyhow, there's no use in having it out with you. I don't blame anyone. What is it that Heidi always says? *The strongest survives.*

(He remembered the way home: the barbed wire, the sentry, then the horseshoe barricades and truncated pyramids of sandbags on Smolensk Street, followed by the door that couldn't quite close, the pitch-dark, icy stairs, the inner door, and beyond that a desperation clotted into darkness that in turn had frozen into grief and sickness where his other wife, his integrity, lay waiting.)

On 27 April 1945, his comrade Zherebkov urged him to flee to Spain by air, to work for the liberation movement in securer surroundings. Vlasov replied that he wished to share his soldiers' fate.

After that, we find him in the midst of the Prague Uprising, issuing his commands on a scarcely audible field telephone. On 8 May 1945, as skeletonized buildings became lyres for flames to play upon, the Czech National Council sent an urgent appeal to Vlasov's troops, begging them to turn against the Fascists, but when he tried to negotiate asylum after the war, the Czechs replied that they could guarantee nothing. That very same day, accepting the entreaties of his soldiers, he turned his attention to the Anglo-American zone. (She was whispering: And then come home to me, Andrei . . .) On 11 May, he demanded to be judged by the International Tribunal, not by any Soviet court. The following day the Red Army broke into his sector. Hanging his cartridge belt from a wrecked girder, Vlasov summoned the spurious protection of an American convoy en route to Bavaria. His hopes resembled corpses frozen with outstretched hands on a plain of dirty melting snow.

38

And so one more time Vlasov found himself compelled to disband his encircled army and advise his men to break out in small groups. Some were lucky enough to reach the Americans and surrender to them. Vlasov, of course, was not.* His stations of the cross remained thoroughly in keeping with the times: first the bridge with a British sentry on one side, a Soviet guard on the other; then the crossroads at the edge of the forest where light tanks and searchlights trained their malice on the "Fascist chaff"; next the barbed-wire compound, followed by the first interrogation in the lamplit tent (NKVD men crowding in to regard him as if he were a crocodile); the first beating; the chain of prisons, each link east of the last; the inspections, tortures, questions; the stifling windowless compartments of Black Marias that lurched down war-cratered roads; the murmur of Moscow traffic; finally, the Lubyanka cells. The very first thing they'd taken away was his memory token (Geco 7.65 millimeter). Punching him in the teeth, they raised that German shell in triumph—literal proof that he was a murdering Hitlerite! Vlasov wiped his bloody mouth. All he wanted now was to get through the formalities.

* The Soviet claim that he was found on the floor of a Studebaker truck, wrapped up in a roll of carpet "like a coward," has not yet been verified.

A photograph of the Soviet military court in Moscow shows him to have become paler than ever after his year of "interrogation," but unlike several of the other defendants whose nude heads bow abjectly, Vlasov stands defiant, his bony jaw clenched, his heavy spectacles (which will be removed on the day when all twelve men get hanged, heads nodding thoughtfully as they sway before the brick wall) occluding our understanding of his eyepits.* Rubbing his bleached blank forehead, he was actually wondering whether some amalgam of planning and determination could save his colleagues. He thought not. Anyhow, he got distracted just then by the hostile testimony of his former commanding officer, K. A. Meretskov, who'd abandoned him (as he now believed) at Volkhov, and who'd never been able to give him any better talisman than that meaningless phrase *local superiority*.

Meretskov looked rather well these days. In his evidence proffered to the court, he referred more than once to "the Fascist hireling Vlasov." With a shadow of his old energy, the accused man smiled upon him, his glasses gleaming like a skull's eye sockets.

The prosecutor demanded to know which of his fellow ghosts and shadows had first recruited him into the anti-Soviet conspiracy. Vlasov cleared his throat. He licked the stump of a newly broken tooth. Remembering how Comrade Stalin had once said to him: Speak the truth, like a Communist! he accepted full responsibility for his actions.

We might say that his mistake was cosmopolitanism, which the *Great Soviet Encyclopedia* defines as the bourgeois-reactionary ideology of so-called world citizenship. Cosmopolitanism pretends to be all-embracing. Really it's but a front for the aggressively transnational surges of capital. Humanistic pacifism and utopianism are other masks of the same phenomenon—which of course differs utterly from proletarian internationalism.

On 2 August 1946, *Izvestiya* announced that pursuant to Article 11 of our criminal code, the death sentence of the traitor A. A. Vlasov had been carried out.

* According to certain émigré sources, whose provenance naturally excludes them from credibility, the accused was warned that he might be tortured to death if he didn't cooperate. —"I know that, and I'm extremely afraid," he is alleged to have replied. "But it would be even worse to have to vilify myself . . ."— The even more mendacious accusation that Vlasov and his cohorts were hanged with piano wire, a hook being inserted at the base of each skull, can be refuted with the simplest extract from the Program of the Communist Party of the Soviet Union: "Communist morality is the noblest and most just morality, for it expresses the interests and ideals of the whole of working mankind."

Contributors

FELICE BEATO was born in the 1820s near Venice, possibly on the island of Corfu, in Greece. He learned photography from the Scottish-born architectural and topographical photographer James Robertson, and was the first photographer to devote himself entirely to working in Asia and the Middle East. His career was long affiliated with images of war: the Indian Mutiny and its aftermath in the late 1850s; the Opium War in China in 1860; and the Sudanese colonial wars in 1885. The photographs he took of the Indian Mutiny in collaboration with his brother are thought to be the first to show human corpses on a battlefield. Beato died in 1908 in Burma, where he was working as a furniture merchant.

BEI DAO is the pseudonym of Zhao Zhenkai, who was born in Beijing in 1949 and lives in Davis, California. He is a Foreign Honorary Member of the American Academy of Arts and Letters. His most recent publications in English translation are a volume of poetry, *Unlock* (New Directions, 2000), and a collection of essays, *Blue House* (Zephyr Press, 2000).

ARTHUR BISPO DO ROSÁRIO was born in Japaratuba in northeast Brazil in 1911 and died in 1989. The first major exhibition of his work, "Registros de Minha Passagem pela Terra" (Records of my passage on earth), was organized in 1989 at the Visual Arts School of Parque Lage, Rio de Janeiro, and traveled to São Paulo, Pôrto Alegre, and Belo Horizonte, Brazil. Subsequent solo exhibitions have been held at the Museu de Arte Moderna do Rio de Janeiro (1992), the Brazilian pavilion of the 1995 Venice Biennale, and the Galerie Nationale du Jeu de Paume, Paris (2003). Bispo do Rosário's work has been included in the group exhibitions "Imagenes del Inconsciente" (Images of the unconscious) at the Proa Foundation, Buenos Aires (2001), and "Brazil: Body and Soul" at the Solomon R. Guggenheim Museum, New York (2002).

ROBERTO BOLAÑO was born in Santiago, Chile, in 1953, and is the author of five novels and five books of poetry. His short-story collection *Llamadas telefónicas* (Lost calls; Anagrama) won the prestigious Santiago de Chile Municipal Prize in 1997, and his novel *Los detectives salvajes* (The wild detectives; Anagrama, 1998) won the Premio Herralde de Novela and Premio Rómulo Gallegos. His writing has appeared in *Grand Street* 68 and 70, and his novella *By Night in Chile* is forthcoming from New Directions in December 2003. Bolaño passed away on July 14, 2003.

INGER CHRISTENSEN was born in 1935 in Denmark and lives in Copenhagen. The winner of numerous European literary awards, she writes in several genres, but it is her poetry that has established her as one of the leading figures in modern Scandinavian literature. An English translation of Christensen's *alphabet* was recently published by New Directions (2001), and a second volume of her poetry, titled *Butterfly Valley: A Requiem*, is forthcoming from New Directions in 2004. Her work has been translated into more than a dozen languages.

MARGARET JULL COSTA was born in 1949 in Richmond, just outside London, and currently lives in Leicester, England. She has been a professional translator since 1987 and has translated works by many Spanish, Portuguese, and Latin American writers. Her awards include the 1992 Portuguese Translation Prize for her rendering of Fernando Pessoa's *The Book of Disquiet*; the translator's portion of the 1997 International IMPAC Dublin Literary Award for Javier Marías's *A Heart So White*; and the 2000 Weidenfeld Translation Prize for José Saramago's *All the Names*. She is currently translating Saramago's latest novel, *The Duplicated Man*, to be published by Harcourt in fall 2004.

CYNTHIA CRUZ was raised in Germany and California. Her poems have appeared or are forthcoming in the *Paris Review*, the *Boston Review*, *Chelsea*, and *Pleiades*, among others. She has received fellowships to Yaddo and the MacDowell Colony and teaches poetry in New York City schools as part of the Teachers & Writers Collaborative.

JOANNE DIAZ received her M.F.A. from New York University, where she was a New York Times Foundation fellow. Her poems have appeared in *Prairie Schooner*, *Crab Orchard Review*, *Poetry International*, and the *Notre Dame Review*. She lives in Chicago and is a graduate student in the English department at Northwestern University.

WILLIAM EGGLESTON was born in Memphis, Tennessee, in 1939. Solo exhibitions of his work have been held at the Museum of Modern Art, New York (1976); the Corcoran Museum of Art, Washington, D.C. (1977, 1990); the Victoria and Albert Museum, London (1983, 1985); the Museum Folkwang, Essen (1992); the J. Paul Getty Museum, Los Angeles (1999–2000); and the Fondation Cartier pour l'art contemporain, Paris (2001–02), among other venues. He was awarded the 1998 Erna and Victor Hasselblad Foundation International Photography Award, and his work was featured in Documenta 11, Kassel, Germany (2002). Eggleston's published collections of photography include *William Eggleston's Guide* (Museum of Modern Art, 1976), *The Democratic Forest* (Doubleday, 1989), and *Faulkner's Mississippi* (Oxmoor House, 1990). "William Eggleston: Los Alamos," opened at the Museum Ludwig, Cologne, in March 2003 and will travel to the Museu Serralves, Porto, Portugal; the Louisiana Museum of Modern Art, Humlebaek, Denmark; the Albertina, Vienna, Austria; and the Dallas Museum of Art.

PAUL FARLEY was born in Liverpool in 1965. He has published two collections of poetry with Picador in Britain: *The Boy from the Chemist Is Here to See You* received the 1998 Forward Prize for Best First Collection, and *The Ice Age* was awarded the 2002 Whitbread Poetry Prize. He is also a recipient of the Somerset Maugham Award and was the Sunday Times Young Writer of the Year in 1999. He lives in Lancashire, England.

ROBERT FRANK was born in Zurich, Switzerland, in 1924, and emigrated to the United States in 1947. His first book of photographs, *The Americans*, was published by Grove Press in 1959 with an introduction by Jack Kerouac. In the late 1950s, Frank turned his attention to cinema: his films include *Pull My Daisy* (1959), which he made with the Beat poets, and *Cocksucker Blues* (1972), a documentary portrait of the Rolling Stones. Frank has had solo exhibitions at venues worldwide, including the Philadelphia Museum of Art (1969); Kunsthaus, Zurich (1995); the Museum of Fine Arts, Houston (1986); the National Gallery of Art, Washington D.C. (1994); the Stedelijk Museum, Amsterdam (1995); the Whitney Museum of American Art, New York (1995); the Yokohama Museum of Art, Japan (1995); and the Museo Nacional Centro de Arte Reina Sofia, Madrid (2001). In 1990 the Robert Frank Collection was established at the National Gallery of Art, Washington, D.C. Frank's numerous awards include the Erna and Victor Hasselblad Foundation International Photography Award (1996), and the Cornell Capa Award of the International Center of Photography (2000). "Robert Frank: London / Wales" opened in 2003 at the Corcoran Gallery of Art, Washington, D.C., and will travel to the Tate Modern, London.

GAO XINGJIAN was born in 1940 in the Jiangxi province in eastern China. He studied French literature at the Beijing Foreign Languages Institute, graduating in 1962. The publication of his *Preliminary Discussions on the Art of Modern Fiction* (Huacheng, 1981; banned 1982) and the Beijing People's Theater's staging of his controversial plays *Absolute Signal* (1982), *Bus Stop* (1983; banned 1983), and *Wild Man* (1985) displeased the authorities, and he was subjected to various forms of harassment. In 1987, he relocated to Paris. Gao received the Nobel Prize for Literature in 2000, marking the first time the prize has been awarded for a body of Chinese-language writings. Among his works, the novel *Soul Mountain* (HarperCollins, 2000) was singled out for special acclaim by the Swedish Academy. Gao's other works of fiction in English include the novel *One Man's Bible* (HarperCollins, 2002) and a forthcoming collection of short stories, *Buying a Fishing Rod for My Grandfather* (HarperCollins, 2004), the title story of which appears in this issue.

ARTHUR GOLDHAMMER has translated more than eighty books from the French. His new translation of Emile Zola's novel *The Kill* is to be published by the Modern Library this winter. He is a Chevalier de l'Ordre des Arts et des Lettres and was awarded the Médaille de Vermeil by the Académie Française.

DIETER M. GRÄF was born in 1960 in Ludwigshafen, Germany, and lives in Cologne. He has published three volumes of poetry with Suhrkamp: *Rauschstudie: Vater + Sohn*, 1994; *Treibender Kopf*, 1997; and *Westrand*, 2002.

TAYLOR GRAHAM's poems have appeared in *Ascent*, *International Poetry Review*, the *Iowa Review*, the *New York Quarterly*, *West Branch*, and elsewhere. Her latest collections are *Lies of the Visible* (Snark Publishing, 2003) and *Harmonics* (Poet's Corner Press, 2003). Graham is a volunteer search-and-rescue dog handler in the Sierra Nevada mountains in California.

HOWARD HALLE is a senior editor at *Time Out New York*.

HERBERTO HELDER was born in 1930 in Funchal, on Madeira Island, Portugal, and lives on the outskirts of Lisbon. He is one of Portugal's leading post-surrealist poets, and his work is well known in France, Spain, and Italy. Helder's poems have appeared in English translation in *Boulevard*, *Barrow Street*, *Cream City Review*, *Confrontation*, and *Osiris*, among other journals.

EMILY JACIR was born in 1970 and currently lives and works in New York and Ramallah, in the West Bank. Her work has been included in numerous group exhibitions, including "Greater New York" at P.S. 1 Contemporary Art Center, New York (2000); "Uncommon Threads" at the Herbert F. Johnson Museum, Cornell University, New York (2001); "Queens International" at the Queens Museum, New York (2002); and the Istanbul Biennial, Turkey (2003). In 2003, she has had solo exhibitions at Debs & Co., New York; Frumkin Duval Gallery, Los Angeles; and the Khalil Skakini Cultural Centre, Ramallah, among other venues.

JOHN KINSELLA's *Peripheral Light: New and Selected Poems* will be published by Norton in November 2003. He is a professor of English at Kenyon College and a Fellow of Churchill College, Cambridge University.

MABEL LEE was born in 1939 of Chinese parents in northern New South Wales, Australia. She majored in Chinese studies at the University of Sydney where she obtained her Ph.D. in 1966 and took up an academic appointment in the same year. In the 1990s she began translating the works of two contemporary Chinese writers, Yang Lian and Gao Xingjian. In 2001, Lee received the New South Wales Premier's Prize for Translation and the PEN Medallion, and in 2003 she received a Centenary Medal "for service to Australian society and literature."

ALEXIS LEVITIN's translations have appeared in the *Partisan Review*, *American Poetry Review*, *Kenyon Review*, and *Chelsea*, among other magazines. He has published twenty volumes of translations, the most recent being *Forbidden Words: The Selected Poetry of Eugenio de Andrade* (New Directions, 2003). He is currently working on the poetry of Herberto Helder and Sophia de Mello Breyner Andresen under a 2003 NEA Translation Fellowship.

JULIO LLAMAZARES was born in Vegamián, Spain, in 1955. He has published two books of poetry, *La lentitud de los bueyes* (The slowness of the ox, 1979) and *Memoria de la nieve* (The memory of snow, 1982), both with Hiperión. His novels, published by Seix Barral, include *Escenas del cine mudo* (Scenes from silent movies, 1993), *El río del olvido* (The river of forgetting, 1995), and *La lluvia amarilla* (*The Yellow Rain*, 1988), which will be published by Harcourt in 2004 and from which the excerpt in this issue of *Grand Street* was taken. Llamazares lives and works as a journalist in Madrid.

CHARLES MEREWETHER is an art historian and curator at the Getty Research Institute in Los Angeles. He has taught at the University of Sydney, the Universidad Autonoma in Barcelona, the Universidad Iberoamericana in Mexico City, and the University of Southern California. He was a 2003 Fellow at the Humanities Research Center, Australian National University (Canberra), and the recipient of a Japan Foundation Research Fellowship.

His writing has appeared in journals and catalogues in Europe, the Americas, Australia, and Asia. He is currently working on exhibition and book projects on art in post-war Japan and contemporary China.

SARAH EMILY MIANO was born in Niagara Falls, New York, in 1974 and recently received an M.F.A. in creative writing from the University of East Anglia in England. Her first novel, *Encyclopedia of Snow*, was published by Picador in spring 2003. Miano currently lives in London.

WANGECHI MUTU was born in Nairobi, Kenya, and received a B.F.A. from Cooper Union for the Advancement of Arts and Sciences, New York, and an M.F.A. from Yale University School of Art, New Haven. Her work has been included in numerous group exhibitions, including the 1997 Johannesburg Biennial; "Out of the Box" at the Queens Museum, New York (2001); and "Africaine" at the Studio Museum in Harlem, New York (2002). Her first solo exhibition was held in September 2003 at Susanne Vielmetter Los Angeles Projects.

SUSANNA NIED is a writer and literary translator whose most recent publications are *Selected Poems* by Søren Ulrik Thomsen (Poetry New York, 1999) and *alphabet* by Inger Christensen (New Directions, 2001). She was the winner of the 1981 PEN/ASF translation award. Her translation of Christensen's *Butterfly Valley: A Requiem*, in which "Watersteps" appears, is forthcoming from New Directions in 2004.

ISAMU NOGUCHI was born in Los Angeles in 1904 and spent his childhood in Japan. In 1924, he abandoned his medical studies at Columbia University to devote himself to sculpture. After being awarded a Guggenheim Fellowship in 1927, he worked as a studio assistant to Brancusi in Paris. During the 1930s Noguchi supported himself through portrait sculpture, while beginning collaborations with Buckminster Fuller and Martha Graham. His first important body of abstract sculpture was made during the 1940s and was exhibited with the New York School. A Bollingen Foundation Fellowship launched a period of international activity for him, with public commissions in Europe and Asia, as well as in the United States. He established a studio in Japan in 1969 and dedicated himself to stone carving. Retrospectives of his work were shown at the Whitney Museum of American Art, New York, in 1968, and the National Museum of Modern Art, Tokyo, in 1992. The Isamu Noguchi Garden Museum in Long Island City, New York, opened in 1985. In 2004, the Whitney Museum of American Art, New York, will present a centenary exhibition of his work, which will travel to the Hirshhorn Museum and Sculpture Garden, Washington, D.C. Noguchi died in 1988.

ADRIANO PEDROSA is a curator, writer, and editor. He is a regular contributor to *Artforum* and *Frieze*, and his work has appeared in *Art Nexus*, *Art+Text*, *Bomb*, and *Flash Art*, among others. Pedrosa has contributed and edited several exhibition catalogues on contemporary art, most recently monographs on Beatriz Milhazes and Ernesto Neto. His curatorial projects include "F[r]icciones" (Museo Nacional Centro de Arte Reina Sofia, Madrid, 2000–01, with Ivo Mesquita); the São Paulo Bienal (1998, adjunct curator); and the "exhibition in a book" titled *Cream 3: 10 Curators—100 Artists—10 Source Artists* (Phaidon, 2003). Pedrosa is cocurator of inSITE 2005 (San Diego/Tijuana), curator of Coleção de Paisagens Paulo A. W. Vieira (Rio de Janeiro, Brazil), curator of Coleção Teixeira de Freitas (Lisbon, Portugal), and curator of Museu de Arte da Pampulha (Belo Horizonte, Brazil), where he is responsible for the exhibition program and the collection.

Artist and architect **MARJETICA POTRČ** lives in Ljubljana, Slovenia. Her work has been featured in exhibitions throughout Europe and the United States, including the São Paulo Bienal (1996); Skulptur Projekte in Münster, Germany (1997); "La casa, il Corpo, il Cuore: Konstruktion der Identitaeten," Museum Moderner Kunst Stiftung Ludwig, Vienna, Austria (1999); "Urban Visions," Worcester Art Museum, Massachusetts (1999); and Manifesta 3, Ljubljana, Slovenia (2000). She has had solo exhibitions at the Center for Curatorial Studies Museum, Bard College, Annandale-on-Hudson (1996); the Solomon R. Guggenheim Museum, New York (2001); the Künstlerhaus Bethanien, Berlin (2001); and the IVAM

Center Julio Gonzales, Valencia (2003), among other venues. Potrč has received numerous awards, including grants from the Pollock-Krasner Foundation (1993, 1999) and the Soros Center for Contemporary Arts, Ljubljana (1994), as well as the Guggenheim Museum's Hugo Boss Prize (2000).

NEIL PRINTZ is the coeditor of the first two volumes of the *Andy Warhol Catalogue Raisonné: Paintings and Sculptures, 1961–1969*, published by Phaidon in 2002. He is currently preparing a catalogue raisonné of Isamu Noguchi's work.

MINNA PROCTOR's translations from Italian include *Love in Vain: Selected Stories*, by Federigo Tozzi (New Directions, 2001), which won the PEN Poggioli Prize; and *Belief, Non-Belief: An Exchange*, by Umberto Eco and Carlo Maria Martini (Arcade, 1999). Her essays and criticism have appeared in the *American Scholar*, *The Nation*, *Aperture*, the *New York Observer*, and *Bomb*. Proctor is currently organizing a special Italian issue of the *Literary Review*, and her nonfiction study of religious calling is forthcoming in 2004 from Viking.

EDWARD W. SAID is University Professor of English and Comparative Literature at Columbia University in New York. His recent books include *Parallels and Paradoxes: Explorations in Music and Society*, with Daniel Barenboim (Knopf, 2002), an excerpt from which appeared in *Grand Street 71*; *Reflections on Exile and Other Essays* (Harvard, 2000); and *Out of Place: A Memoir* (Knopf, 1999).

MARK SCHAFER is a literary translator and visual artist living in Cambridge, Massachusetts. He has translated many Latin American authors, among them novelists Alberto Ruy Sánchez and Virgilio Piñera, poets Gloria Gervitz and Alberto Blanco, and essayists José Lezama Lima and Julio Ortega. His translation of Jesús Gardea's collection of stories, *Stripping Away the Sorrows from the World*, was published in 1998 by Editorial Aldus/Mercury House. He is currently working on translations of Gloria Gervitz's epic poem *Migraciones*, a collection of selected poems by David Huerta, a collection of essays by Antonio José Ponte, and a novel by Belén Gopegui.

ANDREW SHIELDS was born in Detroit in 1964 and has lived in Basel, Switzerland, since 1995. His poems, prose, and translations have appeared in journals on both sides of the Atlantic. In 2004, Harcourt will publish two books that he translated from the German: the correspondence of Martin Heidegger and Hannah Arendt, and *The Cello Player*, a novel by Michael Krüger.

FRANKLIN SIRMANS is a freelance writer, editor, and curator based in New York. A former U.S. editor of *Flash Art* magazine, Sirmans was recently named editor in chief of *Art AsiaPacific*. His writing has appeared in the *New York Times*, *Essence*, *Art in America*, *Artnews*, and *Time Out New York*. He has also edited and contributed to numerous catalogues on contemporary art, including *Transforming the Crown: African, Asian and Caribbean Artists in Britain* (University of Chicago Press, 1998) and *Basquiat* (Tony Shafrazi Gallery, 1999). Sirmans has curated a number of exhibitions in Europe, Asia, and North America, including "One Planet Under a Groove" (cocurator, Bronx Museum), which has traveled to Minneapolis, Atlanta, and Munich.

CHARLIE SMITH lives in New York City and is the author of a dozen books of poetry and fiction, including *Heroin and Other Poems* (Norton, 2000) and *Shine Hawk* (Simon & Schuster, 1988). His new volume of poetry, *Women of America*, is forthcoming from Norton in 2004. He has received grants from the Guggenheim Foundation, the National Endowment of the Arts, and the New York Foundation for the Arts.

ANTONIO TABUCCHI was born in Pisa in 1943. He lived in India and Portugal before settling in his native Tuscany, where he holds the Chair of Literature at the University of Siena. Tabucchi, who writes in Italian and Portuguese, has won numerous awards for his work, including the Prix Médicis Etranger. A new collection of his stories will be published by New Directions in 2004.

KENZO TANGE was born in Imabari, Japan, in 1913, and studied architecture at Tokyo University. Tange's first important commission was the Peace Park in Hiroshima in 1949. The Olympic Stadium in Tokyo, 1961–64, is one of his most admired works, and his urban planning designs have been implemented in Tokyo Bay (1960); Skopje, Yugoslavia (1966); and Bologna, Italy (1967). His works of architectural theory include *Katsura: Tradition and Creation in Japanese Architecture* (Yale University Press, 1960) and *Ise: A Prototype of Japanese Architecture* (MIT Press, 1965). In 1987 he was awarded the Pritzker Prize for Architecture.

DOROTHEA TANNING was born in Galesburg, Illinois, in 1910 and lives and works in New York City. She has also lived in Chicago, Arizona, and for twenty-eight years in France. In addition to her work as a painter, printmaker, and sculptor, Tanning has designed sets and costumes for ballet and theater productions in New York, London, and Paris. Retrospective exhibitions of her paintings, drawings, and sculpture have been held at the Centre National d'Art Contemporain, Paris (1974); the Malmö Konsthall, Malmö, Sweden (1993); and Camden Arts Centre, London (1993). Her work is represented in numerous permanent collections, including the Museum of Modern Art, New York; the Centre Georges Pompidou, Paris; the Menil Collection, Houston, Texas; the Philadelphia Museum of Art; and the Tate Modern, London.

ANN TEMKIN is the Muriel and Philip Berman Curator of Modern and Contemporary Art at the Philadelphia Museum of Art.

WILLIAM T. VOLLMANN is the author of eight novels, three collections of stories, and two nonfiction works. Vollmann's writing has appeared in the *New Yorker*, *Esquire*, and *Granta*, and he is a frequent contributor to *Grand Street*. His new nonfiction book, *Rising Up and Rising Down*, parts of which were featured in *Grand Street* 65, will be published in five volumes by McSweeney's in fall 2003.

Novelist, essayist, and poet **ABDOURAHMAN A. WABERI** was born in Djibouti in northeast Africa in 1965. In 1985, he moved to Caen, France, to study English language and literature. Waberi's first volume of stories, *Le Pays sans ombre* (Land without shadows; Le Serpent à Plumes), was published in 1994 and received the Grand prix de la Nouvelle francophone from the Académie Royale de Langue et de Littérature Française de Belgique and the Prix Albert Bernard of the Académie des Sciences d'Outre-mer de Paris. In 1996, another volume of stories, *Cahier nomade* (Nomad notebook; Le Serpent à Plumes), received the Grand Prix Littéraire de l'Afrique noire. Waberi's first novel, *Balbala*, was published in 1997 (Le Serpent à Plumes). In 2000, his first volume of poems, *Les Nomades, mes frères, vont boire à la Grande Ourse* (Nomads, my brothers, are going to drink from the Great Bear), was published by Pierron and in 2003 his second novel, *Transit*, was published by Gallimard. Waberi's writing has appeared in many international newspapers, including *Africultures*, *Le Monde*, *Libération*, *Le Figaro*, *Le Nouvel Observateur*, *DU*, and *Lettre International*. He lives with his family in Caen, where he works as an English teacher.

ELIOT WEINBERGER is an essayist and translator. His latest books are *9/12* (Prickly Paradigm, 2003), a collection of political articles, and *The New Directions Anthology of Classical Chinese Poetry* (2003), which he edited.

Grand Street would like to thank:
MARIA PAULA ARMELIN, WINSTON EGGLESTON, JACK FEHER, THELMA GOLDEN, STOKES HOWELL, PAMELA S. JOHNSON, EMILIO KALIL/BRASIL-CONNECTS, MICHAEL KANDEL, EDMOND MOUKALA, PEI HONG YE, JIM SAMPAS, EDWARD J. SULLIVAN, DAN TSO, ANN WAGAR, HÅKAN WAHLQUIST, JULIAN ZUGAZAGOITIA, LLOYD ZHAO

This issue of *Grand Street* is dedicated to the memory of
ROBERTO BOLAÑO (1953–2003)
JOSEPH CHAIKIN (1935–2003)
RACHEL CORRIE (1979–2003)
MOHAMMED DIB (1920–2003)
DR. DAVID KELLY (1944–2003)
JEAN-PIERRE MAHOT DE LA QUÉRANTONNAIS (1946–2003)
KIRK VARNADOE (1946–2003)

Illustrations

Front cover William Eggleston, *Untitled*, ca. 1969. Gelatin silver print, 8 x 10". Copyright © Eggleston Artistic Trust. Courtesy of the artist.

Back cover William Eggleston, *Untitled*, ca. 1969. Gelatin silver print, 8 x 10". Copyright © Eggleston Artistic Trust. Courtesy of the artist.

p. 7 Photograph by Robert Frank. Title and date appear with image. Gelatin silver print, 10 x 8". Copyright © Robert Frank. Courtesy of the artist and Pace/MacGill Gallery, New York.

p. 8 Copyright © Roger Ressmeyer/CORBIS.

pp. 24–32 Portfolio: William Eggleston. **pp. 25, 27, 29, 31,** and **32** All photographs untitled, ca. 1973. Gelatin silver prints, 7 x 5". **pp. 26, 28,** and **30** All photographs untitled, ca. 1969. Gelatin silver prints, 8 x 10". All images copyright © Eggleston Artistic Trust. Courtesy of the artist.

pp. 43, 44, 47, 48, 50, 51, and **53** Photographs by Isamu Noguchi. Titles and dates appear with images. Gelatin silver prints, 8 x 10". Courtesy of the Isamu Noguchi Foundation, Inc., New York.

pp. 59–68 Portfolio: Arthur Bispo do Rosário. Titles and dates appear with images. **p. 60** *Presentation Mantle*, n.d.: fabric and thread, 46 5/8 x 55 1/2 x 7 7/8". **p. 61** Wood, metal, glass, plastic, and cotton fiber, 76 3/8 x 29 1/8 x 11 13/16". **p. 62** Fabric and thread, 61 7/16 x 52 3/4". **p. 63** Concrete, wood, and glass, 4 3/4 x 19 11/16 x 2 3/8". **p. 64** Rubber, plastic, wood, and fabric, 42 15/16 x 24 13/16 x 11 13/16". **p. 65** Fabric, wood, and plastic, 33 1/16 x 15 9/16". **p. 66** Fabric, thread, and wood, 57 1/2 x 77 3/4". **p. 67** Spindles, fabric, wood, and plastic, 46 7/16 x 9 7/16 x 29 5/16". **p. 68 (left)** Assemblage with purses: Wood, cardboard, wool, plastic, fabric, straw, and metal, 66 15/16 x 24 13/16 x 7 7/8". **(center)** Blue jacket: Fabric and plastic, 26 x 18 1/2 x 7 1/16". **(right)** Assemblage with objects: Wood, metal, plastic, rubber, ceramic, glass, fabric, and leather, 78 3/4 x 31 1/2 x 6 5/16". **pp. 60** and **68** Photographs by Walter Firmo. Copyright © Walter Firmo. Courtesy of the photographer. **pp. 61–67** Photographs by Fernando Chaves, for exhibition catalogues for "Mostra do Redescobrimento: Brasil +500" (Ibirapuera Park, São Paulo, 2000) and "Brazil: Body & Soul" (Solomon R. Guggenheim Museum, New York, 2001–02), both organized by BrasilConnects Cultura. Copyright © Fernando Chaves. (**pp. 61, 63,** and **64** Photographs courtesy of BrasilConnects Cultura. **pp. 62** and **65–67** Photographs courtesy of Fernando Chaves.) All works collection of the Museu Bispo do Rosário/Instituto Municipal de Assistência à Saúde Juliano Moreira, Rio de Janeiro.

p. 70 Hubert P. Dubois, *Cheminot de Djibouti à Addis-Abeba: Le Chemin de Fer Franco-Éthiopien* (Paris: Librairie académique Perrin, 1959), plate 17. Photo credit: C.F.E. General Research Division, The New York Public Library, Astor, Lenox and Tilden Foundations.

pp. 76–80 Portfolio: Marjetica Potrč. Eight untitled drawings, 2003. Marker on paper, each 12 x 9". For "CaracasCase and the culture of the informal city," a project of the Federal Cultural Foundation of Germany and the Caracas Urban

Think Tank. Courtesy of the artist and Max Protetch Gallery, New York.

pp. 82 and **86** Photographs by Felice Beato. Titles and dates appear with images. **p. 82** Albumen silver print, 12 x 10". **p. 86 (top)** Albumen silver print, 9 3/4 x 11". **p. 86 (bottom)** Albumen silver print, 9 x 11 3/4". All images courtesy of the Michael and Jane Wilson Collection, Santa Barbara Museum of Art.

p. 90 Collection of the Poly Museum, Beijing.

p. 93 Copyright © Carl & Ann Purcell/CORBIS.

pp. 95–105 Portfolio: Emily Jacir. From the series "Where We Come From," 2002–03. Color photographs and text, dimensions variable. Courtesy of the artist and Debs & Co., New York.

p. 108 Photograph by Sven Hedin. Title and date appear with image. Copyright © Sven Hedin Foundation, Stockholm.

pp. 126–139 Portfolio: Dorothea Tanning. Titles and dates appear with images. **p. 127** Photocollage, 7 3/4 x 10 1/2". Collection of the artist. **p. 128** Graphite on paper, 5 x 12 3/8". Collection of the artist. Photo: Christian Carone. **p. 129** Fabric, synthetic fur, door, wool, metal, and wristwatch, 70 7/8 x 37 3/8 x 44 7/8". Private collection, Milan. Photo: J. P. Augerot, Nice. **p. 130** Graphite on paper, 19 1/4 x 17 1/8". Collection of the artist. Photo: Christian Carone. **p. 131** Fabric, wool, synthetic fur, cardboard, and Ping-Pong balls, dimensions variable. Collection of the Musée National d'Art Moderne, Centre Georges Pompidou, Paris. Photo: J. Faujour. **p. 132** Fabric, wool, synthetic fur, cardboard, and Ping-Pong balls. **(left)** 39 3/8 x 25 1/8 x 16 1/8". **(right)** 27 1/2 x 16 1/8 x 12 5/8". Collection of the Musée National d'Art Moderne, Centre Georges Pompidou, Paris. **p. 133** Upholstered chair, tweed, and wool, 31 1/2 x 47 1/4 x 33 1/2". Collection of the Musée National d'Art Moderne, Centre Georges Pompidou, Paris. **p. 134** Watercolor on paper, 8 3/4 x 11 3/4". Private collection, New York. **p. 135** Fabric, wool, cardboard, and Ping-Pong balls, 14 1/2 x 45 1/4 x 19". Collection of the Tate Modern, London. Photo: Christian Carone. **p. 136** Velvet, paint, gun pellets, plastic, and pins, 15 3/4 x 17 15/16 x 15 3/4". Collection of the Tate Modern, London. Photo: Christian Carone. **p. 138** Ink, watercolor, and wash on paper. Image: 6 3/4 x 5 1/4", paper: 9 1/2 x 6 1/4". Collection of the artist. **p. 139** Fabric, metal, and wool, 69 5/8 x 19 3/4 x 20 1/2". Collection of Galerie Jan Krugier, Geneva. Photo: J. P. Augerot, Nice. All images copyright © Artists Rights Society (ARS), New York. Courtesy of the artist.

pp. 156–160 Portfolio: Wangechi Mutu. Titles and dates appear with images. **p. 157** Ink and photocollage on paper, 60 x 44". **p. 158** Ink and photocollage on Mylar, 24 x 36". **p. 159** Ink and photocollage on Mylar, 20 x 16". **p. 160** Ink, paint, and photocollage on Mylar, 20 x 17". All images courtesy of the artist and Susanne Vielmetter Los Angeles Projects.

pp. 168, 170, and **173** Photographs courtesy of the author.

Back Issues

36

Edward W. Said on Jean Genet • Terry Southern & Dennis Hopper on Larry Flynt • Saul Steinberg • Elizabeth Bishop • William T. Vollmann • William Eggleston • John Ashbery • Antonio Tabucchi • Bei Dao • Jeannette Winterson

37

William S. Burroughs on guns • John Kenneth Galbraith on JFK's election • Pierrette Fleutiaux • "Blackboard Equations" • John McIntosh • Clark Coolidge • Suzanne Gardinier • Charles Simic • Robert Creeley

38

Kazuo Ishiguro & Kenzaburo Oe on Japanese literature • Robert Rauschenberg • a lost chapter of Julio Cortázar's *Hopscotch* • Linda Connor • Fernando Pessoa • Charles Wright • Ben Sonnenberg • Jimmy Santiago Baca

39

Nadine Gordimer: *Safe Houses* • James Miller on Michel Foucault • Hervé Guibert • Dubravka Ugrešić • Mark di Suvero • Amiri Baraka • Michael Palmer • John Yau • Theodor W. Adorno • Ammiel Alcalay • Jonathan Franzen

40

Gary Giddins on Dizzy Gillespie • Toni Morrison on race and literature • Yehudit Katzir • Marcel Proust • Gretchen Bender • Arkadii Dragomoshchenko • Brice Marden • Tom Paulin • Umberto Eco

41

Nina Berberova on the Turgenev Library • Ben Okri • Mary-Claire King on tracing the "disappeared" • Louise Bourgeois • Kurt Schwitters • Jean Tinguely • Eugenio Montale • Rae Armantrout • David Mamet

42

David Foster Wallace: *Three Protrusions* • Henry Green: an unfinished novel • Félix de Azúa • Eduardo Galeano • Sherrie Levine • Jorie Graham • Ariane Mnouchkine & Ingmar Bergman—two productions of Euripides • Gary Snyder

43

Jamaica Kincaid on the biography of a dress • Stephen Trombley on designing death machines • Victor Erofeyev • Christa Wolf • Kabir • Joseph Cornell • Robert Creeley • Kenzaburo Oe • Sue Williams • Jorge Luis Borges

44

Martin Duberman on Stonewall • Andrew Kopkind: *Slacking Toward Bethlehem* • Georges Perec • Edmund White • Fred Wilson • William Christenberry • Lyn Hejinian • Theodor W. Adorno • Sharon Olds

45

John Cage's correspondence • Roberto Lovato: down and out in Central L.A. • David Gates • Duong Thu Huong • Ecke Bonk • Gerhard Richter • A. R. Ammons • C. H. Sisson

46

William T. Vollmann on the Navajo-Hopi Land Dispute • Ice-T & Easy-E: L.A. rappers get open with Brian Cross • David Foster Wallace • Italo Calvino • Nancy Rubins • Dennis Balk • Michael Palmer • Martial

47

Louis Althusser's *Zones of Darkness* • Edward W. Said on intellectual exile • Jean Genet on *The Brothers Karamazov* • Barbara Bloom • Junichirō Tanizaki • Julio Galán • Jospeh Lease • John Ashbery • Stig Larsson • Ovid

48 OBLIVION

William T. Vollmann: *Under the Grass* • Kip S. Thorne on black holes • Heinrich Böll • Charles Palliser • Saul Steinberg • Lawrence Weiner • Mahmoud Darwish • Antonin Artaud

49 HOLLYWOOD

Dennis Hopper interviews Quentin Tarantino • Terry Southern on the making of *Dr. Strangelove* • Paul Auster • Peter Handke • William Eggleston • Edward Ruscha • John Ashbery • James Laughlin • Tom Paulin

50 MODELS

Alexander Cockburn & Noam Chomsky on models in nature • Cees Nooteboom • Graham Greene's dream diary • Rosario Castellanos • Katharina Sieverding • Paul McCarthy • Robert Kelly • Nicholas Christopher

51 NEW YORK

William S. Burroughs: *My Education* • Terry Williams on life in the tunnels under NYC • William T. Vollmann • Orhan Pamuk • Richard Prince • David Hammons • Hilda Morley • Charles Simic • Ecke Bonk on Marcel Duchamp

52 GAMES

David Mamet: *The Room* • Paul Virilio on cybersex and virtual reality • Fanny Howe • Brooks Hansen • Walter Benjamin • Robert Williams • Chris Burden • Miroslav Holub • Dennis Hopper on Golf • Georganne Deen

53 FETISHES

John Waters's film fetishes • Colum McCann • Samuel Beckett's *Eleuthéria* • Georges Bataille • Simon Armitage • Helmut Newton • Yayoi Kusama • Taslima Nasrin • Man Ray • Rosmarie Waldrop

54 SPACE

"Born in Prison": an inmate survives the box • Jasper Johns's galaxy works • Vladimir Nabokov • Irvine Welsh • Vito Acconci • James Turrell • W. S. Merwin • John Ashbery • Alberto Giacometti • Robert Venturi

55 EGOS

Dennis Hopper • David Foster Wallace • Kenzaburo Oe • Amiri Baraka • Julian Schnabel: *The Conversion of St. Paolo Malfi* • Suzan-Lori Parks on Josephine Baker • Susie Mee • Brigid Berlin's *Cock Book* • Pierre Boulez

56 DREAMS

Edward Ruscha: *Hollywood Boulevard* • Lydia Davis • *Terry Southern and Other Tastes* • Jim Shaw • ADOBE LA • Luis Buñuel • Bernadette Mayer • Saúl Yurkievich • Franz Kafka • Karlheinz Stockhausen

57 DIRT

John Waters & Mike Kelley: "The Dirty Boys" • Rem Koolhaas on 42nd Street • Mohammed Dib • Sandra Cisneros • Langdon Clay • Alexis Rockman • Robert Creeley • Thomas Sayers Ellis • Alan Warner

58 DISGUISES

Anjelica Huston on life behind the camera • D. Carleton Gajdusek: *The New Guinea Field Journals* • Victor Pelevin • Arno Schmidt • Kara Walker • Marjorie Welish • Hannah Höch • Vittorio Sereni

59 TIME

John Szarkowski: *Looking at Pictures* • Mike Davis on the destruction of L.A. • Naguib Mahfouz • Nina Berberova • Spain Rodriguez • Adonis • Charles Ray • James Tate • William S. Burroughs • Luis Buñuel

60 PARANOIA

Fiona Shaw on life in the theater • Salvador Dalí on the paranoid image • David Foster Wallace • Nora Okja Keller • Tom Sachs • David Cronenberg • Fanny Howe • Lawrence Ferlinghetti • Michael Hofmann • Antonin Artaud

61 ALL-AMERICAN

William T. Vollmann tracks the Queen of the Whores • Doris Salcedo • Peter Sellars: *The Director's Perspective* • Aimé Césaire • Reinaldo Arenas • Guillermo Cabrera Infante • Rubén Ortiz-Torres • Octavio Paz

62 IDENTITY

Edward W. Said on Mozart's dark side • Robin Robertson • Marcello Mastroianni explores his past • Can Xue • Marcel Beyer • Mona Hatoum • Christopher Middleton • Robert Rauschenberg • Shirin Neshat's "Women of Allah"

63 CROSSING THE LINE

John Waters interviews drag king Mo B. Dick • Elias Canetti's aphorisms and adages • Franz Kafka • Patrick Chamoiseau • Lygia Clark • Justen Ladda • Guillaume Apollinaire • Hilda Morley

64 MEMORY

David Mamet recalls his *Salad Days* • A lost play by Tennessee Williams: *Not About Nightingales* • José Saramago • Tony Smith • Murathan Mungan • Nancy Spero • John Ashbery • James Laughlin • Pablo Neruda

65 TROUBLE

William T. Vollmann's treatise on violence: *Rising Up and Rising Down* • Fiction and reportage from Algeria • Einar Már Gudmundsson • Christopher Fowler • Larry Burrows • Sam Taylor-Wood • Zbigniew Herbert

66 SECRETS

An interview with Ingmar Bergman about his childhood demons • Peter Brook's meditation on *Don Giovanni* • António Lobo Antunes • Victor Pelevin • Rianna Scheepers • Susan Meiselas • Joseph Cornell • Bruce Nauman • Bertolt Brecht

67 FIRE

José Saramago's Nobel Prize lecture • prose poetry by Cees Nooteboom • Bilge Karasu • Linda Lê • Ben Okri • Ana Mendieta • Yves Klein • Nari Ward • John Ashbery • Sándor Csoóri • Ryan Oba • Roberto Bolaño

68 SYMBOLS

Mike Davis on Pentacostal L.A., with photos by William Eggleston • a scene from Andrei Tarkovsky's unrealized film *Hoffmanniana* • Ozren Kebo • Lídia Jorge • Alberto Guerra Naranjo • Willie Cole • Alfred Jensen • Nizar Kabbani • Vladimir Nabokov

69 BERLIN

Cees Nooteboom's *Return to Berlin* • Bertolt Brecht's *War Primer* • an excerpt from Heiner Müller's autobiography • Ingo Schulze • Günter Grass • Emine Sevgi Özdamar • Hannah Höch • Hans Haacke • Albert Ostermaier • Judith Hermann • John Heartfield

70 AGAINST NATURE

Edward W. Said & Daniel Barenboim discuss music and exile • Roberto Bolaño • Shelley Jackson • Kiki Smith • Lucinda Devlin • Durs Grünbein • Volker Braun • Michael Longley • Enrique Vila-Matas

71 DANGER

James Rosenquist's meteor paintings • A. L. Kennedy • René Char • Alan Warner • Mike Davis on the Los Angeles Fine Arts Squad • William T. Vollmann • Neo Rauch • Vija Celmins • Alice Oswald • Isabella Kirkland • Roman Signer • Vladimir Sorokin • Harun Farocki

Some of the bookstores where you can find Grand Street

Charles H. Scott Gallery, Vancouver, Canada
Magpie Magazine Gallery, Vancouver, Canada
Vancouver Art Gallery, Vancouver, Canada

Bailey Coy Books, Seattle, WA
Elliott Bay Book Co., Seattle, WA

University of North Dakota Bookstore, Grand Forks, ND

Powell's Books, Portland, OR

Berkeley Art Museum Store, Berkeley, CA
Black Oak Books, Berkeley, CA
Cody's Books, Berkeley, CA
Laguna Art Museum, Laguna Beach, CA
Armand Hammer Museum of Art, Los Angeles, CA
Dutton's Brentwood Bookstore, Los Angeles, CA
Skylight Books, Los Angeles, CA
Depot Bookstore, Mill Valley, CA
Vroman's, Pasadena, CA
Richard L. Press, Sacramento, CA
The Booksmith, San Francisco, CA
City Lights, San Francisco, CA
MuseumBooks–SF MOMA, San Francisco, CA
Arcana, Santa Monica, CA
Hennessey & Ingalls, Santa Monica, CA
Reader's Books, Sonoma, CA
Small World Books, Venice, CA
Book Soup, West Hollywood, CA

Boulder Bookstore, Boulder, CO
Books Buffs, Denver, CO

Asun Bookstore, Reno, NV

Sam Weller's Zion Bookstore, Salt Lake City, UT

Ergo Books, Santa Fe, NM

Ceres Books, Dallas, TX
SMU Bookstore, Dallas, TX
Menil Collection Bookstore, Houston, TX

David Mirvish Books on Art, Toronto, CANADA
Pages, Toronto, CANADA

University of Maine Bookstore, Orono, ME
Books Etc., Portland, ME
Casco Bay Books, Portland, ME

Hampshire, Amherst, MA
Boston University Bookstore, Boston, MA
ICA Boston, Boston, MA
Brookline Booksmith, Brookline, MA
Harvard Book Store, Cambridge, MA
BNI College, M.I.T. Bookstore, Cambridge, MA
M.I.T. Press Bookstore, Cambridge, MA
Nantucket Bookworks, Nantucket, MA
Broadside Bookshop, Northampton, MA
Bunch of Grapes Bookstore, Vineyard Haven, MA
Rainbow New England, Worcester, MA

UConn Co-op, Storrs, CT

Brown University Bookstore, Providence, RI
College Hill Store, Providence, RI

DIA/BEACON, Beacon, NY
Bookcourt, Brooklyn, NY
Spoonbill & Sugartown, Brooklyn, NY
Talking Leaves, Buffalo, NY
Shop Naked, Hudson, NY
Book Revue, Huntington, NY
The Bookery, Ithaca, NY
Ariel Booksellers, New York, NY
Columbia University Bookstore, New York, NY
DIA Center for the Arts, New York, NY
Global News, New York, NY
Gotham Book Mart, New York, NY
Kim's Mediapolis, New York, NY
Language, New York, NY
Lenox Hill Bookstore, New York, NY
Museum of Modern Art Bookstore, New York, NY
New York University Book Center, New York, NY
St. Mark's Bookshop, New York, NY
Shakespeare & Co., New York, NY
Whitney Museum of Modern Art, New York, NY

University of Minnesota Bookstore, Minneapolis, MN
Walker Art Center Bookshop, Minneapolis, MN

Northshire Books, Manchester, VT
Bear Pond Books, Montpelier, VT

Shaman Drum Bookshop, Ann Arbor, MI
Book Beat, Oak Park, MI

Prairie Lights, Iowa City, IA
University Bookstore, Iowa City, IA

Toadstool Bookshop, Peterborough, NH

Indiana University Bookstore,
Bloomington, IN

Avril 50, Philadelphia, PA
U. Penn. Bookstore, Philadelphia, PA
Andy Warhol Museum, Pittsburgh, PA

Mayuba Bookstore, Chicago, IL
Museum of Contemporary Art, Chicago, IL
Seminary Co-op Bookstore, Chicago, IL
Quimby's, Chicago, IL
University of Chicago Bookstore, Chicago, IL

UC Bookstore, Cincinnati, OH
Columbus Museum of Art, Columbus, OH
Ohio State University Bookstore, Columbus, OH
Student Book Exchange, Columbus, OH
Kenyon College Bookstore, Gambier, OH

Maryland Institute Bookstore, Baltimore, MD

Cooper Enterprises, Washington, DC
Politics & Prose, Washington, DC

Left Bank Books, St. Louis, MO

Carmichael's, Louisville, KY

Studio Art Shop, Charlottesville, VA
William & Mary College Bookstore, Williamsburg, VA

Regulator Bookshop, Durham, NC

Square Books, Oxford, MS

Tulane University Bookstore, New Orleans, LA

Books & Books, Coral Gables, FL
Goerings Book Center, Gainesville, FL
Inkwood Books, Tampa, FL

And at selected Barnes & Noble and Borders bookstores nationwide.

SARAJEVO MARLBORO

by Miljenko Jergović

translated from the Bosnian by Stela Tomasević

"This classic of anti-war writing is a warning about the immense human cost of following those who would have us hate others."

—RICHARD FLANAGAN

THE VANISHING MOON

by Joseph Coulson

"This novel captures the collective memory of an American working class family, with all its pain and poetry. . . .So many unheard voices speak and sing through his voice. Listen."

—MARTIN ESPADA

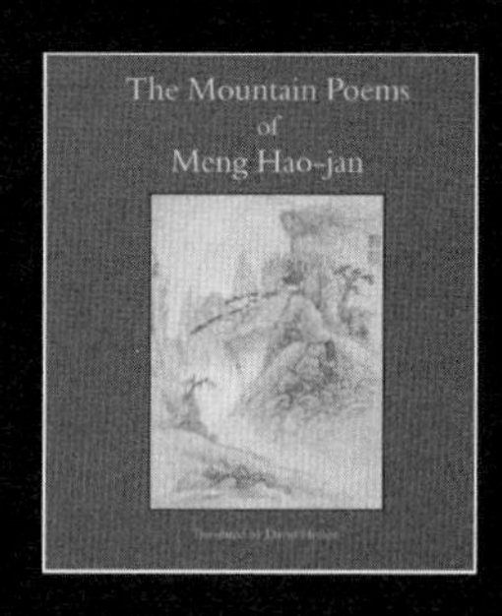

THE MOUNTAIN POEMS OF MENG HAO-JAN

translated from the Chinese by David Hinton

"Hinton's music is subtle, modulated. . .poems that breathe another culture into our English."

—THE ACADEMY OF AMERICAN POETS

AUGUSTE RODIN

by Rainer Maria Rilke

translated from the German by Daniel Slager

photographs by Michael Eastman

introduction by William Gass

Lyrical meditations on Rodin that illuminate the profound psychic connection between the two artists.

distributed to the book trade by Consortium Book Sales and Distribution
visit us at: www.archipelagobooks.org

CHELSEA

PHILIP-LORCA DICORCIA

A STORYBOOK LIFE

SEPTEMBER 4–OCTOBER 11

57TH STREET

HARRY CALLAHAN

EARLY EXPERIMENTS

SEPTEMBER 6–OCTOBER 18

DUANE MICHALS

THE HOUSE I ONCE CALLED HOME

OCTOBER 23–DECEMBER 6

George Plimpton Hawking the Foremost Literary Magazine of Our Day. Photographed by Chris Buck. Subscribe Today! (760) 291-1553